The Virus

Damien Lee

Edited by Linda Nagle

Cover art designed by Matt Seff Barnes

Prologue

The farmhouse floorboards creaked as Ronald Carter made his way upstairs, the worn carpet doing little to muffle the sound of his faltering steps. His hands trembled as he tried to balance the laden breakfast tray in front of him, the mouth-watering scent of sausages and bacon rising from the plate, mixing with the aroma of freshly-brewed coffee. A lone, spotted orchid stood proudly in a tall, transparent vase next to the breakfast.

Ronald smiled as he reached the top of the staircase. Although the contents of the tray had caused his arms to ache, it would be worth the toil if it would make his dear wife feel better. In over fifty years of marriage, he could not recall the last time she had taken ill. Alice was the healthy one in the family. Their daughter and grandchildren would often remark that she would outlive them. Yet, for the past couple of days, she had been bedridden with the flu. Casting a final, appraising eye over the contents of the tray, he nudged open the bedroom door.

The room felt clammy, with an air of sickness. Red matter covered everything around his shuddering wife. He stared at her with wide eyes as she cradled her head in her hands, rocking backward and forward on the soiled bedding.

"Alice?"

The breakfast tray shook violently in his hands. Coffee spilled over the rim of the mug; the vase tilted. Fell. Shattered. Ronald didn't seem to notice, eyes transfixed on his wife. Her nightdress hung loose from her skeletal body; her silver hair, normally thick and glossy, had fallen out in clumps, exposing her raw scalp.

Her eyes suddenly bulged as a geyser of blood gushed from her mouth, forming a pool on the mattress. Ronald stood motionless, frozen to the spot as Alice retched. Gobbets of meat spattered amongst the gory procession, bringing with them a rotten stench.

The flow of blood ceased, and Alice slumped back onto her pillow.

A squelching sound came from the carpet and Ronald looked down past the tray at his soiled slipper. A spurt of vomit came up his throat. He swallowed it and took a deep breath, composing himself as he neared the bed.

His wife's pallid skin seemed to thin out before his eyes, stretched tight over her tiny, shuddering frame. Her hair littered the pillow beneath her. Deep lesions criss-crossed her skin. With a jerk, Alice swung a hand to her neck and began scratching ferociously. The tray clattered to the floor. Strands of flesh peeled away under her probing fingernails.

"Alice!"

His wife lurched upright, her eyes snapping open and instantly locking on her terrified husband. Ronald backed away slowly as her mouth stretched into a wide, freakish grin. She let out a growl, springing forward onto her hands and knees, and darted towards him. She reached out her arms, but her lunge fell short and she landed in a heap. She growled, swiping out as she got to her feet.

Ronald turned and ran, pulling the door closed behind him. An almighty crash followed, and Alice screamed in anger before throwing herself against the door. The handle started to turn, but he kept hold from the other side and fought hard to retain control of the door. Finally, Alice's efforts subsided. Ronald placed an ear against the wooden pane, listening as she moved back to the sodden bed. Maintaining his grip on the handle, he pressed his head against the door and wept.

1

The sound of laughter and jeering inundated the halls of HMP Harrodale. The coppery stench of blood was rife in the prison, mixing with the scent of stale sweat. The two prisoners in the centre of the crowd faced each other after being separated from their clinch on the ground.

Frank Lee stared at his opponent through one eye. A gigantic swelling covered the other. Blood flowed from his broken nose and ran into his mouth, only spurring him into fighting harder. He spat it toward his rival, raining a pair of blows to his midriff. The crowd booed and hissed as his opponent doubled over, only to be kicked in the face by one of Frank's old, worn-out trainers.

"Get up, Hardy!" one prisoner shouted as the man slowly began to rise.

"C'mon, Hardy, shake it off!"

Hardy made it onto his knees, swaying, dazed. Frank could tell the fight was over. If his opponent managed to get to his feet, a well-aimed punch would send him straight back down. Flickers of relief coursed through his body. The money he would earn from the fight would pay off a good portion of his debt.

He watched as Andrew Hardy rose to his feet, shaking his head and blinking hard. Frank advanced, eager to keep the man down. As he neared, a firm hand from within the crowd grabbed his shoulder and he felt himself being dragged back. He turned as a fist smashed into his face. The roar of the crowd intensified as Frank reeled away. Tears stung his eyes, blurring his vision as more blood gushed out of his nose. He could see his attacker being subdued by members of the crowd, prisoners and corrupt guards alike. A barrage of punches rained down on the foolhardy assailant as he was dragged away.

Frank composed himself, wiping away the warm blood with the back of his hand. He glanced back at his opponent and saw that he was now bouncing on the balls of his feet. Twin lacerations adorned Hardy's lip, and he had a deep cut above his left brow. Blood trickled from the wound into his eye, causing him to squeeze it shut. With the temporary distortion to his opponent's vision, Frank had to act fast.

He raced forward, throwing a flurry of punches to Hardy's face. The man dodged and weaved, successful at evading some, but not all of the blows. One fist caught him in the mouth, snapping his jaw sideways. Blood and spit sprayed the jeering onlookers. The man's fractured jaw hung limply as Frank finished him with a powerful uppercut. The force of the punch snapped Hardy's head back and he fell, hitting the ground hard.

The crowd roared with a mixture of emotions. Some cursed, others cheered. The punters quickly exchanged cigarettes, drugs, and other commodities, then dispersed. Those who had profited from the brawl hung around to congratulate the victor. Those who had backed his opponent slunk away, muttering obscenities under their breath. Frank turned when he felt a pat on his back.

"You did well, Frankie."

Gus Razor grinned as he passed him a shirt. Frank took the garment and used it to wipe his bloody face. He tossed it back to Razor's bodyguard who remained still, allowing the garment to fall to the ground. At almost seven feet tall and thirty stones, 'Big Tony' Swales was a man-mountain and one of the toughest inmates in Harrodale.

"I made quite a bit out of you today," Razor continued. "Not many thought you'd get the better of Andy Hardy. He used to be a cage fighter until he got banged up in here."

"Yeah, well, you know me, I'd fight anything." Frank eyed the huge man next to Razor. Tony sneered and cracked his knuckles. Whether it was a threat or out of habit, Frank was unsure.

"Indeed," said Razor. "Well, I'd say about eight more fights and your debt should be clear."

"Eight?" Frank snapped. He lowered his voice as the guards returned to their duties. "You know it won't take eight fights to get your money back."

"It's just business, Frankie. Have you heard of *interest?*"

"Have you heard of *broken legs?*" Frank stepped forward, glowering. Razor burst out laughing.

"Oh, Frankie, you're a hoot. I'll be in touch when I want you to fight again."

Chuckling to himself, he walked away with his henchman in tow. Frank turned to leave, grabbing his shirt from the floor.

"Frank Lee!"

Barry Henderson was a typical screw. He would play everything by the book, but was more than willing to look the other way if the price was right. The prisoners had paid him to turn a blind eye for months whilst they gambled on the bare-knuckle fights. His companion, Michael Jones, was even more corrupt, and the two often made wagers of their own.

"That was some fight, Lee," Henderson said. "Didn't think you'd have it in you!"

Frank put on his shirt.

"You've surprised everyone with your recent fights. You've only lost against Big Tony, which was an obvious conclusion. Then there was Charlie Clapton, but that wasn't your fault."

"Get to the point."

"Don't get snappy with us, son," said Jones. "We can put you in segregation at the drop of a hat."

"All we're saying is that people around here think you're pretty tough," Henderson continued, smoothing his thick moustache. "They'll be betting in favour of you winning your next fight. And we want in on the action."

"What?"

"I think this guy has had too many blows to the head," Henderson said. "Shall I spell it out for him, Michael?"

"I think you might have to, Barry."

Frank regarded the charade with disgust.

"We want you to throw your next fight," Henderson said. "A lot of value will be wagered, and we stand to earn a considerable amount by betting on the other guy."

"Forget it." Frank made to walk away.

"I don't think you understand," Henderson urged, raising a hand to halt him. "It wasn't a request."

"Look, I need the money to pay Gus back!"

"We'll give you a share of our takings."

"Oh yeah, I'm sure that'll go down well with the other lads, especially when they find out I helped a couple of screws cheat them."

"Who'll know?"

Frank cast an appraising eye around the room. Most of the inmates had dispersed, but there were still some within earshot.

"They always find out."

"Well, I guess you better watch your back then, Lee." Jones sniggered, clapping the prisoner on the shoulder.

"And if I refuse?"

"We'll make your life hell." Henderson rocked on the heels of his feet with a smug grin.

"Okay," Frank sighed. "I'll sleep on it. Now can I get my face seen to?"

"They're doctors, not miracle workers, Lee."

The pair cackled as Frank pushed past them and made his way towards the hospital wing. If he threw the fight, Gus Razor would have him eating out of a straw for the rest of his life. If he won, the guards would torment him until he served his time, or until he committed suicide, whichever came first.

Decisions, decisions.

2

"Amy, I need your help here!"

At the sound of her name, the nurse dashed out onto the corridor, almost tripping over a motionless body at her feet. The man appeared to be in his sixties, judging by his grey hair and aging skin. Amy glanced over at her colleague, who was tending to a second unconscious patient. The young woman, barely out of adolescence, was curled up in the foetal position as Joyce Khaliq tried to help her.

A coughing sound from the man caused Amy to tear her gaze away from her colleague. He began to choke. His face adopted a purple hue before a spray of blood erupted from his mouth. It drenched the surrounding area, coating the white walls and floor. Amy dropped to her knees and pulled him onto his side, placing a comforting hand on his shoulder as spasms racked his body. His eyes rolled back in their sockets as bloody foam spilled from his lips.

"We need help over here!"

Quickly scanning the alarmed faces of the gathering crowd, she could see they were only patients and visitors. The man's convulsions abated. His swollen tongue lolled from his mouth. He wasn't breathing. The crowd of onlookers whispered to one another as Amy checked for a pulse.

"I need help!"

She started CPR compressions until she heard her colleagues arrive with a trolley.

"What have we got?" the doctor asked as they lifted the unconscious man onto the stretcher.

"He's gone into arrest. I don't have a pulse."

"Okay, we'll handle this. Go and help Joyce, another set of wheels are on the way."

With that, the medics pushed the man through the crowd and down another corridor of Sunnymoor Hospital. Amy ran over to her colleague. The young patient shuddered violently, bucking and writhing.

"Hold her," Joyce urged.

Amy pinned the woman's arms to the ground. Joyce gripped her head firmly and studied the woman's eyes, which had rolled back in their sockets.

"She's crashing. Are they sending another trolley?"

"It's on its way."

Amy looked on as the patient's convulsions stopped. The young woman lay still, her tongue lolling from her mouth. Joyce leaned in to check for a pulse.

The patient suddenly heaved, covering the nurse in a nauseating cocktail of blood and vomit. Joyce recoiled as the young woman slumped back to the ground. She hurriedly wiped the crimson matter from her face, gagging from its putrid stench. Amy held a hand to her mouth, eyeing the fleshy tendrils clinging to Joyce's hair as she resumed her search for a pulse.

"She needs a defib right now."

Amy nodded, trying to ignore the smell of rotten meat. As she stood, she spotted a pair of doctors rushing a stretcher through the crowd.

"She needs—" Amy began.

"We know, she needs a defib. Just like the rest of them," one doctor muttered.

They stopped next to Joyce. Together, the quartet lifted the unconscious woman onto the trolley. Her arm swung loosely off the side, but the doctors didn't seem to notice as they pushed her down the corridor.

The crowd of onlookers began to disperse as the two nurses left to get cleaned up.

"What the hell's going on?" Amy asked once they were in the refuge of the staff washroom.

"I don't know. It's been happening all morning: people coming in complaining of headaches, nausea, and dizziness. Next thing we know, they end up on life-support in ICU."

Joyce splashed cold water on her face. Diluted droplets of blood trickled over her dark skin until she wiped them away. She cast an eye at her reflection. The fleshy tendrils still clung to her black curls. Amy watched as she plucked them out and dropped them into the running water. They swirled around the basin, leaving behind a cherry-coloured trail before coming to an abrupt stop in the plughole. With a groan of disgust, Joyce scooped up the bloody pieces and dropped them into a biohazard bin. She returned to the sink and scrubbed her hands.

"Some kind of food poisoning?" Amy suggested, turning to the mirror and examining her pallid features. Her long brown hair, normally tied in a tight bun, had fallen loose and hung at her shoulders. She looked pale and aged, no doubt an effect of the morning's events, the usual tan and freshness no longer apparent.

She did the same as Joyce, washing her hands and face. The water was cool. She longed for more, splashing herself a few more times.

"Not like anything I've ever seen," Joyce said. "That meat smelled rotten." She cast a disgusted glance back to the biohazard bin. "I guess you wish you'd stayed at Brackton, huh?"

The shift marked only her second at Sunnymoor. She had started her career at Brackton University Hospital. Although Sunnymoor was a lot smaller, she had been looking forward to working within the close-knit community. After the morning's events, though, she was starting to regret her decision to transfer.

"But then again, Brackton has all those riots going on."

Joyce looked up in surprise. "Really? I didn't know they were that close."

Amy recalled the news report she had watched that morning. Following a sweep of unexplained violence, the riots had spread. At first centralised to the major cities, the random acts of aggression were now occurring in the smaller towns as well.

"So, if it's not food poisoning, what else could it be?"

Amy studied her reflection. Her features had become flushed from the water's harsh touch. Her cheeks glowed red and her blue eyes sparkled. She smiled, relieved to have her fresh-faced appearance back.

"I don't know," Joyce said. "Once we've examined the patients, we might establish a cause. But, until then, your guess is as good as mine."

The two women made their way down the corridor, approaching the bloody scene once more. The onlookers had dispersed, with only the bloody pools serving as a grisly reminder of their ordeal. 'Wet floor' signs had appeared at opposite ends, with a lone cleaner mopping up the mess. Exhausted, his face had adopted a grey hue, and dark rings circled his bloodshot eyes. The mop handle trembled as he leaned heavily on it for support. Amy watched as more of the white floor was painted red by the cleaner's efforts.

"Gary, are you okay?"

A tall, middle-aged doctor approached. The cleaner didn't respond, but went about his task in the same sluggish manner.

"I don't mean to pry, but shouldn't the rest of the cleaning team be dealing with this?"

They looked at the red pool, which had significantly expanded since they had arrived, despite the efforts of the lethargic cleaner.

"I guess they're all tied up," Joyce said. "There have been situations like this all morning: vomiting blood, seizures, the lot."

"I know. I've just examined a patient who came in earlier with those symptoms."

"Have you established what's causing it?" Amy asked, tearing her gaze away from the cleaner.

"No. But there will be a post-mortem. That should establish a cause."

"Wait, post-mortem?"

"Yes, the gentleman died. He suffered a seizure and went into cardiac arrest. We tried to revive him, but his heart had given up."

"The same thing happened here," Joyce said. "Two patients with the same symptoms and both went into cardiac arrest."

Amy's eyes were fixed on the gory pool that was gradually creeping closer. The cleaner mopped in a figure of eight, sending waves of liquid rolling towards the walls. The trio stepped back as the bloody ripples threatened to flow around the soles of their shoes.

"Where the hell did all this blood come from?" Joyce said, taking in the scene with a newfound awareness. Amy stared at the cleaner's feet, just as a fresh stream of gore poured from his mouth.

"It's coming from *him*." She gasped, pointing at the man's bowed head. The three of them watched as a thin strand of blood oozed down, dripping onto his shoes.

"Gary, you need help!"

The doctor rushed forward, his feet splashing amongst the blood. He put his hand on the inflicted man, who suddenly sprang to life. The doctor screamed as Gary clamped his teeth into his hand. He tried to get away, but within seconds, the demented man was on his back, dragging him to the ground.

Amy leapt forward as the doctor fought to push the man off him. Both men were coated in blood as they wrestled for the upper hand, the doctor whimpering, the cleaner growling. Amy grabbed the cleaner's left arm whilst Joyce knelt on his back, forcing his head to the side. Gary snarled, fighting to be free. The doctor staggered to his feet, grabbing the right arm and pinning it behind his back.

"Amy, get security!" Joyce said. "We'll hold him."

The doctor took over from Amy and seized the left arm, allowing her to move. She sprinted down the corridor, her heart hammering, her breath catching as she went. She turned a corner, greeted by a row of closed doors in another empty corridor. She tried each door as she ran down the hall, crying out in frustration when none of them would open. Finally, the last door granted her entry.

The well-lit room was an office. Twin desks stood up against the wall, with computers and paperwork atop both. Amy caught sight of the phone and grabbed the handset. She wracked her brain, desperately trying to remember the number for security. Her memory failed her, and she had to contact the operator.

"Hello, Sunnymoor Hospital," a female voice crooned.

"Security, please."

"One moment."

The line went silent. Amy tapped her fingers against the desk anxiously, willing someone to pick up the phone. Her heavy breathing whooshed down the line. She toyed with the phone cord as a high-pitched scream echoed down the hall. Amy spun round. It sounded like Joyce. Finally, a voice sounded on the other end of the phone.

"Security."

"We need help. There's someone attacking staff in the main corridor outside the nurse's station!"

"Everyone is responding to a call at the minute," the man replied. "I'll send a message for the nearest person to attend once they have dealt with their call-out."

"But he's *biting* people!"

"Biting?"

"Yes!"

"Look, there's nothing I can do at the minute. I'll ring the police and I'll send a member of the team as soon as they're free."

Amy slammed down the receiver and darted out of the office. If security wasn't coming, then she would have to help Joyce and the doctor herself. She sprinted back down the corridor. Her heart hammered in her chest, the blood-curdling scream still fresh in her mind. She dared not imagine what sights would greet her as she turned the corner.

She stopped in her tracks, trying to muster a scream. Her legs softened, her body trembled, and her lungs ached from the breath trapped inside.

The doctor's body lay a few feet from his killer, who was kneeling with his back to Amy. She realised with horror that he was hunched over the still form of Joyce Khaliq. Her colleague stared at the ceiling as the cleaner busied himself tearing chunks out of her face. The squelching of flesh being ripped from bone met Amy's ears, and the putrid stench of excrement and decay invaded her nose. It was too much. The hot spurt of vomit erupted from her mouth, and she retched as it showered the floor.

The cannibal whirled around, regarding her with wide eyes. Clasped in the man's teeth was a lump of brown flesh, which swayed as he jumped to his feet, an evil grin creasing his face. The flesh fell to the ground with a splat as he let out an almighty roar.

Without warning, he sprinted towards her, arms outstretched, eyes hungry. Amy turned and bolted back around the corner. The rapid footfalls behind her drew near. She ran as fast as she could, pushing her body to its limit. Her legs felt heavy and her breathing laboured, but she pushed on.

Her footsteps filled the empty corridor. The cannibal screeched. He was faster than her. He was getting closer—

A tall man stepped into the corridor ahead. He held a large sports bag and a jacket draped over his arm.

"Help!"

A frown creased the man's face as he turned. She grabbed hold of his shoulder to slow herself.

"He's killing people!" Amy cried.

The man dropped the sports bag as the cannibal lunged at them. "What the fuck?"

The lunatic squealed in excitement as he collided with the pair. The impact pushed Amy aside as the other two fell to the ground. She gasped as the cannibal wormed his way on top of the man. He lurched forward, trying to bite his struggling victim. The man held the lunatic under the chin, forcing his mouth shut and his head backward.

"The bag," he said. "Open the bag."

Amy grabbed the holdall. Inside, there were several items used in cricket. She could see balls, wickets, shin guards, and two cricket bats. She grabbed the first bat and turned to face the pair. Although the man was holding his attacker by the throat, the cannibal was only inches from his face. In a swift motion, Amy lifted the bat over her shoulder and swung it sideways with all her strength. She hit the cleaner above his temple, sending him hurtling into the wall.

The man jumped to his feet.

"Quick!"

He snatched the bat from her. Raising the weapon above his shoulder, he swung it in a downward arc. It cracked on top of the lunatic's head. The blow sent him crashing to the ground, smashing his face into the tiled floor. They watched as he twitched for a few seconds before lying still. Amy stared in silence, waiting for any signs of movement. The man with the bat eyed the maroon stain on the edge of his makeshift weapon.

"I think I killed the bastard." He dug into his pocket and produced a two-way radio. "Geoff, it's Ben, we've got an incident outside the East Wing changing rooms."

"We've got incidents everywhere, Ben." Static tainted the voice on the other end.

"Yeah? Well, I've got a psycho here who could be dead or just unconscious. We need some more security, police, and medics."

"Jesus, Ben, I don't have anyone to spare! The police are on their way, though. I just had a call from some woman saying there's a bloke biting people!"

Amy felt Ben's gaze on her, but her eyes were fixed on the motionless corpse.

"Yeah, I think I got him. Just send them to the East Wing corridor when they get here."

Ben returned the radio to his pocket and rounded on Amy.

"What the hell's going on?"

3

The harsh buzz of the alarm stirred Frank from his slumber. The clatter of opening cell doors came from a distance; he could hear the laughter and chatter of the inmates as guards ushered them down to the canteen. He winced at the searing pain in his ribs, squeezing his eyes tight in response to the powerful overhead lights. His body ached from the fight. His knuckles were sore and his nose throbbed as he lifted himself up.

The whitewashed walls adorned with medical charts seemed unfamiliar at first. He glanced around, taking in the alien environment, before he realised he was lying in an in-patient bed. He'd only been there twice in the past. The first time was after his futile brawl with Big Tony. He could remember that day well, and the excruciating pain even more.

The second time had been a few months later after another of his fights, with a prisoner called Charlie Clapton. The man had been a supposed 'easy opponent' to make Frank a bit of money. It was true, the fight was over in less than twenty seconds after a few well-timed body shots that had instantly floored Clapton. But as Frank turned his back, his downed opponent produced a shiv and attacked him in a fit of rage. Frank had suffered multiple stab wounds from the vicious onslaught and had spent over a week in hospital. Charlie Clapton had not been seen since.

Not much had changed except for a few new light fittings and two extra beds in the corner. His roaming eyes eventually fell upon a guard stood in the doorway. The man's dark moustache stretched across his face as he grinned, baring yellowed teeth, his cold brown eyes fixed on Frank.

"How are you feeling, Lee?" Henderson asked, stepping forward.

"Like a nun in a brothel. What the hell do you want?"

"That's no way to talk to a concerned well-wisher." The guard sneered, stopping a few feet away. "I'm only here to check how you're doing."

"Of course you are." Frank glanced around the room. "I don't see any grapes, flowers, get-well-soon cards, nothing."

"What can I say, the prison gift shop isn't well-stocked." Henderson sniggered, perching on the side of the bed. "No, I'm just here for your answer."

"What?"

"Well, I've let you sleep on it, now I want to know how you're going to lose your next fight."

"Drop dead, Henderson. There's nothing you could do that's worse than what Gus and his boys would do if I threw the fight."

"You disappoint me, Frank. And I don't think Jones will be happy, either." Henderson rose from the bed.

"Oh yeah, I forgot about your bitch. Where is he? Humping the governor?"

"No, he had to go home; family emergency."

"What happened? His old lady been caught fucking the postman?"

"Now there's no need for crudeness, Lee," Henderson chided in mock surprise. "Jonesy's missus is a faithful, devoted housewife. And, she's an ugly cunt; the postman wouldn't go near her."

"Yeah, I bet. Now, if you don't mind, Henderson, I believe visiting times are non-existent on this ward, I think you should leave."

"Karma's a bitch, Lee. Remember that. Now, are you sure there's no changing your mind?"

"Not a chance."

"Well, that is a shame. I suppose I'll have to take matters into my own hands."

"What do you mean?"

The guard strolled to a nearby cupboard. He reached inside and produced a pump-action shotgun. He held the weapon admiringly before aiming it at Frank's face.

"Still adamant you won't change your mind?"

"What the fuck's that doing in here?"

"I stashed it while you were sleeping. I didn't want to turn nasty if you were willing to co-operate."

"Well, you'll have to kill me, Henderson. I'm not rigging the fight."

"Oh, this won't kill you, it's just a little something to tip the odds in my favour."

Frank looked on in horror as the guard aimed the weapon at his arm. He pulled the trigger, sending a shooting pain up Frank's shoulder. He roared in agony as the rubber bullet bounced away. The crack of the shotgun reverberated in his ears as he doubled over, clutching his injured arm. He thought he'd gone deaf until he heard Henderson's voice from afar.

"By the way, your next fight is tonight. You'll be up against some shitty-arse so it'll all appear in your favour. Be sure to make it seem legit."

The guard's laughter droned through his skull as Henderson turned and walked away. Frank tried to flex his fingers, sending another wave of pain shooting up his arm. He knew if he *was* fighting that night, it would be impossible to win. He felt himself succumb to unconsciousness as approaching footsteps announced the doctor's arrival.

***

The warm rays from the sun blanketed the newlyweds as they lay in a field of lush grass. The trickle of water from a nearby stream provided a natural soundtrack for the couple's day out. They had returned from their honeymoon, and, with four days holiday remaining, had decided to take a walk in the country. Following a stroll through the winding trails of forests and fields, they finally rested at their favourite beauty spot.

"What a lovely day."

Leigh smiled, lying back on the tartan blanket. She adjusted her sunglasses and closed her eyes, savouring the warmth of the sun on her skin. Adrian sat down at her side. He picked at the blades of grass and ran one of the long, green strands over his wife's bare midriff. Leigh squirmed under the touch and slapped his hand playfully.

"Quit it!"

Adrian grinned and continued tickling her with the grass, running it over her denim shorts and down her right leg until it reached her shoes.

"I said quit it."

She sat up and snatched the blade of grass. Adrian chuckled as she lowered herself back against the blanket.

"Isn't it peaceful here?"

"Sure is," he said. "And look: no signal."

He raised his mobile phone into view.

"It's one of the best things about being out here," Leigh said.

"Yeah, your mother can't interrupt."

Adrian rolled away as his wife swatted him. They lay apart, Leigh basking in the sun and Adrian plucking more blades of grass.

"There's one thing that's not so good about this place," he said, rubbing his hands. "All the damn spiders."

"Oh, you have to ruin it, don't you?" Leigh shifted uneasily, dusting her arms and legs.

The couple fell silent again, the slow-running stream and the twittering of birds creating a calm ambience. Adrian glanced at his wife. He grinned when he saw her eyes were closed. He plucked another piece of grass and shuffled closer.

"You should see the size of this spider I've found," he said. "Here, look."

Leigh shrieked as he dropped the grass on her forehead. She jumped up and shook it away, running her fingers through her long, golden hair. She glared at her husband as a blade of grass drifted to the ground.

"You twat!"

Adrian jumped to his feet as his wife chased him towards the stream. The birds fled their nests and soared high into the air as the couple's shrieks of laughter drew near. Adrian jumped into the stream, feeling the cool touch of the water, which rose as high as his ankles. Leigh stopped short and stared at him with her arms crossed.

"You can't stay in there forever," she said, her eyebrows raised.

"You're not coming in?"

"No, I'm not. God knows what you'll catch in there!"

"You're more likely to catch something out there than in here."

Adrian stooped down and rubbed the water up and down his arms. The cool touch soothed his tender sunburned flesh. He cupped some water into his hand and splashed his face, to the dismay of his wife.

"Urgh, I'm not kissing you again."

"C'mon, it's fine."

She shrieked as he hurled a handful of water in her direction.

"Don't," she said, as the second wave showered her legs.

Adrian laughed as he soaked her for the third time. This time, her shriek was diminished by a louder one. They both looked up as a massive bird circled above them. It called out again, staring at the couple with its beady eyes.

"I think we should go back."

Adrian stepped out of the water, ushering Leigh away from the stream. Both kept their eyes glued to the bird as they cautiously made their way up the bank. All at once, it stopped circling. With an ear-splitting screech, it darted towards them.

"Run!" Adrian urged, but Leigh had already raced back to their blanket. He ran after her, just as the bird swooped over his head. He felt a gush of wind as its talons grazed his ear. It flew ahead of him towards his wife. Leigh shrieked as the bird attacked her. She swung her arms, slapping its heavy wings as it tore at her face. She dropped to the ground, shielding her head and rolling onto her stomach as Adrian ran over.

"Leigh!"

He grabbed the bird by its breast and wing, but it continued its frenzied attack. Leigh cried out as razor-sharp talons tore open her back. Driven by the strands of flesh, the bird darted forward, tearing into her with its beak. Adrian grabbed its throat and heaved backward. The creature let out a squawk of dismay before turning on him. He dodged the eager beak as it went for his eyes. He pushed the bird to the ground and stomped on its throat. It screeched as he pushed all of his weight down, snapping its neck.

"Ade."

He whirled around and rushed over to his injured wife.

"I feel—"

"Shh," he said. "Don't talk. We'll get you to the hospital."

He scooped his wife up and rushed back onto the dirt track. Leigh's blood saturated his shirt, oozing out of the remains of her face. He tried not to look. He kept his eyes focused on the path ahead, ignoring the aching in his legs and the tightness in his back.

"Ade."

"It's okay, darling."

The sound of her guttural breathing made him increase his pace. He was desperate to reach the end of the track, hoping for a signal on his mobile phone. He tried to ignore his wife's frenzied gasps, tried to disregard the damp touch of her blood on his skin. Her last breath rattled before she died.

"Leigh?" He gasped, shaking his wife in his arms. "Leigh!"

Panic seized his lungs in an icy grasp. His heart raced and he could feel the tears well up. He trembled as he made to lower her limp body to the ground, his mind starting to cloud. Her sudden frantic inhalations brought him back to his senses and he breathed a sigh of relief.

"Oh, thank god."

He adjusted her body in his arms as he rushed toward a familiar point in their trek. It was the last place they'd had a signal. He gently lowered his wife as she started to thrash.

"I'm going to ring for help."

He tried to prise her hand from his T-shirt. She held tight, causing the fabric to stretch.

"Just lie back."

He tried to disengage her fingers with one hand whilst holding his phone with the other. But it was no use. Leigh's grip was firm, and he felt himself being pulled closer.

"Darling, please lie down."

His request fell on deaf ears. As his wife drew near, Adrian had to look at her disfigured features.

"Sweetheart, you have to—"

His words caught in his throat when he glimpsed her wide eyes, staring at him with an insatiable hunger. He barely had time to react before she was on top of him, tearing a chunk out of his neck. Blood spurted from the gaping wound as she chewed on the flesh. He stared through blurred eyes as his blood rapidly drained from his body. He watched in silent horror as his wife swallowed the meat before leaning back in to rip more from his throat. It only took ten seconds for Adrian to die, but it took over ten minutes for his wife to finish eating him.

Her meal was cut short when the cadaver began to twitch. Adrian's eyes regained focus as he started to move. Swallowing the last morsel, Leigh's corpse staggered to its feet and set off in search of more meat, closely followed by the remains of her late husband.

4

A roaring crowd filled the wing as Frank made his way into the main hall. Several guards lined the walls; an unusual sight during the organised fights. Ordinarily, they were paid to give the inmates a sixty-minute amnesty, with only one or two of the guards loitering to place a bet. But not tonight. All eyes were fixed on the fight in progress. The air was warm, with the familiar smell of blood and sweat. Frank tried to catch a glimpse of the fighters, but the boisterous crowd blocked his vision. He stopped at the back of the hall, his left arm hanging limply by his side.

Whilst his arm wasn't broken, he had sustained significant muscle damage thanks to Henderson's foul play. He knew that if his foe were to discover his weakness, he would be in trouble. With this in mind, he'd declined a sling whilst in the hospital ward. Any sign of vulnerability and his opponent would target that spot.

The crowd suddenly roared with vigour, signalling the end of the bout. Frank watched the usual exchange of commodities, noticing that several guards stepped forward to collect their winnings as well. He looked from face to face, trying to spot Henderson amongst the crowd. With his distinct features, it wouldn't be hard to locate him. After scanning the area, Frank determined he was not amongst those in attendance. Gus Razor was easily visible, as was Tony Swales, who stood almost a foot taller than everyone else.

Frank tore his eyes from the crowd and began looking around at each of the posted guards. He couldn't see Henderson *or* Jones. It was surprising, as neither had ever missed a fight. The teeming crowd spread out as they waited for the next bout to begin.

"Frankie!"

Frank turned to see Gus Razor holding out his arms as if greeting a long-lost son. "We were wondering where you'd gone off to."

"I was in the hospital wing. Is it true that I'm fighting tonight?"

"It certainly is, hair of the dog and all that. The best way to recover is to take another beating."

"Henderson talked you into it, didn't he?"

"Sure did. I gave him stupid odds as well, and he still placed a whopping wager."

"It's because he knows I'm going to lose, you prick!"

"That's why I put you up against a new kid," Gus said. "Some punk who had a problem with Mummy and Daddy and beat them to death with a shovel."

"Oh, great."

"Don't sweat it; the kid's a scrawny midget. He won't stand a chance."

"Gus, I'm *not* fighting."

The gangland boss stopped scanning the crowd. He fixed Frank with an icy glare.

"I'm sorry, I didn't catch that," he said. "Tell me, Frankie, does this ring a bell? 'Oh, Mr Razor, can you please help me? My horrible wife was being shafted by a young stallion. Can you get your boys to kill him?'"

Frank didn't answer.

"I responded with kindness," Gus continued. "I said 'Of course, Frankie m'boy, I'd be happy to help, for the princely sum of thirty thousand British pounds.' You couldn't afford that, could you? So, you agreed to fight for me to pay off the debt. Do you remember?"

Frank nodded.

"I held up my side of the bargain. Casanova's dead. So, in response to your insolent comment, yes, you *are* fighting, and you dare question me again, you'll end up in the ground with your slag wife and her fucking toy boy."

"You don't understand, Gus, I—"

Razor ignored Frank's retort as he spied an inmate in the crowd.

"Oy, Craddock! You owe me a gram!"

Within seconds, Razor and his thug had left Frank behind.

Frank sighed. Despite Gus's reassurances that his opponent was only a kid, he couldn't dismiss the feeling that Henderson had more up his sleeve. His fears increased tenfold when he finally spotted the guard conversing with a small teenager away from the crowd. They were too far away for him to hear, but Frank could tell by Henderson's body language what he was saying. He was patting his left arm, revealing to the kid where to aim his punches. A sense of dread developed in the pit of his stomach as he tensed the muscles of his left arm. Searing pain shot up to his shoulder.

"Shit."

He flexed his fingers, gritting his teeth through the pain. His left hand would be no use in the fight, not without causing more harm to himself. He sighed as Gus Razor yelled at him, beckoning him over to the centre of the room.

"Frankie! Get over here, you're up!"

The milling crowd formed a circle once more as Frank made his way into the makeshift ring and watched his young opponent emerge from the mass of spectators. He barely looked old enough to shave, yet he hopped confidently on the balls of his feet. He shot Frank an acid glance as he stopped next to Gus, who held the two fighters apart.

"You girls ready?"

Frank remained silent. He stared at the teenage inmate. The youngster's eyes met his, before flitting to his injured arm. There was no doubt about it: he knew his weakness. The babble of the crowd intensified as they placed their bets. The chatter was almost inaudible, but Frank could make out some wagers. All were on him to win, some stating it would be after the first punch, and others predicted two minutes into the fight. *Oh, how wrong they are,* he thought as he lifted his shirt over his head. He winced as he stretched out his arm, but tried not to show pain as he hurled the garment aside. He locked stares with his opponent as the crowd fell silent.

"Right then, you know the rules," Gus said. "Are you both ready?"

The two opponents gave quick nods, maintaining their icy stare.

"Good. Then beat the shit out of each other!"

He stepped to the side as the crowd roared. No sooner was Gus out of the way than the young prisoner dashed forward, focused on one area. He threw a flurry of punches towards Frank's disabled arm. One punch connected, spreading a wave of pain up to his shoulder. The crowd jeered as Frank sidestepped the rapid punches, all directed at the same spot.

"What the fuck are you doing?" Gus bellowed. "Knock his fucking head off!"

Frank continued to sidestep, parrying some of the punches and dodging others. He could see the frustration in his opponent's eyes as he persistently retreated. An abrupt shove from a spectator in the angry crowd sent Frank staggering forward. He quickly recovered, pivoting to the right as his opponent advanced. The young prisoner continued aiming at the weak spot, but with Frank standing side-on, his right shoulder forward, he could not reach.

With a roar of frustration, he targeted other parts of Frank's body, giving him the opening he was looking for. As the prisoner aimed for his face, Frank caught his fist in an open hand. A brief look of surprise came over him as

Frank lunged forward, breaking his opponent's nose with his forehead. The crowd cheered in delight as the prisoner staggered back.

"Yes! Knock his fucking teeth out!"

Razor's voice was barely audible over the hollering crowd. Frank stepped forward and threw a powerful jab, keeping his injured arm out of reach. The young prisoner reeled back as blood pumped from his face. He stared wide-eyed as Frank came at him again, throwing punch after punch with his right hand. He tried to block the attacks, but his efforts were futile. Jab after jab struck his mangled face. In an act of desperation, he lurched forward and grabbed Frank's left arm. His effort was short-lived, as Frank sent a knee into his midriff and he doubled over before a second knee crashed into his face with crushing force. The crowd roared in delight as his head snapped back. His legs buckled and he crumpled to the ground.

"Get up, you piece of shit!"

The angry outburst had come from Barry Henderson, who had pushed his way through the jeering spectators. The teenager didn't respond. Henderson turned a dark shade of scarlet. Veins throbbed in his temples as he glared at Frank.

"Lee! You've had it!"

"Bite me."

"Oh, I'll do more than that."

He lurched forward, thrusting a baton into Frank's abdomen. Frank doubled over, coughing and wheezing as Gus Razor made his way into the circle.

"Take your frustrations out on someone else, Barry. It won't get you your money back."

The guard turned on Razor, who folded his arms as his colossal bodyguard stepped beside him.

"Well, well, Gus, it seems we have a bit of a situation here," Henderson said. "You must have, what? A century? Two centuries on you? You can't walk around with that much product. You might get hurt!"

The smile slid off Razor's face as the guard held out his hand.

"Why don't you hand it over and we'll keep it safe for you?"

"Put your hand away, Barry, or I'll have Tony rip it off."

"Well, I tried to play it peacefully." Henderson shrugged as he turned away. Frank watched as he unclipped a two-way radio. "C'mon then, boys."

The walkway above them clanged under a flurry of footfalls as an army of officers entered. They all wore riot gear, some carried large Perspex shields, and others held firearms. Frank looked up to see more officers pointing weapons at them. The guards already in attendance had drawn their batons.

Razor looked back at the smug guard.

"You slimy cunt," he said, as Henderson held out his hand again. "You're a dead man. You know that, right?"

"Sure, Gus, whatever helps you sleep at night."

He waited as Razor produced a large transparent bag containing a variety of individually-sealed drugs.

"You're a dead man."

"We're all dying, Sunshine." Henderson winked as he pried the bag from Razor's chubby hand. "My, my, you *have* been a busy boy."

He inspected the contents of the bag before stuffing it into his pocket. He looked past the seething gangland boss and down at Frank, who had propped himself up on one knee, still struggling to catch his breath. The mass of armed security began leading the protesting convicts back to their cells as Henderson approached him.

"Just think, Lee, all this could have been avoided if you had just sat down like a good little dog."

Henderson swung a boot into Frank's face, knocking him sideways.

"Take this piece of shit to segregation."

"What about the kid?"

A guard pointed at the young prisoner, who still lay motionless.

"Take him to the in-patient beds. If he wakes up, throw him in the seg. If not, bury him outside."

Frank felt rough hands clasp him under the arms, hauling him to his feet. He watched as Gus Razor and Big Tony were forced out of the hall at gunpoint.

"Get that fucking pellet gun out of my face!" Gus turned on the guard who had motioned for him to move. "I'm going to get you, Henderson!"

Frank tried to pull his arm free of the pincer-like grasp, but the guard was unmoving.

"Fancy loosening your grip?"

The officer responded by squeezing Frank's arm tighter.

"Oh, you little bitch."

Frank glanced from room to room as he was led down a corridor which housed the segregation cells. The majority were empty.

"Am I not good enough for these cells?"

The guard ignored him, leading him farther down the corridor.

"Does it matter which one I'm in? It's just four walls and a shit-bucket. Put me in any." They stopped at the end of the corridor.

"You made me walk all this way just to come in *here*?" He laughed as the guard shoved him into the room and slammed the thick metal door.

The room was identical to all those he had passed. The thin mattress on the floor was the only luxury offered. Aside from the primitive toilet in the corner, the room was empty. He sat on the edge of the mattress, listening as the rest of the cells became occupied with spectators from the fight. The segregation block was designed to be soundproof, a psychological measure to punish unruly inmates. Yet, time and lack of maintenance had left countless gaps in the brickwork, rendering that measure ineffective.

"You can fuck off if you think I'm going in there!"

Gus Razor's voice boomed down the corridor. A series of tirades came from the other prisoners as, one by one, the guards slammed the cell doors. After a while, silence enveloped the corridor, with only the odd dissatisfied murmur coming from the cells. Frank lay back on the mattress, contemplating the night's events. Henderson was becoming more and more reckless. It was starting to make him feel uneasy. The guard's actions would be reported eventually, but how much damage would he have caused by then?

Frank flexed his arm, wincing as the pain shot up to his shoulder again. The shotgun attack was a clear example of Henderson's deteriorating mental state. Trying to throw the bout was a dangerous move, even for the arrogant guard. Frank replayed the fight in his head. The knee to the face was a crushing blow, but something the teenager should recover from.

A sudden footfall from the end of the corridor caused Frank to sit up. He listened hard as one of the cell doors was quickly unlocked. *Probably Gus being released before the shit hits the fan,* he mused. He soon realised that he was right about the cell belonging to Gus Razor, but wrong about his release.

"What?" Razor's voice boomed down the corridor.

"Keep your voice down," a guard said.

"What do you mean they failed? I told them to intercept that cargo nearly two weeks ago! Why am I only finding out now?"

Frank strained his ears, trying to hear the indecipherable whispers of the guard, but it was no use. If his cell were closer, he may have had a chance, but being at the end of the corridor meant he was more isolated than anybody. He leaned back on his mattress, musing at Razor's ability to keep his criminal empire running from within the prison. He had observed the man dealing drugs, arranging protection, and now he was clearly involved in the acquisition of some kind of cargo. The number of screws on the crime boss' payroll seemed endless.

The sound of the cell door slamming shut indicated the end of the conversation. Frank briefly wondered whether Gus was still in segregation until the loudmouthed inmate shouted after the guard.

"You've got two days!"

5

Amy shuddered as she held a mug of coffee. She could feel the gaze of her manager and the security guard, but she didn't look up. It had been over an hour since she'd witnessed her colleague being eaten. Since then, she had cried uncontrollably, spoken to the police, cried some more, been given a mug of coffee, and now she felt like crying again. Nothing in her life even came close to the massacre she had witnessed that morning.

"Can I get you anything else?"

It was Ben, the security guard. He had a warm smile as he sat down next to her, but she could see the torment in his eyes.

"No thanks, I'm fine."

"Amy, with everything that has gone on today, I think it best that you have the next few days off."

She looked at her manager. "Are you sure? This place is hectic."

"I've got a dozen agency nurses drafted in to help. We should be fine."

Amy nodded.

"But stay here for as long as you want. Have your coffee, sit and rest, and when you feel well enough, you can go home."

"Thank you," she said as her manager left the room. She took a sip.

"Are you going to be okay?" Ben asked. "Do you need a ride home?"

"No, I drove here," said Amy, staring at the cup.

"Oh, right."

She blinked, breaking her reverie, and smiled at him.

"Are you going home too?" she asked, trying to clear her mind of the gruesome images it was harbouring.

"Yeah, my shift finished an hour ago. I was leaving when you caught up with me. Lucky I didn't sneak out early, huh?"

Amy's head filled with the sight of the demented cleaner.

"What was with the bag you were carrying?"

"I was supposed to be playing cricket with some lads from work. I guess that was lucky, too."

"Yeah, I guess. But won't you be missed?"

"I should hope so. I was the one bringing all the gear."

Amy managed a weak smile.

"I'm Ben."

"I know, I heard you on the radio. I'm Amy."

"I know, your manager just told me."

"Right."

"So, Amy, I've not seen you around here before. Are you new?"

"Yeah, today's my second day."

"I guess it doesn't leave a good impression of the place then, huh?"

Amy shook her head, returning her gaze to the cup.

"Well, I hope the incident hasn't scared you off. This kind of thing never happens here. I've... never had to stop anyone like that before."

Ben stood and put on his jacket.

"So, have the police cleared you of everything? Did they not want to question you?"

"No idea. They got a call halfway through speaking to me and had to dash. They told me to stay put, but they've got my address. If they want to speak to me, they know where I am."

"I see. So what are you going to do now?"

"Well, the police took my bat, and you can't play without one of those. It's just not cricket."

Amy smiled as Ben raised a hand in farewell. He left the room, leaving her alone with her thoughts. The images her brain replayed were unsettling, and she quickly drained the cup before getting to her feet. She had to take her mind off the carnage. She grabbed her bag and walked out of the room. The hospital seemed empty. It was no longer visiting time, but she wasn't used to seeing the corridors so deserted. Feeling a chill creep up her spine, she hurried down the hallway and went to turn the corner.

She flinched as a gurney raced past, cutting off her path. The elderly man atop it was coated in blood, his limbs twitching. A doctor examined him whilst two nurses and a porter rushed the trolley down the corridor and around a corner.

So many patients had been admitted to the hospital with the same symptoms. Yet, they still could not establish a cause. Even more worrying was how the infected people seemed to deteriorate rapidly until their demise. Although the symptoms were similar, there didn't appear to be a link between any of the patients. Everyone seemed to be vulnerable.

Amy left through the main entrance and shielded her eyes. The sun shone from a clear blue sky. She dug into her handbag and produced a pair of sunglasses on her way to the car park. Most people were strolling around in summer wear. She even saw the porters wearing navy shorts as they went about their work. One of them grinned at her as she passed, casting a lecherous eye over her tight-fitting attire. She strode past him without making eye contact.

"Going home already?" he called after her.

"Sure am."

"Alright for some, eh? Going to do a little sunbathing?"

He cast another eye over Amy's white skirt and navy-blue T-shirt.

"I highly doubt it."

She turned her back on the man and made her way over to her car. Sunbathing was the last thing on her mind. After the morning's events, all she wanted to do was relax in a cool shower and curl up in bed. Even though it was only mid-afternoon, she felt exhausted. Locating her keys, she unlocked her car and pried open the door. She groaned as the suffocating heat billowed out, engulfing her as she slid behind the wheel. She lowered the windows and adjusted the air conditioning as she started the car.

Cool air caressed her face and toyed with her hair as she made her way out of the car park. The roads were empty; a welcome alternative to those she was used to back home. Minutes passed and Amy saw only four other road users as she left the town and accelerated along the country road.

Her home was almost twenty miles from Sunnymoor, in the neighbouring town of Cranston. She had considered moving closer to work, but she had never been able to bring herself to part from the beautiful countryside. Yet, today, there was something about the rural landscape that didn't feel right, something that threatened to overshadow the serene beauty.

Amy's eyes narrowed as she tried to determine the source of her unease. Whether it was the cloying feel of the air, the stench that worsened the farther she drove, or the sheer silence that was unusual even for the countryside, she could not tell. She glanced out of her windows at the empty fields on either side of her. Normally filled with grazing sheep, the grassland contained no visible life at all.

A gradual movement in the distance caught Amy's attention. It seemed to be two people running across the moors, but she was going too fast to be able to tell. She didn't slow, but kept her eyes rooted on the figures. From their position, it almost seemed as though the one at the front was fleeing the other. She watched the pair run until they disappeared from view. It was the first time she had seen anybody on the moors other than sheep and cattle—

She looked back to the road and slammed on her brakes. The vehicle screeched as it skidded towards the edge of the road, narrowly missing the animals in the centre. The world seemed to spin as her car lurched to a stop. Amy groaned as she released her grip on the wheel. She blinked hard, trying to clear her distorted vision. She didn't feel hurt, nor could she identify any visible injuries as she examined herself in the mirror.

She turned in her seat. The fox remained where it was, undaunted by the near-fatal collision. It stared at Amy for a few seconds before burying its head back into the sheep's carcass. Tufts of wool littered the road, and a crimson trail showed it had been dragged. Wide areas of ribcage and bone had been exposed. The fox tore a section of neck away from its prey and looked back at Amy. It chewed the gristly meat, fixing her with an unblinking stare. Amy shuddered.

The animal didn't seem to notice her starting the car. It turned back to its meal, tearing off another morsel. Amy drove ahead, giving the fox a wide berth. She checked the rear-view mirror one more time as she continued her journey. The fox stared after her, watching as she drove into the distance.

6

A metallic clatter filled Frank's cell, rousing him from his slumber. He squinted towards the source of the noise as his eyes tried to adjust to the light. With his blurred vision, he could just make out a small bowl that had been left on the floor. He staggered to his feet, wincing as the pain in his arm resurfaced. Events of the previous night swarmed around his mind as he made his way over to his breakfast. He wondered what had happened to Gus and his thugs, how long Henderson had left to live after the stunt he'd pulled, and whether the kid he'd fought was in a stable condition or buried outside in the recreation yard. He almost hoped for the latter. The kid would be in for a rough time if Henderson were to get his hands on him.

He stooped down and picked up the porridge. The bowl was cool to the touch, and its contents were even worse than the rations he had consumed in the army. He pounded on the metal door and listened for the approaching guard. A few seconds passed before a small, eye-level compartment on the door snapped aside.

"What do you want, Lee?" the guard said, peering through the gap.

"What the hell is this?"

"Sorry, bacon and eggs are only for the obedient cons. Troublemakers like you get standard-issue gruel."

The guard chuckled as he snapped the tiny door closed. Frank listened to his footsteps down the hallway before looking back at the bowl of grey sludge. A small air bubble had formed on top of the mixture, gradually easing the lumps aside. It popped after a few seconds, sending ripples through the murky liquid. Dropping the bowl in disgust, Frank returned to his bunk.

The segregation unit was designed to punish inmates for stepping out of line. But keep them in too long and it served as a torture device, destroying their mind until they went insane. Frank wondered how long Henderson planned to keep him locked away. Not giving the guard what he wanted usually had drastic consequences. He half expected to spend the rest of his sentence staring at the same four walls.

A roar from down the hall made Frank smirk.

"I told you I'm not eating that shit!"

He strained his ears, listening to the rest of Gus Razor's tirade.

"I don't care what Henderson said! I want my fry-up and newspaper in five minutes or I'll be using your bollocks as castanets!"

The guard must have declined, as moments later a clattering sound met Frank's ears. He imagined the plastic porridge bowl hurtling through the air and colliding with the observation panel on the door.

Silence descended on the wing once more. What would be the consequences of such an action? How could they punish a con beyond putting him in the seg? What else could they do? Since it was Gus Razor, not a lot. The gangland boss had nearly every screw under his thumb. Apart from leaving, Gus could do whatever he wanted, which made it even more surprising that Henderson had ordered him into the cooler. Segregation was the one area that Gus Razor had never found himself in, and he clearly didn't take kindly to being there.

Frank closed his eyes and tried to think of something to keep his mind occupied for the duration of his stay. He journeyed back to his childhood: the acres of farmland, the calls of various animals, the sweat and toil of labouring with his father, and the mouth-watering reward of dinner at the end of the day. For as long as he could remember, he had always worked on the farm. Even from the moment he could walk, he had helped herd the chickens back into their pen. It was only once he had hit early adolescence that he decided on a different path.

His father had originally expressed disappointment at his decision to join the army. He had intended Frank to take over the farm. But, after lengthy discussions, he had wished him well before his departure at sixteen.

The horrifying sights Frank had witnessed during his service quickly replaced the heart-warming images of his farmyard upbringing. He had trained for two years, enjoying every minute of his military lifestyle, until, at eighteen, they sent him to fight in Iraq. It was an ordeal he would never forget.

Twelve men he'd trained alongside were killed in the first week, some right in front of him. He could still smell the mud, chemicals, and excrement, and hear the deafening blasts that came from all around. He saw one man's head exploding inches from where he stood, and another whose entire right side was obliterated in a cloud of blood, flesh, and entrails.

A slamming door made Frank sit bolt upright. His body trembled and his clothes were sodden with sweat.

Shit! How long was I asleep?

Trying to control his ragged breaths, he sat on the end of the bed and listened once again as raised voices filled the wing. He heard a series of metallic snaps as the viewing panels were pushed aside on every door. Frank listened as the guards got closer, trying to decipher what they were saying. Eventually, the beady eye of Barry Henderson peered into his cell.

"It must be the meat." Henderson turned to someone standing beside him. "These arseholes are fine."

"That's what you get for serving ungraded pork, Henderson," Frank yelled at the disgruntled guard. A howl of laughter came from the cells back down the corridor.

"You tell him, Frankie!" Gus Razor chuckled.

"Shut it, Lee. Or I'll bury you right next to that kid you killed."

Frank felt a knot develop in the pit of his stomach. So the kid *had* died. He knew the impact had caught the teenager off guard, but he never thought it would kill him. He looked down at the ground through his trembling hands, something which seemed to delight the smug guard.

"Oh, so you do have a conscience?" Henderson sneered. "Where was that when you killed your wife?"

The comment was too much for Frank to handle. He jumped to his feet and slammed against the metal door, causing Henderson to jump back.

"Easy, Lee," Henderson said. "The in-patient beds might be full to bursting with all those sick dogs, but I'll still beat you within an inch of your life!"

"Try it!"

Frank fixed his eyes on the guard. Henderson looked away and turned to his silent companion.

"C'mon, McAllister, let's leave these scumbags to rot."

He made his way down the corridor, duly followed by the second guard. A few of the inmates jeered at the pair as they passed, but all Frank could do was stare after them until they were out of sight. He returned to his bunk, his conscience at war with his brain. With the teenager dead, that meant he'd murdered two people, three if he counted the hit he'd arranged through Gus Razor. *Nice going, Frank.*

He examined his small enclosure. Scrawls from previous inmates covered the white walls. He tried to estimate how many prisoners had sat there before him. He knew the majority showed no remorse for their crimes. In fact, most would still murder, rape, and torture if they were released. People like that should never be let out. *People like me*. He looked down at his hands again, only this time he could see his wife's blood dripping from them. He could see her mutilated corpse lying face-down on their marital bed. She was naked, her body glistening with sweat and blood. He felt rage burn in his stomach again. Adrenaline coursed through his body. He clenched his teeth as he relived her murder, feeling a sense of elation wash over him as he struck her again and again. The bloodied hammer had clumps of hair and flesh stuck to the side, something he had only noticed in hindsight.

He jumped to his feet and approached the wall, eager to expel the massacre in his mind's eye. He read the untidy scrawls. Most were made up of pornographic sketches and obscene words. There were some terms, however, that caught his eye: '*Bless me O' Lord for I have sinned*', '*Help me God*', and '*Forgive me*'. The religious sentiments took him by surprise. During his stay at the prison, he had witnessed many inmates spouting religious drivel. But they usually reserved their pleading for salvation in front of authoritative figures. Given the choice, the majority would rather worship Satan, Loki, or the seventy-two Spirits of Solomon than revere a divine god. Yet, many believed the appeal board would more likely consider a prisoner reformed if he had embraced religion.

Frank traced his finger over the paintwork, checking for other religious quotes. There were more, many written in a different hand. He sat back on his bunk. He had never expected any of the prisoners to seek redemption, even in the confines of their cell. Segregation was just that: being alone. If these prisoners were still pleading for forgiveness when nobody was around, perhaps they weren't as bad as he first assumed. He sat back and stared at the ceiling, all the while mulling over the possibility of convicts repenting for their crimes. He found it hard to take in. Nobody he had met so far in the prison had shown any remorse.

"Soup's up, ladies!" a guard yelled down the corridor.

A crescendo of unlocking doors echoed through the silent confines. Frank looked up as his door opened. Henderson entered the cell holding a plastic bowl and wearing an enormous grin.

"What're you so happy about?" Frank asked, as the guard stopped beside his bed.

"Some of the boys in the in-patient beds are dying."

"What?"

"Oh yeah, looks like a bad case of food poisoning."

"Food poisoning?"

"Okay, a *very* bad case of food poisoning," Henderson said. "Let's just hope it's nothing to do with the meat."

Frank eyed the bowl warily as the guard lowered it to the floor.

"Chicken soup. Cold, of course. We don't want to waste any energy on you troublemakers, do we?"

"Probably tastes like shit, anyway."

Frank lay back on his mattress and stared at the ceiling. From the corner of his eye, he saw Henderson stoop down. A hocking sound filled the room as he spat in the bowl.

"There's a bit of spice for you."

Henderson winked as he left the cell, slamming the door behind him. Frank sighed and closed his eyes, listening as the guard walked away. A few seconds passed, then another disturbance started.

"I'm not eating this shit!" Gus Razor bellowed.

A splattering sound accompanied a round of indignant cursing. Another guard had experienced one of Razor's tantrums.

"You can clean this shit up," the guard yelled, his voice youthful and faltering.

"Do I look like a fucking housewife?"

"You're gonna regret that!"

"C'mon boy, that soup isn't going to clean itself up. Mop and bucket, on your way!"

The laughter and ridicule of the prisoners followed the young guard as he stormed away.

The sound of dull footsteps indicated a second guard walking down the corridor.

"Hey, McAllister, how come you haven't battered that prick Henderson yet?" one prisoner shouted. The footsteps stopped outside Frank's cell and the door flew open, revealing the hulking form of McAllister.

"What d'ya want?" Frank asked as the guard entered the cell.

"Henderson's got it in for you."

"Tell me something I don't know."

"You didn't kill the kid, Henderson did."

Frank stared at the guard with wide eyes.

"What?"

"I'm telling you something you don't know. Right after they took you away, he dragged the kid out to the rec yard and caved his head in."

"Are you sure?"

"Yup. He made me dig the grave."

Frank fell silent for a moment. "And why are you telling me this?"

"Because we're not all corrupt. Some of us know exactly what Henderson's like and we want rid of him."

"Then why don't you report him?"

"It's not that easy. He's got enough people scared of him; he'll always have an alibi."

"So what do you want me to do about it? Who the hell is gonna believe a con?"

"Nobody."

Frank frowned. "So why bother telling me?"

"Like I said, he's got it in for you. I don't know how, I don't know when, but he *will* find a way of getting rid of you. You may want to consider a pre-emptive strike, so to speak."

Frank massaged his temple, the gravity of his predicament starting to become clear.

"Here," McAllister said, reaching into his pocket for a protein bar. "I doubt you're going to eat that shit." He pointed at the bowl of spoiled soup.

Without waiting for Frank to respond, he threw the snack onto the bed and closed the door. The guard stopped every so often on his way back down the corridor.

"It's about fucking time," Gus said. "Nice one, McAllister."

"Oh yes! You legend," another yelled.

Frank grabbed the protein bar and tore away the wrapping. The sugary aroma had barely met his nose before he shovelled it into his mouth. He chewed mightily, savouring its sweet taste. The flavour lingered, and he longed for more, but knew he had to be thankful for the rations. Henderson was a first-class prick, but McAllister seemed to be one of the few screws the inmates could tolerate.

Frank lay back on his bunk, listening to the appreciation of the other cons: their cheers of gratitude and moans of fulfilment.

Soon, the inmates became silent once more. Frank despised the still atmosphere. His nightmares resurfaced, and with nothing to distract him, they lingered. He ignored his wife's pleas for mercy and turned on his side. Once again, several scrawls zigzagged across the wall. Some had been written in ink, whilst others were carved into the paintwork. Frank read them with interest. Many more sexual statements were present, as were the crude drawings. As he looked closer, he found a gem of a list, hidden amongst the artwork.

'1987 Andy Emerson, strangled a prostitute. She charged extra'

'1988 Simon Reaves, merded a famly, I am sory'

'1988 Paddy Glover, raped two girls and killed a third. I should be dead.'

'1988 Jimbo Smith, cut up nine bimbos, they only found three.'

'1990 Charlie Robson, killed my father and stepmother, God forgive me.'

The list continued halfway down the wall, all in the same format. It made Frank feel better reading the crimes committed by past inmates. Although he was right in his earlier assumptions, the scumbags seemed almost like friends. He read on until he came to the last entry:

'2002 David Anderson, shot four men and two died, I'm so sorry.'

The names meant nothing to Frank. The prison housed over six hundred inmates, with countless being transferred in and out since he'd been there. Reading the line gave Frank an uncontrollable urge to contribute. He rose from his bunk and glanced down at the bowl of soup. The lumps of meat swam lazily in the yellow water, the green gob of sputum floating in the centre. He eased the spoon out of the bowl, careful to avoid the phlegm, which drifted dangerously close to the utensil. Once clear, he wiped the remaining drops of soup onto his blanket and approached the wall. The paintwork broke away effortlessly as he carved his line at the next available space. After he had finished, he sat back to admire his input. He had made his mark on the prison, and if he were ever released, there would always be a memory of him within the walls.

He grinned as he read his contribution:

'2004 Frank Lee, butchered my wife with a hammer, she deserved every strike.'

7

Cranston was bustling with activity. Everywhere she looked, Amy saw excited crowds milling about. Police cars made their presence known by their blinking red and blue lights, and it was only as she approached the barricade she found the source of the commotion.

Past the barrier, a multitude of medical personnel were attempting to revive a lone figure in the middle of the road. A bus driver was being questioned next to his vehicle. The underside of the bus was dripping with blood, a trail of which also glistened on the road, a sign of how far the huge vehicle had dragged the body. Amy tore her gaze from the scene as a police officer motioned for her to perform a U-turn. She complied, and drove back the way she had come, taking an alternate route home.

The detour added only a couple of minutes to her journey, but Amy was glad when she arrived home. She swung the car door wide and stepped out into the warm summer air. A pleasant smell of geraniums and daffodils shrouded her as she neared the house. Norman Collins stood in the neighbouring garden, spraying a multitude of flowers with a hosepipe. He raised a hand in greeting as she approached her front door.

"Afternoon, Amy."

"Good afternoon, Norman. The flowers are coming along lovely."

"Why, thank you." He beamed. "They always smell beautiful during early summer."

"I must pay you to do my garden sometime," she said, as she retrieved her door keys. "By the way, how's your dad? Is he feeling any better?"

Norman's smile faded.

"No, he's getting worse," he said. "He can't keep anything down. I'm waiting for the doctor. I called a few hours ago, but nobody has come out to see him yet."

"I'm sorry to hear that. Do you want me to check him over?"

"You're too kind," he said. "But I doubt the old man would ever forgive me. He'll be mortified when he finds out I've called a doctor. He's a proud man."

Amy chuckled and nodded.

"I blame that meat he insists on buying from the farmer's market," Norman continued. "He's been under the weather ever since he made that beef stew!"

"Did he cook it thoroughly?"

"I couldn't tell you. I'm a vegetarian. I can't even go near the kitchen when he's cooking."

"You and me both." Amy laughed. "Well, if you need anything at all, you know where I am."

"Thank you."

A shriek in the distance caused them both to flinch. Amy looked in the direction of the noise, but houses concealed the source. She looked back at Norman, who grimaced as another noise reached them.

"I hope it doesn't escalate here," he said.

"Hope what doesn't escalate?"

"Haven't you heard? The riots might have spilled into Cranston. Some guy was causing trouble, attacking random people, just like everywhere else. I heard he was trying to bite people!"

Amy felt the knot in her stomach tighten as images of the massacre came back to her. She saw her colleague's lifeless eyes staring up at the ceiling as the cleaner tore into her flesh.

"I know," Norman said, reading Amy's look of horror. "I couldn't believe it. He was dragging people out of cars and everything. But apparently he was hit by a bus. My sister's there now. I've just got off the phone with her."

Amy clasped a hand to her mouth. She had witnessed the aftermath of the carnage, but if she had been any earlier, she might have been attacked as well.

"I wouldn't worry," he said. "As far as I know, the police have the matter under control."

Amy offered him a weak smile. "I'll see you later, Norman."

He raised a hand in farewell as Amy stepped through her front door. The air inside the shady confines of her house was cool. She sighed, feeling more at ease under its medicating touch. Although the demented cannibal was still fresh in her mind, she felt all the better for being in the refuge of her own home and away from the hospital. Just distancing herself from the massacre was a step towards recovery.

Dropping her keys on a nearby unit, she made her way up the stairs, glancing out the window as she reached the top. She saw her neighbour tending to a new patch of his garden, apparently unconcerned about the noise they had heard. She took a deep breath and tried to convince herself he was right. The police had had the situation under control when she arrived at the accident.

She headed to her room and slumped on the bed. The morning sun had warmed the covers, instilling a sense of drowsiness as it permeated her skin. Despite only working half her shift, she felt exhausted. Too drained to remove her clothes or even close the curtains, she drifted off to sleep.

She awoke with a start several hours later. The sun had moved position, but its warmth still lingered in the room. She was unsure what had stirred her, but decided against going back to sleep. If she slept through the rest of the afternoon, she would be awake until the early hours. She dragged herself out of bed, undressing as she made her way to the bathroom. A chill swept up her back, causing her to shiver as she started the shower. She ran her hands through her long brown hair, savouring the fresh touch of the spray. The patter of water hitting her feet eradicated all other noise. All except a distant, panicked cry coming from outside. Amy turned her ear towards the window. There was no further noise.

Ten minutes later, she felt revitalised. She stepped out of the shower with her mind almost free of the horrors she had witnessed. She wrapped herself in a towel and tied another into a turban on her head before heading out of the bathroom. The sound of her mobile phone downstairs split the silent atmosphere. Amy made for the staircase but felt the fold of her towel come loose. Catching its end before it fell, she wrapped the towel tighter and ignored the call. Whoever it was could wait five minutes until she got dressed. With that, she entered her bedroom and slipped into a pair of tracksuit bottoms and an old T-shirt.

The sun's rays glared through the open window, and it was only then she realised she had not drawn her curtains. She shot an anxious glance towards Norman's house and the window level with hers. Thankfully, his curtains were closed, with no sign of a voyeur. She looked down into the yard and saw he had finished his gardening and had started his other favourite pastime, sunbathing. She looked back at his house. A stumbling figure came into view, emerging from the conservatory. It was Norman's father. He appeared groggy as his faltering steps took him into the garden.

The ringing of her mobile phone stole Amy's attention. She bounded downstairs to answer the call. She located her handbag at the bottom and retrieved the handset from within. The ringing stopped.

"Damn."

A frown creased her face as she read the screen. She'd had four calls from the hospital and two from her mother. There was also a voicemail. Perplexed, Amy sat down and listened to the message.

"Hello, Amy!" The frantic voice was that of her manager. "I know you've been through a lot today and I'm sorry to ask, but we need you back here! People are collapsing all over the place, the agency nurses haven't turned up, and there's nobody to help at all! Please get back here as soon as you get this message."

The line went dead. Amy stared at the phone in disbelief. It had only been four hours since she had left. What was happening? Images of the crazed cleaner resurfaced. She massaged the bridge of her nose with her thumb and forefinger. Chewing her fingernail, she returned her mother's call. The phone immediately went to voicemail. With a sigh of disdain, Amy waited for the interminable message to end.

"Hi, it's me," she said, adopting a faux positivity. "I'm just returning your call. Give me a ring back when you get this."

She hung up the phone and looked down at her shaking hands. Returning to the hospital was the last thing she wanted to do, but with it being only her second shift, she was reluctant to refuse. With an agonised groan, she got to her feet and traipsed back upstairs to dress in more appropriate clothing. She cast a cursory glance out of the window and saw that both Norman and his father had gone. Making her way back to the bedroom, she undressed, this time drawing the curtains.

Things must have turned pretty bad for her manager to have asked her to return. The notion worried her. If the man she had treated earlier was anything to go by, then many people must be seriously ill. She examined her appearance in the mirror. The black leggings, T-shirt and cardigan were not as comfortable as her loungewear, but they would have to do until she reached work.

A gnawing pain in her stomach reminded her she hadn't eaten. With everything that had happened, food had been the last thing on her mind. She proceeded downstairs, making a detour to satisfy her hunger.

The kitchen was cleaned to an immaculate finish, something Amy had always dedicated her time to. She made her way to the refrigerator, conscious she had not been shopping in over a week. Despite this, she still peered inside, confirming the lack of food. With a sigh, she closed the door and glanced around her kitchen for another alternative. Being a vegetarian was hard for somebody living in Cranston. Most stores endorsed the meat of local farmers. There were few that catered to those who didn't eat animals.

The fruit bowl in the corner of the kitchen caught her eye. She chose an apple before leaving the house for the second time that day. The heat hit her as soon as she stepped outside. She made her way to the parked car, glancing back at her neighbour's garden as she passed. Norman hadn't returned. It was only once she reached the car she remembered she had left her keys in the hallway. Exhaling through gritted teeth, she retraced her steps back into the house.

Retrieving her keys, she returned to the car, half expecting to see Norman sunbathing. Yet, the garden was empty. She inhaled deeply, enjoying the sweet aroma of her neighbour's flowers, only this time, another scent invaded her senses. She inhaled again, deeper this time, trying to identify the foreign smell. It was almost like perfume tinged with copper, or daffodils tainted with blood. She stopped in her tracks and stared at the garden with newfound concern.

"Norman?"

Amy made her way to the bordering hedge and peered into the garden. There was no sign of her neighbour or his father. She looked over at the conservatory door and found it ajar. It would only take a few seconds to call in and see if Norman was okay—

A sound in the distance displaced her thoughts. A whirr of alarms immediately followed the sound of shattering glass. She looked out towards the town and saw two clouds of smoke rising in the distance.

What's going on?

She got into her car and reversed out of her drive as a scream pierced the air. She set off back towards the hospital, all the while debating whether returning to work was a sensible idea. It didn't take long for her to find the answer.

Reluctant to travel through the town with all the sounds of distress in the air, she opted to take the longer route through the country lanes. The first alarming sight she encountered was the ravaged corpse of a cow along the side of the road. She tried not to look as she veered around the animal, but she couldn't help but notice the savagery of its demise. Huge craters in its flesh exposed ribcage and parts of its skull. There was no sign of its killer.

The next concerning sight came as she returned her gaze to the road. The speeding saloon blared its horn as it raced down the middle of the lanes. Amy shrieked and swerved, narrowly avoiding a collision as the vehicle shot past. She fought for control of her car as it veered off the road, but the momentum took over. The car's spin came to an abrupt end when the driver's side smashed into a tree. Amy's head hit the window and it shattered, showering her in flecks of glass and rendering her unconscious.

8

Frank awoke to his second day in segregation. At first, he struggled to work out what had roused him. But after a few seconds of deliberation, the cause was apparent.

Gus Razor's poor rendition of 'Mustang Sally' boomed down the corridor. The other inmates cheered the crooner on as Frank groaned into his hands. He knew what effects segregation could have on a prisoner, but he had never expected them to set in so quickly. Yet here he was, listening to the most feared inmate in prison belting out the sixties classic. A guard's heavy footsteps were almost drowned out by Razor's performance.

"Gus!" It was the voice of the young guard Frank had heard the night before. "What the hell are you doing? Stop singing! Stop dancing!"

Razor ignored the command as he reached the peak of his song. Frank could only laugh in disbelief as the tone-deaf chorus reached his ears.

Hysterics broke out all along the corridor as Gus started his second verse. The only person not amused was the young guard.

"I'm warning you, Gus! Shut up or I'll come in there and silence you!"

The singing continued, with no heed paid to the guard's warning. Frank heard a rattling of keys as the guard opened Razor's door. The singing stopped as a loud thud sounded down the corridor. After a few muffled thumps, Gus Razor's voice boomed louder than ever with his second chorus. He made his way along the corridor, jingling a set of keys merrily as he went. Frank sat up, listening as all the doors were opened.

"Nice one, Gus!" the prisoners exclaimed as Gus released them, and he eventually made his way to Frank's cell.

"Rise and shine, Frankie." He grinned through the viewing compartment. "Fancy a walk?"

"Why? We'll only get banged up again in a few minutes."

"True, but don't you want to see something other than these four walls?"

"I rather like these walls," Frank retorted, looking around at the scrawls on the white paint.

"Well, I'll still open the door. Feel free to leave if your big head can fit through." With a rattle of keys, Frank's door swung wide. He regarded Gus with raised eyebrows. He looked haggard. His greying hair was unkempt, and the bags under his eyes were darker than ever.

"Henderson's gonna have your balls for this," Frank said, as Gus twirled the key chain around his finger.

"You let me deal with Henderson."

Gus left the cell and went to join the rest of the prisoners. Frank heard them laughing and joking at the end of the corridor. He hesitated for a moment and stepped out. The rest of the men had convened at the barred gates at the end of the hall. Frank slowly walked over, aware they were being watched by at least two overhead cameras.

"So, are we going to break out of here or what?" one man asked, running a hand over his beard.

"Don't be a fuckwit all your life, Craddock!" Gus snapped. "This is a *high-security* prison. You can't just clonk a guard on the head and stroll out through the front doors."

"What's stopping us? We've got the keys!"

The gangland boss frowned.

"Have a word with this one, will you, Tony," he said. "There are hundreds of locked gates, CCTV at every turn, and enough guards to fill a Pink Floyd concert, twice-over!"

"So what are we doing here?"

"Waiting."

"Waiting? For what?"

Gus looked from face to face. "I just thought you boys would like to stretch your legs a bit. I know I didn't want to stay in that cell any longer."

"You know they're gonna drag us right back in there," Frank said from the back of the group. "Why waste your time getting into more trouble?"

"Well, truth be told, I was sick of that smarmy cunt staring at me." He motioned to his cell where the unconscious guard lay sprawled on the floor.

"And what else?"

Gus ignored Frank's question and looked back through the barred gate expectantly.

"So don't any of those keys open the gate?" one prisoner asked. His Polish accent was strong, distinguishing him from the rest of the crowd.

"Have you seen how many keys are on here? I can't be arsed to sift through them all. We'll only get a few feet before we hit another barrier!"

"Let me try."

"There was more chance of your boys escaping Auschwitz than getting out of this place, Zielinski." Gus tossed the key chain to the prisoner.

Zielinski ignored the remark. Catching the keys, he made his way forward.

The group watched as he tried five keys, all to no avail. He was halfway through trying the sixth when a rubber bullet struck him in the chest. The crowd backed away as Zielinski fell to the ground, writhing in agony. A few seconds later, an array of armed guards came bursting through the gate.

"C'mon then, lads, back in the hole."

Gus motioned for the prisoners to head back to their cells. Frank watched him curiously as he scanned the rabble of guards spilling into the corridor. Henderson was among them, yet Razor paid him no heed as he continued to search the crowd. Eventually, he strode over to one of the guards. Watching their exchange, he guessed it was the same person Razor had spoken to the previous night. He watched as Gus handed the man a piece of paper. Before he could see anything else, one of the guards grabbed him.

"Back to your cell, Lee!"

"I'm not gonna lose my way, you prick," Frank snapped, shrugging off the guard's grip.

"Get in there!" The guard shoved Frank into a new cell.

"What the hell is this?" he yelled as the door slammed shut behind him. He looked around at his new abode in disgust. Someone had pulled the bed apart, with blue foam strewn across the floor. The room smelled heavily of urine, with a dark yellow puddle in the corner. Frank longed for the homely environment of his previous cell.

"So, you ladies fancied an early morning walk?" Henderson shouted over the commotion. None of the cons responded, leading the smug guard to his next question.

"Where's Daniels?"

"Unconscious." Razor chortled from his locked cell.

"Well, that *is* a problem."

"Yeah, it is! Why don't you come in here and get him, Henderson?"

"No, he got himself into this mess, he can get himself out. If he dies, that's on him."

"You gonna bury him next to the kid you killed, Henderson?"

Frank's query caused a hush to spread amongst the inmates. Only the guard's ominous footsteps could be heard until he reached his cell. Henderson's keys rattled in the lock and he stormed inside.

"What did you say?"

He stopped within an inch of Frank's face.

"You heard me. You tried to make me think *I'd* killed the kid. We both know that isn't true, and I'm sure the governor would be interested to find out."

"You think the governor would entertain a piece of shit like you?"

"It doesn't have to be me, Henderson. Surely you know how many enemies you have here. All I have to do is let my mouth run and you'll have a major problem on your hands."

He watched with satisfaction as the guard took a step back, his lips forming a thin line.

"There'll be investigations," Frank continued. "Who knows how many more you've bumped off in the past. You'll probably end up in here with the rest of us. Imagine that, Henderson, being hated by the cons *and* the guards. You wouldn't stand a chance."

Henderson managed a smile and shook his head.

"Watch your back, Lee," he whispered as he left the cell. "You never know what might happen."

Frank ignored the comment and watched the heavy door swing shut.

"Someone get Daniels out of that cell!" the guard roared as he stormed out of the wing.

Frank was sure there was no weight to Henderson's statement, but he knew he'd have to keep looking over his shoulder for the next few weeks.

***

"Good to see you, Gus. Have a seat." Henderson motioned for the gangland boss to sit in the chair opposite him.

"What do you want, Henderson?" Gus asked.

"I want you to sit down. Don't make me ask you again."

Gus hesitated for a moment before taking his place in the chair. He glared at the guard through narrow eyes while McAllister looked on from beside the door.

"What do you want?" he repeated. "Don't make *me* ask again."

He watched as Henderson leaned forward, his hands clasped together.

"What do you think I want, Gus? I've invited you to this secluded place, in the middle of the night, with only McAllister witnessing what's about to happen."

Razor maintained his frosty glare as Henderson continued.

"You boys have been playing up big time; disrespecting me, the other guards, and you even got poor Daniels hospitalised."

"So you're going to kill me?"

"Oh, there will be blood." Henderson grinned. "Just not yours."

Razor's glare turned into a frown. "What are you talking about?"

"I want you to arrange a hit. You know everyone in this joint. I want one of them to wipe out Lee."

"Frank?" Razor retorted. "Why?"

"He's rubbed me up the wrong way these past few days; saying things out of turn, being rowdy, disruptive."

"You've just described every bloke in here. You can't kill us all, Henderson."

"I'm not killing anyone. *You* are."

"We all know you have your own ways of getting rid of people. Why ask *me*?" Gus leaned back in his chair.

"Since Lee killed that teenager, I've been asked certain… questions. Awkward questions I don't like to answer. If I went and killed him *now*, I'll be in deep shit."

"But if one of my boys gets caught, *they'll* be in deep shit. That's no incentive for anyone."

"First, you're all gonna die in here. You know this. Don't kid yourselves with early release or any of that shit. So, what more can they do to you? Second, I'll make it worth your while."

The guard reached into an inside pocket and produced a wad of bills. He placed the money on the table and pushed it towards the prisoner.

"Twenty grand," Henderson muttered as Gus flicked through the notes. "That's the profits from the drugs I took off you the other day, and a lot more. Kill Lee and it's all yours."

Razor sighed in dismay as he pushed the money back across the table.

"Sorry, Henderson, it's not happening. First, Frank is my best fighter. Second, he still owes me. It's bad practice to kill a man who's in your debt. You'll just have to live with Frankie's taunts a little longer."

He rose from his seat, satisfied at the look of indignation creeping across Henderson's face.

"Fine," the guard snapped. "I'll do it myself."

"Just try it, Henderson. You go anywhere near Frank while he owes me money, and McAllister will be digging *your* grave."

He glared at the guard as he passed. McAllister didn't make eye contact, but fought hard to suppress his smirk.

9

Joe Longmoor wiped a film of sweat from his brow as he stepped away from the corpse. His mortuary had become overrun with the bodies of countless patients. He had examined the most recent cadaver in the mortuary's corridor. He had known before he'd even looked under the sheet what he would see. All morning, deceased patients had been wheeled in, all with the same fatal symptoms and no apparent cause. As he peeled back the sheet, his speculation was confirmed.

A young woman stared through Joe as he removed his latex gloves. He guessed her cause of death would be the same as the rest. Her pallid skin was tight over her face, angry sores covered her body, and the blood vessels in her eyes had ruptured. He had worked with the deceased for nigh on twenty years, and in that time he had learned to repress any feelings of grief. Whether it was fear of the unknown virus, the hectic workload of that morning, or the promise of more bodies by the end of his shift, Joe could not decide, but his occupation was starting to get the better of him.

He wiped his brow again and pulled the sheet over the corpse. Hunger had set in, and he needed nourishment before he could continue his grisly task. With that, he left the corpse in the corridor and made for the kitchen. With his co-worker calling in sick, Joe had to examine the dead patients on his own. He had worked alone frequently during his time at the hospital, but never at a time of such dire need. If there were any more fatalities, the examinations would have to wait until the next day.

Dread merged with the gnawing sensation in his stomach. If he didn't eat soon, nausea would overpower him and he would not complete his tasks. With this in mind, he entered the kitchen.

The overhead lights cast a harsh glare around the room, the sterile surfaces glimmering as he retrieved his lunch from the refrigerator and sat at the table. Various magazines lay scattered on the surface, most of which had been there for the past six months. Few people ate in the kitchen during their lunch break, opting to venture out to the canteen or the hospital café. Yet, Joe had always preferred to eat his meals in the comfort of the mortuary. It made him feel more at ease to eat alone with the deceased, rather than face the living.

A muffled thud in the corridor disturbed the solitude of the morgue. Joe put down his sandwich and gazed at the door. The sound came again, only this time it was more prominent. A heavy slap met his ears, followed by a low groan. He rose from his seat with visions of an undead corpse shuffling towards the kitchen. It was impossible, but he failed to think of an alternative. The morgue was closed off to most staff, and the only living person in there was him. There were no windows, and the only way into the department was through a secure door.

The sound of shuffling footsteps drew closer. He glanced around, looking for something to defend himself with. He knew it was illogical, but something at the back of his mind told him he was in danger. The footsteps approached, getting louder and louder until they were right outside the door. But then the intruder passed. Joe exhaled deeply as the footsteps faded to nothing.

He took a slow, deep breath and crept over to the door. Despite his apprehensiveness, he had to find out who was there. With trembling hands, he gripped the handle. It felt slippery under his sweaty palms; he cringed as the hinges squeaked in protest. He stopped and listened again. There was no sound. He eased the door open and slipped into the corridor. *There's nobody here.* Upon inspection, Joe realised how literal his observation was. The corpse had gone. The examination trolley was empty.

Visions of a naked, shambling cadaver roaming the corridors filled his mind. He dismissed the idea. *Dead people don't come back to life. Somebody has moved the body.* He couldn't decide which was worse: an undead corpse wandering the corridors, or a twisted body-snatcher looking for an escape route. It didn't take long to find out which it was.

The rhythmic slapping of bare feet met his ears. Joe made to turn, but was seized in a fierce embrace. Before he could scream, a portion of flesh was ripped from the back of his neck. Now he found his voice. With a cry of agony, he whirled around, hurling his attacker aside. The woman's corpse screeched and lunged at him once more. This time he was ready and seized her head with both hands. She fought against his grip. Twisting her head, she ripped off a section of his thumb. Joe screamed for a second time as the crazed woman feasted on his flesh.

Blinded by pain, he shoved her aside and made for the exit. He could hear her in pursuit, her bare feet slapping against the floor. He knew he'd never outrun her. Cradling his injured hand, he shouldered open the nearest door. A rectangle of light briefly illuminated the area before he slammed the door behind him and the room was plunged into darkness.

The dead woman pounded the door, shrieking with every strike. Joe stood firm, using all his strength to keep the monster at bay. He tried to search for a weapon, but his eyes could not penetrate the vast darkness of the windowless room. At the back of his mind, he wondered where he had escaped to, but this thought was superseded by another: how was he going to survive?

Seconds passed and the woman's attempts grew futile. Joe tried to slow his breathing, but fear still gripped him. Worse still, the blood loss had started to make him light-headed. Finally, the pounding stopped and he could hear the zombie shamble away down the corridor. He eased the pressure on the door but didn't vacate it completely. For all he knew, the woman was still close by, waiting for him to leave. He fought the urge to collapse in a heap as he touched the scathed flesh on the back of his neck. He needed medical attention, and fast.

He put an ear against the cold steel door and listened for movement outside. There was none. Or at least nothing he could hear over the rapid beating of his heart. He closed his eyes and tried to picture his escape route. It proved difficult, as he was still unsure where he was. Replaying the scene in his head, it slowly dawned on Joe which part of the morgue he was in. The realisation hit him. He screamed as a sea of hands grabbed him, pulling him farther into the darkness. Joe had not found sanctuary at all. He had fled into the lion's den. As a dozen eager mouths began to feed, the door to the chapel of rest opened. A silhouette of the young, dead woman appeared before she joined in the feast.

***

Amy's world gradually came back into focus as her eyes flickered open. For a moment, she was unable to determine where she was. The crushed steel to her side seemed alien, and the silence had her fearing she had gone deaf. She moved her arms and flexed her legs. There was no immediate pain. She reached down and tried to open the ruined door of the car. It remained shut, hindered by the bulk of the tree. Amy groaned as the throbbing pressure in her head intensified. She clambered over to the passenger side and swung the door open.

The road remained empty as she stepped out of the wreckage. There were no signs of vehicles, people, or any life at all. Even the fields were void of animals. She looked back at her car and felt her heart sink. The entire right side had caved in. She felt tears well up in her eyes as she ran a hand over her hair. Her breath became ragged as she tried to compose herself.

She had two options: either call a breakdown service, or try to drive to work. Glancing back up the road, she saw she was close to Sunnymoor. As the hospital was on the border of the town, the drive would only take another two minutes. She reached into her pocket and found nothing. She had left her phone at home.

"Oh, great," she muttered.

With the decision made for her, she flexed her arms as she approached the car. The only pain was the relentless throbbing in her head. She leaned over the passenger seat and turned the key. The engine roared to life. With a sigh of relief, she slid behind the wheel. The scrape of metal and the patter of glass caused her to wince as she veered back onto the road. There was still no sign of any other vehicles; something which wasn't irregular, but was still unsettling. She put the car into first gear and trundled forward.

After a few minutes, Amy pulled into the car park beneath the hospital, letting out a long sigh as she shut off the engine. The prospect of venturing back to work so soon was daunting. She closed her eyes tight and tried to concentrate on something other than the wild eyes of the cleaner. She took a deep breath in an attempt to calm her nerves, but a distant shriek countered her efforts. Keeping her eyes shut, she took another breath, trying to rationalise the noise.

Another scream sounded, and her eyes snapped open. This one was closer, almost as if it had come from within the hospital. She stepped out of her car, into the vast, dimly-lit carpark, every sound bouncing off the walls as she strode over to the lift, a sense of unease creeping up her spine. She heard movement behind her. Jabbing the button to call the carriage down, she turned and scanned the gloomy confines. Nobody was there, at least not within the limited glare of the overhead lights.

There was no sign of the lift. She turned and jabbed the button again. Movement within the shadows caught her eye. She stared at the far end of the car park, certain the darkness had changed shape. She strained her eyes, trying to permeate the blackness, looking for a figure, a silhouette, anything. The concealing darkness remained in place, but she did hear a sound. It started low, almost like a drawn-out exhalation. It sounded like somebody groaning. But there was a longing to the sound, a hunger.

Amy flinched as the lift announced its arrival. The metal doors slid open, revealing an unoccupied carriage. She cast a glance back at the shadow as she stepped inside. It moved again, but this time it wasn't subtle. With an almighty roar, a figure leapt out of the darkness. Amy gasped, jabbing the button for the sixth floor, willing the doors to close. The man sprinted towards her from the other side of the car park, his staccato footfalls echoing around the enclosed space. He drew closer. Close enough for Amy to see the ruby foam spilling from his mouth. He bounded over the parked cars, eager to reach her.

"Come on!" she cried, punching the button again and again.

He let out a yearning cry as he cleared the last of the parked cars. He rounded toward the lift, his bloodshot eyes fixed on the terrified nurse.

Finally, the doors began to slide shut. The crazed man reached out as he neared. Amy stepped back, unsure if the painfully slow doors would actually grant her refuge from the lunatic. The gap was barely an inch wide when the man slammed against it. The impact caused him to stagger back, allowing the doors to close. Amy heard his indignant roar as the lift began to rise.

She exhaled, unaware she had been holding her breath. She watched the numbers above the door light up, one after the other. As each second passed, fear gripped her stomach tighter. The lift ascended past the fourth floor, where a scream preceded an almighty thud against the doors. The sounds diminished as the lift climbed higher but she could still hear the agonising cry. Her body shook as she reached her destination. With a prompt ding, the lift arrived at the sixth floor.

The doors slid open and Amy braced herself for scenes of bloody carnage on the other side. What she actually saw was a picture of normality, a stark contrast to what she had envisioned. The whitewashed walls weren't tainted with blood, the tiled floor wasn't encumbered with bodies, and the sterile air had no traces of copper, excrement, or any other aromas associated with death. The only discrepancy was the sound. Usually filled with the bustle of medical staff, the beeping of electronic monitors, and the din of chatter, the ward was silent. Outside, she could hear the muffled din of sirens. On the floors below, she could hear a tumult of shouting and screaming. But on this floor, she could hear only her thumping heart and faltering steps as she left the lift.

"Hello?"

She cringed at how loud her voice seemed on the desolate ward. The doors behind her closed as the lift descended to another floor. She watched the illuminated figures fall to number four. There, it stopped. Amy stared, waiting for it to move again.

A gentle clatter down the ward displaced any further notion of the lift. She turned and made her way down the corridor.

"Hello?" she repeated. There was no response.

She cast an inquisitive glance into each room as she passed. All were empty. She stopped beside one of the doors and peered into the dark room. The curtains were drawn. It was the only room she couldn't see into, but she doubted anyone was there. The clatter came again, closer this time.

Amy turned and made her way to the far end of the ward. *Where is everyone?*

She reached the nurses' station only to find that it, too, was vacant. A desktop fan slowly rotated, its path obstructed by an overturned computer monitor. It clattered against the obstacle again before turning back, expelling cool air to the rest of the empty ward.

Disheartened, Amy returned to the lift. Countless questions danced around her mind. Her manager had seemed so anxious for her to return, yet where was she? And where were all the patients? What was going on?

She looked up at the illuminated figures and saw the lift was still on the fourth floor. She pressed the button to call it and stepped back. The noises on the lower levels had ceased, at least as far as she could hear.

She tried hard to justify the strange events. Nothing made sense. Had the hospital been evacuated? If so, why? There was no evidence of fire damage or smoke. And *where* was everyone at? She sought a reason, but there was nothing that didn't defy logic. She pressed the call button again and turned back to the ward.

Nothing seemed out of place. The beds in the side rooms were unmade and the computer monitor was upturned, but there was nothing that evidenced a mass exodus—

A distant scream startled her. It sounded like it was coming from outside. Leaving the lift behind, she made for the nearest window. The view wasn't ideal, only offering sights of the rear of the hospital. She could see the vast, desolate moors and distant hills, but not a single person.

Discouraged, she resumed her vigil by the lift. Seconds turned to minutes with still no movement from the fourth floor. She pressed the button again. The number four continued its mocking glow.

With a sigh, Amy made her way over to the fire exit. She didn't like the idea of descending six flights of stairs, and even less the idea of walking past the fourth floor, but she had to leave one way or another.

She pushed the fire door wide and left the sixth floor behind. The air on the back stairs was cool, similar to that of the underground car park. A pang of fear swept through her when she remembered the lunatic. The stairs led down into the bowels of the hospital. Down into the car park. What if he was waiting? What if he came *up*?

She peered over the railing, into the abyss that led to the lower ground floor. The feeble light of the car park did little to illuminate the base of the stairway, but she could not see any movement.

As she made her way down, the silence was almost too much and she increased her speed. She cleared the fifth floor and apprehensively approached the fourth. There was no further noise, but she could still hear the screams in her head. She watched the door as she approached, half expecting it to be thrown open.

The cleaner appeared in her mind again. His eyes. His grin. She gripped the handrail as she reached the fourth level, her eyes still fixed on the door. The images were displaced by the man in the car park. The foaming mouth, the longing roar. She reached the door and turned towards the next stairway. Her fear eased its grip on her lungs and she exhaled deeply.

The reprieve was only short-lived. A fire door on one of the lower levels broke the silence like a discharged gun. The door crashed against the wall as a series of footfalls bounded up the stairwell. Amy looked over the railing, catching sight of a pair of men sprinting up towards her.

She made to flee, but stopped when she heard panicked, heavy breathing. The two weren't working in unison. One was pursuing the other.

She looked over the railing again. The pursuer was closing in. They had reached the second level and were approaching the third. Amy looked around for anything she could use to defend herself. But the stairs were empty. Within seconds, the pair would reach her. She made to turn, but stopped as a loud thud echoed from the level below. The man had been caught. A delighted screech bounded off the walls as a scuffle broke out.

Instinct took over, and without thinking, Amy bounded down and turned to the next flight. She found the pair clinched on the stairs, both grappling to gain the upper hand.

"Ben?"

She gasped as the security guard's face came into view beneath his frenzied attacker. Another noise sounded below as a door crashed open. With it came the squeak of rubber soles as more sprinted to join the fray.

Amy darted forward and swung a kick at Ben's assailant. She struck the man's head, sending him reeling down the stairs. She saw him land in a heap at the bottom before he was joined by others. A multitude of men, women, and children, all foaming at the mouth, stared up at the pair.

"Move!"

Amy yanked Ben to his feet as the crowd bounded up the stairs towards them. They ran to the fourth floor, where

Ben shouldered open the door. Amy followed, aware it was too late to voice her concerns.

"We need something to barricade it!" Ben said. He slammed the door shut and applied the thumb-turn lock.

Amy spotted a large metal filing cabinet down the hallway. It was then she saw the gore-filled corridors for the first time. Blood had spattered nearly every inch of white paint, while gobbets of flesh and muscle were strewn across the floor.

"We could use that," she said.

Not waiting for a response, she ran across the corridor. Ben followed, assisting her as she wrenched the cabinet away from the wall.

An almighty bang filled the ward. Their pursuers had reached the door.

"Do you think it'll hold?" she shouted over the wailing and pounding coming from the stairwell.

"I don't know. Let's just get it over there."

They shoved the cabinet, making slow progress across the floor. Yearning cries accompanied the assault on the door. They were primitive. More animal than human. When the cabinet was almost in place, Amy felt flickers of relief in her stomach. That was until the sound of splintering wood accompanied the banging.

"Hurry!" Ben yelled as cracks spider-webbed through the door. Amy pushed with all her might until the cabinet completely covered the wooden frame. She staggered away, gasping for breath. The hammering was still prominent, but muffled behind the steel cabinet. The blood-drenched corridor seemed almost trivial against the terror that lurked on the back stairs. She glanced over at Ben, who was leaning against the wall, struggling to catch his breath. Regaining her composure, Amy approached him as he mopped his brow.

"Tell me what the hell's going on," she urged.

"You don't know?"

"No, tell me!"

"Come over here."

He made his way over to one of the windows that looked out towards the front of the hospital. She joined him, peering out as Ben stepped aside. She felt the breath seize in her lungs as the scene of slaughter and destruction met her eyes.

Everywhere she looked, people were being ripped apart, dragged out of cars, or tackled as they tried to flee. Fires consumed overturned vehicles and even some assailants as they pursued the survivors. Standing on the fourth floor gave her a good view of Sunnymoor, and an even greater idea of how far the infection had spread. Plumes of smoke drifted high in the distance at various points throughout the town. Everywhere, it seemed, had succumbed to the bouts of violence.

Amy turned away. With an anguished cry, she sank to the ground, hugging her knees.

"How could this happen?"

"I don't know," Ben replied, glancing around the blood-soaked corridor. "But we can't stay here."

"I have to get out of here. I need to check my family is safe."

"Wait. Did you hear that?"

A clattering sound caused Amy to flinch.

"I don't think this floor's empty."

Ben's eyes remained fixed on the end of the corridor. She held her breath as a tiptoeing sound reached them from around the corner. Whoever it was, they were trying to avoid detection. Ben grabbed a fire extinguisher from the wall and pressed onward. Amy followed, her anxiety increasing with every step as the footsteps drew nearer. She looked on, prepared to meet the wild stare of a demented stranger. But the man that came into view seemed just as surprised as them.

"Terry?" Ben lowered his makeshift weapon as the older man recoiled.

"Ben?"

"You two know each other?"

"Yeah, Terry's one of the maintenance guys."

"I'm the *only* maintenance guy now," Terry said, cupping the back of his neck. "Keith and Trevor are dead, and we will be too unless we get out of here. What are you even doing here, I thought you went home?"

"I'm looking for my sister," Ben said. "She was admitted to the fifth floor this morning, but I've not seen her since they evacuated the hospital."

"Have you seen what's happening out there, Ben? Of course there's no sign of her. Half of Sunnymoor is missing."

"Which is why I came back here. This was the last place I saw her."

"How did you get in?" Amy asked. "We barricaded the door."

"The lift," Terry replied.

"You managed to call the lift?"

"No, I was on the floor above, I had to climb down."

"Climb?" Ben and Amy exclaimed in unison.

"Yeah, I obviously couldn't *call* the lift."

"Why not?"

"Haven't you seen?"

He motioned for them to follow him back around the corner. Immediately, Amy could tell why the lift wouldn't move. The first sign was the pair of legs jutting out into the corridor. As they got closer, she could see it was the body of a man, preventing the lift doors from closing.

"My god," she said. She rushed forward, but Ben held out an arm and stopped her.

"Wait!" he urged. "He might not be dead."

"Exactly, I can help him." She approached the corpse but found a gaping hole in his stomach.

"No, I mean he might be one of those things. He might get up."

"He's got a massive hole in his chest!" Amy said, pointing out the fatal wound.

"He might get up. They've been doing it all morning."

"He's got no insides."

"That doesn't matter!" Terry snapped, pulling her from the corpse. "The dead have been coming back to life. And we don't know how long this guy has been here. He could get up at any moment."

"I think we should move him," said Ben.

"You mean shove him into the lift?"

"Yeah."

"Wait, you want us to drag him inside?" Amy asked.

"Don't worry, we'll do it, c'mon."

As the two men set to work moving the corpse's legs into the lift, Amy approached the window. The carnage had finally ended. Bodies lay strewn across the road outside with only one or two of the lunatics lingering around. She wondered where the rest of the pack had gone, and how long it would be before they reached more of the population.

The two men stepped back as the sliding doors closed, concealing the corpse. Amy felt a brief sensation of relief to be free of the dead man. That was until the lift whirred into motion and descended.

10

The dull clamour of opening locks woke the prisoners. Frank, however, hadn't slept at all. The soiled mattress and overwhelming stench of urine were less than inviting, but it was Henderson's threat that had deprived him of sleep. He'd spent the night pondering what the guard could be planning. He didn't believe there was any truth to Henderson's statement, but as the minutes had passed, his torment increased. When he heard Gus Razor being led away from his cell in the dead of night, Frank's paranoia only intensified.

Despite his returning no more than half an hour later, Frank couldn't help but wonder what Gus was involved in. Was he being ordered to kill him to keep the heat off Henderson? Or was it more dodgy deals he was conducting outside the walls? The possibilities were endless, and it was only once his cell door burst open that Frank was given something else to occupy his mind.

"You've got some serious problems, Lee," McAllister said.

Frank shifted in his perch on the ground, the only portion of the cell not stained or tainted by bodily fluids.

"McAllister, why don't you take a seat?" He patted the soiled linen on the mattress.

"I think I'll pass," the large guard replied, leaning against the door frame. "Henderson's going to kill you."

Frank rose to his feet, shaking his head. "That bloke isn't happy unless he's surrounded by death. First the kid, and I'm guessing he's poisoned the lads in the hospital wing?"

"Mortuary," McAllister said. "They're dead."

"Dead?"

"Yup, the last one died twenty minutes ago. The mortician's van has seen more miles than a London cabbie these past few days. We've still got a heap of bodies waiting to be taken away."

"I bet Henderson's thrilled."

"I wouldn't concern yourself with them. Four of them were rapists, and the rest were murderers."

"And what do you think *I* am, McAllister? I'm hardly a fucking saint."

"Look, you need to watch your back. It won't be long before—"

McAllister's words were cut short by a distant agonised scream. The two men stared at each other when the pained outburst came again, louder this time.

"Now what's he done?" McAllister groaned. He slammed the cell door and ran to the end of the corridor.

"What's going on?" a voice called from one of the cells.

"Sounds like someone's finally had enough of that bastard cook." Razor chuckled. Frank turned his ear to the door. The shrieks of pain were chilling. And the roars? They sounded more animal than human. He had no idea what was happening elsewhere in the prison, but the chaos seemed to be escalating.

Then he heard the gunshots.

***

McAllister ran through the empty corridors as the hysteria intensified. He had no idea whether the prisoners were rioting or his colleagues were dishing out some severe punishment. He rounded a corner, faced with a guard running towards him.

"What's going on?"

"They're killing each other!" the guard yelled.

"Have you phoned it in?"

"There's no response anywhere!" he shouted, sprinting past his colleague. "We've gotta get down there now!"

With that, he vanished from sight. McAllister went to follow, but curiosity kept him rooted to the spot. As more gunshots echoed around the large room, he ran towards the end of the corridor and looked down at the carnage below.

He froze. Bodies were strewn all around the hall, with entrails and organs splayed across the prison floor. He had observed the cons fighting in this same spot, but not like this. Prisoners were running free, attacking each other as well as the guards. He watched dumbfounded as a group of cons overpowered one of his colleagues. The man screamed in agony as they burrowed deep into his gut. McAllister felt his body tremble. The crazed men chewed like animals as others lunged in, ripping organs from the man's stomach.

McAllister's heart lurched as he spotted one of the cons. Yesterday, he had seen the man sprawled on a gurney, dead. Now, he sprinted like an athlete, darting back and forth, ripping the few surviving men to pieces.

The corpse of one of his stricken colleagues began to rise; the gaping hole in his torso did not seem to trouble him as he got to his feet. McAllister felt nausea overpower him as the guard's internal organs spilled from the huge crevice, hitting the floor with a soft splat. The zombie, seemingly unaware, continued to stagger forward.

McAllister turned and ran into the office overlooking the hall. He seized the phone and dialled 999, his eyes fixed on the chaos below. He could barely hear the monotonous ring tone over the shrieks and wails of the prisoners. After the tenth ring, he slammed the handset down and scanned the printed list of contacts on the desk.

A hand slapped the window in front of him and he flinched. He looked up, straight into the bloodshot eyes of Andrew Hardy. The prisoner was still sporting the black eye and distorted nose administered by Frank Lee a few days earlier. The yawning hole in his neck was new, as were the strands of pink saliva spilling from his mouth. He regarded McAllister with an evil grin before striking the glass again.

McAllister stepped back as the man hurled himself forward. He feared the glass would break—until the prisoner stopped in his tracks. His head snapped to the side as another con ran into the hallway.

"Oh shit." The newcomer whimpered as Hardy raced toward him. McAllister watched the man flee, with the deranged prisoner at his heels.

"C'mon," he whispered, running a finger over the list of names. He stopped on 'National Operations Unit' and quickly dialled the number. The ringtone sounded again as he looked back through the window. There was nobody else on the floor, with most of the screams coming from the lower levels. His hands trembled as the ringing tone continued to torment him. Eventually, he slammed the phone down.

Cautiously, he stepped back out onto the walkway. He inspected the carnage once again, as somebody else joined the fray. The guard he had passed earlier entered the room, looking around in terror as the last of the survivors was brought down. Before he had time to react, one of the cannibals had attacked, tearing a sizeable chunk from its hapless victim's throat.

"No!"

McAllister looked on as blood gushed from the fatal wound. The crazed zombie paid him no heed and took another bite. The rest of the congregation, however, stared up at McAllister. After a shriek of excitement, they raced through the open door and out of sight.

"Shit!"

He turned on his heel and sprinted back down the corridor, producing his baton as he went. There was no sign of the lunatics anywhere. He didn't know what was happening, nor did he want to wait around to find out. He darted down a second corridor with only one room in mind. He needed riot gear.

***

Frank sighed in frustration. It had been several minutes since the last gunshot, and they were still unaware of what was happening. Had the insurmountable force of the guards finally been beaten? Or had the rioting prisoners been put back in their place? The rants and speculations from the other cons didn't help, as Frank desperately strained his ears. He flinched as the prison gate leading into the corridor clanged open. The cons fell silent as somebody approached the nearest cell. There was an urgency in the rattle of keys as Frank heard the first door swing open.

"Get out!" McAllister ordered.

Frank stepped back as more doors were opened. The guard was making his way down the hallway, releasing every prisoner in confinement.

"What the fuck's going on?" Gus Razor said as he left his cell.

"We've gotta go."

Eventually, Frank's door swung wide. He stared at the guard's huge frame in the doorway. Decked out in full riot gear, McAllister's ashen face was barely visible beneath his helmet. In one hand, he held a ring full of keys, and in the other, a shotgun.

"What's happening?" Frank asked, exiting his cell and joining the other cons in the passageway. McAllister ignored the query as he searched his chain for the next key.

"Hey, he asked you a question," Razor snapped, grabbing the guard's shoulder.

"The prison has been compromised," McAllister stammered, his wide eyes laced with fear. "Most of the guards are dead. Everyone's ripping each other to pieces!"

"Pull the other one." Gus laughed, along with the rest of the prisoners.

"It's the truth, Razor!"

"Bullshit." He smirked, but the mocking tone had vanished from Razor's voice.

Frank remained silent. The guard's sincerity concerned him. The idea seemed ludicrous, but watching the huge man tremble as he searched for the next key made him uneasy. A spirited shriek caused the men to whirl around.

"Shit, they're here," McAllister said.

"What the fuck was that?" Razor demanded. He took a step back as another screech filled the air.

"I told you, we need to get out of here."

McAllister opened the last cell as a wide-eyed guard lurched around the corner. His blood-spattered uniform was torn in several places, exposing gaping wounds to his abdomen. He quivered in excitement as he lunged towards the nearest prisoner.

"What the f—" the man started, but his words were cut short as the guard dragged him to the ground.

The group retreated to the back of the hallway as the zombie tore into its screaming victim. Blood sprayed the surrounding walls as it feasted, ending the dying man's cries in seconds. Their fearful gasps caused the creature to jump to its feet, observing the cowering group.

"Get him, Tony!" Gus said, shoving his bodyguard forward. The flesh-hungry guard ran at them with a piercing roar. Tony grabbed him, slamming his head against the wall. He snarled before the man-mountain struck again, clamping a giant hand around his head, and smashing it against the brickwork. A final crunch accompanied the guard's eyeballs launching from his head. The organs sprung out from their sockets like a grisly jack-in-the-box, dangling by maroon optic nerves. The eyeballs swung as Tony hurled the corpse aside.

"Good boy."

Gus approached the disfigured corpse. Brain matter and skull fragments oozed out of the eye sockets. With a look of disgust, Razor turned back to McAllister.

"Why the fuck didn't you shoot the bastard?"

"These are only rubber bullets," McAllister snapped. "I'd need a point-blank shot to do any serious damage."

"Then why don't you put live rounds in there?"

"This isn't an army base, you prick. These are only used for crowd control."

"Well, I'd feel better if we tried to escape with *real* bullets."

Frank looked on as the body of his fellow inmate began to twitch.

"Is he still alive?" Frank asked.

"No," McAllister replied. "He's one of them."

"What do you mean?"

"I mean, I've seen it happen already. You die, and then you come back as one of them. Have you never seen a zombie film?"

McAllister made his way over to the downed man with the rest of the prisoners in tow. Frank watched the twitching prisoner curiously.

"This isn't a fucking film," Razor said.

They stopped close to the dead inmate as McAllister aimed the shotgun at his head. The presence of the men sent the prisoner into a rage. He jumped onto all fours and eyed them hungrily. A high-pitched growl barely escaped his mouth before McAllister pulled the trigger. The man's head smashed against the floor, causing his body to convulse. The men watched, entranced, until the twitching subsided.

"We've gotta get out of here," McAllister said.

"Yeah? And go where?" Frank asked.

"We're evacuating, Lee. It's standard procedure."

"There's nothing *standard* about this, McAllister. How do we know the same thing isn't happening outside? There could be an army of them out there."

"Speaking of the army, where the hell are they?" Craddock asked, scratching his beard. "There's a base twenty miles away. Last time we rioted, you called them in!"

"This isn't a riot!" McAllister snapped. "This is... something else. Besides, it's been vacant for the last couple of months now."

"What?"

"Yeah, they've sent loads more troops out to the Middle East. It's left most of the garrisons in the country short-staffed. The one nearby is empty, as far as I know."

Another distant screech reached their ears.

"Look, can we get the hell out of here?" the Polish prisoner asked.

"That's the smartest thing you've said all day, Zielinski." Razor chortled as he pushed past the inmate. "C'mon, McAllister, you're leading!"

McAllister made his way through the prisoners until he reached the front.

"It'll take about five minutes to get out," he said. "Keep an eye out for any of those freaks. If anyone attacks, kill them without thinking twice."

"We're murderers," Zielinski said. "It's what we do."

With that, McAllister led the men out of the confinement area. Frank followed at the rear of the procession. Never in his wildest dreams had he expected to be evacuated. Never in his wildest nightmares had he considered the reason behind it.

11

"You think they're gonna use the lift?" Amy asked. They stared at the illuminated figures. It was on the ground floor.

"I'm not sure," Ben replied.

The carriage had been there for almost a minute, with no indication of moving.

"You still didn't tell us how you got here." Ben frowned, turning to Terry.

"What?"

"Earlier, when you were telling us how you got here. You climbed down the lift shaft?"

"Who cares? We've got bigger things to worry about. Like how the hell we're gonna get out."

"I care. If there's another way those things can get in, I want to know about it."

"I pried open the doors on the fifth floor and looked to see where the lift was. Luckily, it was trapped on this floor so I just lowered myself on top of it, and slipped in through the hatch."

"But if the dead are coming back to life, weren't you scared of the body in the lift?" Amy asked.

"I thought about it. But I figured the longer I wait, the more time the guy has to come back to life. So I went for it."

"Now all three of us are stuck," said Ben.

"So what do you suggest we do now?" Terry retorted. "We have no way of getting out of here and we're surrounded by zombies."

"Well, there are only two ways off this floor. We can either call the lift or take our chances down the staircase."

Amy didn't favour either option.

"Don't be stupid," Terry spat. "Both will get us killed. We can go down in the lift and die, or, we could take the stairs and die."

"You got any other ways off this floor?"

"Yeah. We can break a window and climb down a drainpipe."

Ben burst out laughing. "Now I know you're kidding. That might work for Amy, but I doubt the plastic drainpipes could support your fat arse."

"Fine!" Terry snapped. "Then let's just stay here and starve to death. Either that, or we could resort to a bit of cannibalism; those guys seem to like it!"

"Sounds good to me! Why don't we start by eating you, you fat bastard. You could keep us going for weeks!"

"Stop!" Amy yelled, jumping between the two men, who had almost come to blows. "We need to think clearly, otherwise we're going to end up killing each other."

"Fine by me," Terry said. "It seems to be survival of the fittest anyway."

He paced over to the lift and pressed the call button. Ben strode over to him.

"Survival of the fittest? You won't last five minutes on your own."

A prompt ding announced the lift's arrival and the doors slid open.

"We'll see."

Terry turned to enter the carriage, only to be grabbed by the eviscerated corpse they had disposed of earlier. Ben jumped back in surprise.

"Help!" Terry stammered, struggling against the creature's grasp. Ben lunged forward, pushing the eager corpse away from its victim. In a fit of rage, the snarling attacker whirled around. It ran at Ben, but was met with a forceful right-hook, sending it reeling into the wall. It collapsed in a heap.

"You got the fucker," Terry said, rushing over to the downed corpse. He booted it in the head.

"Terry, stop," Ben said, but he continued to stomp on the corpse.

"Try to bite *me*?" he snarled, through kicks.

"Get away from it!"

Finally, with the sound of cracking bones, Terry ceased his brutal assault, breathing heavily.

"I had to make sure it was dead."

"We don't know what kills these things."

"Relax, it's dead."

As if to mock Terry's judgment, the zombie lurched forward and tore into his leg. Amy and Ben rushed to his aid, kicking out at the assailant. Its grip on Terry was lost, and it rolled onto its back. In an instant, Ben stomped on its head. Once, twice, the third attempt crushing its face in. It was still, but Ben kept stomping.

Terry staggered away from the lift, whimpering as blood poured from his leg. Amy helped him to the ground.

"You're going to be okay," she said as he lay back on the floor.

She delicately rolled up his trouser leg. The wound was the size of a tennis ball and was close to the bone. She looked over at Ben, who was still stomping on the head of the corpse. Its features had been smashed into a bloody pulp, the skull shattered into fragments.

"Ben, I need your help over here!"

She took off her cardigan and wrapped it around Terry's wound. The white fabric instantly shone red as the blood seeped through.

"What do you need?" Ben panted.

"I need gauze and bandages."

"We haven't explored this floor yet. There might be more of them."

"I need bandages otherwise he could die," she whispered through gritted teeth. Terry's face had adopted a pale white hue, his breathing laboured.

"Okay, I'll go," Ben said. "Where will I find them?"

"Look for a supply trolley. I need gauze, bandages, and sterile water."

Ben rushed away, leaving Amy with the stricken man. She crouched beside him.

"Stay conscious, Terry."

"It hurts," he mumbled, his eyes beginning to falter.

"I know. Ben has gone to get bandages. In the meantime, focus on your breathing. I want you to take slow, steady breaths."

She monitored his inhalations, breathing in time with him as he began to calm.

An almighty bang echoed around the ward. The pair flinched. Amy stared at the barricaded door. Another crash shook it in its frame, causing the metal cabinet to rock.

Terry gasped. "What the hell is that?" He tried to look up as a third strike echoed around the room, louder than ever.

"Shit!" Ben sprinted past the door holding a handful of materials. "They're going crazy out there."

Amy tried not to listen as she gathered the supplies. She flushed the wound with the sterile water, causing Terry to hiss in pain.

"We're nearly done," she said, raising her voice over the clamour. She packed the wound with gauze and wrapped it in bandages. Satisfied the blood was no longer seeping through, she looked around the ward and saw an upturned wheelchair in the corner.

"Ben, I need that wheelchair."

He nodded and duly retrieved it before helping Amy lift the wounded man. Terry hissed in pain as they lowered him into the chair, but the crescendo of blows from the door drowned out his protests.

"We need to do something fast," Ben said. "The door won't hold much longer."

The door began to buckle, and the upper part started to crack.

"Fuck!"

Ben darted over and pressed his weight against the cabinet, using all his strength to keep the door in place.

"I can't hold it!" he yelled as another strike sent him reeling back.

Amy scanned the ward, looking for anything that might be useful to create a barricade. Her gaze fell on one of the many beds in the side room. Leaving Terry behind, she ran inside and manoeuvred the gurney out into the corridor.

"Move!"

Ben leapt aside as she slammed the bed into the metal cabinet. Applying the brakes, Amy stepped back to observe the durability of the barricade with the addition of the heavy bed. The door still shook in its frame, but the added bulk held it in place.

"We need to move," Ben said. "That barrier won't last."

"What do you suggest?"

"The lift," he said. "It's our only way out."

"No way!" Terry snapped from his perch on the other side of the room. "If those things are waiting for us down there, we'll be dead as soon as the doors open."

"You were all for the idea a few minutes ago!"

"That was before I got crippled by that fucker," he spat, pointing an accusatory finger at the corpse next to the lift.

Amy felt the tension rise again and for a second time she resorted to playing mediator.

"Stop!" she shouted, partly out of frustration, but also so she would be heard over the thunderous banging at the door. "Isn't there a way we can just climb on top of the lift and send it down? Then, if the doors open and a bunch of those things come pouring in, we would be safe."

"And suppose they *do* come in, we'll be trapped there," Terry said. "At least here, we have room to breathe."

"Not for long," Ben said. "In a few minutes, they'll be in here with us."

Not waiting for a response, Amy ran towards the lift and stepped inside.

"Hold on!"

She ignored Terry's outburst and glanced at the roof of the carriage. The hatch was closed.

"Need a hand?" asked Ben. Amy stepped aside, allowing him in. She watched him reach up and push the hatch.

"It won't open."

"Of course it won't open," Terry yelled. "It can only be opened from the top side. Otherwise, anyone could get in there."

"You said you climbed down?"

"I did, but there's a latch that locks once it's closed."

"Fine, we'll take our chances in the lift."

"Wait," he said. "There's a way you could get above the carriage."

"How?"

"You two climb through the ceiling and make your way over to the lift shaft. There's a maintenance hatch that will give you access to the lift. I'll wait inside the carriage and then just pull me up."

Ben almost managed a contradictory remark, but the sound of splintering wood stopped him. All three stared at the door as it started to come away from its hinges.

"Okay, what do we do?" Amy urged.

"Ben, stand on that desk and push one of the ceiling tiles aside."

Ben complied and scaled the desk. He reached up and punched a hand through one of the square tiles.

"They're foam! How the hell is that going to hold us?"

"You climb on the pipes," Terry said. "Look through the gap, there are loads of thick pipes up there."

More snapping wood came from the buckling barricade.

"I see them."

"Jump up, grab onto the biggest pipe, and lift yourself in."

"Will it hold?"

"As long as you grab it near the brackets fixing it to the wall."

"Are you sure?"

"I service these pipes, of course I'm sure!"

Ben nodded and jumped through the gap in the ceiling. Amy watched as he dragged himself up, his legs dangling momentarily before they vanished.

"C'mon!" Ben's voice sounded muffled above them.

Amy stepped over to the desk.

"Be careful not to put any of your weight on the ceiling tiles," Terry said. "They won't hold you. And don't put any weight on the middle of the pipes. Stick to the fixings."

The second hinge on the door broke.

Amy climbed onto the table. She looked through the gap in the ceiling and saw Ben's face appear out of the gloom.

"Let's go."

"I can't jump that high," she stammered, panic starting to surface.

"Just jump," Ben said. "I'll help you up."

A large gap appeared in the corner of the door. A dozen eager hands reached through, groping the air.

"Move!" Terry roared. His outburst spurred Amy into action. She leapt high into the air; Ben caught her by her outstretched arms.

"Gotcha." He hoisted her through the gap until she could feel the cool touch of the pipe.

"Pull yourself up, I'm heading to the lift," Terry shouted.

Amy wormed her way up through the multitude of pipes until she was comfortably perched on the largest one. She looked back through the gap as Terry wheeled himself along.

With a final crack, the door gave way, providing a gap big enough for the eager attackers to gain entry. The shrieks of delight screeched through the air as the undead poured into the room. Amy closed her eyes tight and clapped her hands over her ears; she couldn't bear to hear the man being eaten alive. It was too much. Sitting on the pipe for what seemed like an eternity, she hummed to herself to drown out the murmuring chorus below. She shrieked as a hand clasped her shoulder. She looked through the gloom at Ben.

"It's fine," he said. "He made it."

"What?"

"He got into the lift. The doors are closed. He's fine."

They listened to the sounds below. The zombies had found another barricade. She felt the tightness in her lungs loosen. Although Terry was an obnoxious old man, she was thankful he was still alive. Her relief turned to wonderment as a thought entered her mind.

"Why don't they just press the button?" she whispered, almost as if the creatures might overhear and take her advice.

Ben shrugged. "They've been at it for a few seconds and not one of them has pressed it so far."

Before she could question the intellectual capacity of their attackers, Terry's voice echoed through the shaft.

"Are you two coming to help me or what?" he shouted. "I can't stay here forever."

Amy looked past Ben and down their intended escape route. The crisscrossing pipes allowed little room for manoeuvrability, and she couldn't even see the hatch leading to the lift shaft.

"I'm not sure we'll be able to get across here!" she shouted back. "There's not much room to move."

"You need to get over here."

"It's fine," Ben said. "They can't open the doors. We'll get to you soon."

"Never mind *soon*. You need to get here now!"

"We can't see a way across yet."

"Well, you need to *find* a way across. At three o'clock, there's a hot water release on the pipes. You'll be burned alive in there!"

The pair cast each other a worried glance. Amy looked at the illuminated hands on her watch. It was 14:50.

12

The prison was filled with the gleeful shrieks of the undead and the screams of those they were feasting on. Gunshots sounded from a distance as more of the guards were devoured.

"We'll go above the hall," McAllister told the prisoners behind him. "It's a bloodbath down there."

The six men quietly rushed through the corridors, listening for any sign of the zombies. There didn't seem to be any nearby, at least none that could be heard. Frank glanced behind them as they turned down another corridor. The last thing he wanted, being at the rear of the procession, was to be attacked by somebody chasing them. He looked back towards the front of the group where McAllister stood, his shotgun poised. In the middle of the congregation, Gus spoke in a hushed whisper to Tony. The hunched man was nodding in response. Frank frowned. *Now what's he planning?*

"How much further, McAllister?" Gus hissed. "We're sitting ducks out here."

"Just over this balcony and then down to the fire doors," the guard replied.

He glanced both ways before stepping onto the metal grid overlooking the great hall. The rest of the cons followed, staring in disbelief at the massacre below. Strewn limbs, innards, and pools of blood concealed the prison floor. The macabre display served as a grisly memento from Frank's army days, memories he longed to repress. A shriek filled the air.

"There's another one," Craddock yelped as an undead con darted over the walkway. Frank strained to see upfront, looking past the countless bodies. The sound of the demented man filled the air as his feet slapped against the metal grid. McAllister levelled his weapon, waiting for the creature to get close.

"Don't be wasting bullets on this piece of shit!" Razor snapped. "Let Tony deal with it." He pulled McAllister aside. "Do me proud, Tony."

The colossus remained silent, his arms outstretched. When the attacker reached him, Tony grabbed the man by his shirt and lifted him off his feet. The undead prisoner snarled before Tony hurled him over the railings. He fell through the air, hitting the ground with bone-crushing force.

"Good boy." Gus grinned, patting the huge man on the back. "I think we should let Tony stay upfront with you, McAllister."

The guard raised his hands in submission and led the men onwards. Frank followed, looking down at the shattered remains of the crazed prisoner. His heart skipped a beat when four undead guards ran beneath the bridge. They exchanged a glance between themselves and looked up at the escaping prisoners. Seeing their prey crossing the walkway, they emitted a gleeful screech and sprinted through a door.

"I think we've got company," Frank told the rest of the group as they neared the end of the hallway.

"Where?"

"Four of them just went through the door down there." He pointed to the spot where the men had vanished.

"Then they're going to cut us off before we can reach the exit." McAllister groaned. "C'mon, we've got to be quick."

The men increased their pace as they left the metal walkway and made their way down another hall and around a corner, the screaming and gunshots getting closer. Frank looked on as Gus pulled Zielinski close, whispering something in his ear. Frank tried to lean in to overhear what was being said as they reached the top of a staircase.

"We're almost there, it's—"

The sound of hurried footsteps stole McAllister's tongue. Frank watched as he aimed the shotgun down, towards the source of the noise. The men waited, all staring at the foot of the stairway, hoping to catch a glimpse of any potential attackers. The sound came again, only this time accompanied by four flesh-hungry guards racing up the steps towards them. McAllister didn't wait for them to approach. As soon as they fell into his line of sight, he fired the shotgun. The rubber bullet struck the first zombie in the head, sending it staggering back into the others. He reloaded as the remaining three clambered over the motionless corpse and continued towards their prey. Another shot rang out as McAllister fired a second bullet.

"C'mon lads, there's only two left," Gus Razor yelled as the second zombie fell. "We can take them!"

He shoved Tony and Craddock forward as the remaining attackers reached them. With the prisoners farther down the steps, Frank could see the turmoil unfold. Tony grabbed one by the head, repeating his previous spectacle by slamming him into the wall. A crunch split through the air and the corpse slid down into a crumpled heap on the floor. The final zombie lunged at McAllister, only to be deflected by the barrel of his shotgun. Frank stared with wide eyes. The undead corpse was none other than Daniels, the scrawny guard Razor had knocked unconscious the previous day.

A right hook from Tony thwarted a second lunge at McAllister. The men watched as the undead guard lost his footing and stumbled into Craddock. Without warning, a high-pitched scream came from the prisoner as the zombie tore off part of his cheek. Chewing hungrily, the monster seized Craddock in a pincer-like embrace, dragging him to the ground.

"Fucking hell, don't just stand there, Tony!" Razor snapped. "Give the lad a hand."

The giant made his way over to the grappling men, just as the zombie's eager teeth ripped away Craddock's nose.

He screamed louder as Tony dragged the flailing attacker away. Frank looked on as Zielinski rushed to aid Craddock.

"Is that the last of them?" Gus asked, stepping over the two men and making his way down the staircase. Frank followed, watching as Tony crushed the zombie's head underfoot.

"I think so," McAllister muttered, reloading his shotgun. "How's Craddock?"

"Looks like John Travolta in Face/Off." Razor chuckled, stepping past the guard. "He'll live."

Razor looked down the corridors, which each led to a different section of the prison.

"He's dead."

Frank turned to look at Zielinski, who had joined them. The motionless body of Craddock lay on the steps.

"What do you mean *dead*? He only lost his hooter," Razor said, marching up to the Polish inmate.

"Yeah, and now he's dead."

"How?"

"I don't know," Zielinski replied. "He might've had a heart attack? Go and check him if you want."

"Tony, check him," Gus said, running a hand through his greying hair.

The giant strode over to the staircase as Razor spoke again.

"I can't believe this is happening. You lot are dropping like flies."

"We have to keep moving," Frank said.

"And what annoys the shit out of me is how we haven't found Henderson yet. I'd love to give his corpse a good kicking."

"He should be here," McAllister said. "Unless he's already escaped."

"I wouldn't be surprised if he's behind all this," Razor continued. "Seems like something he'd do."

A yelp of pain caused them all to flinch. Frank whirled around as Tony jumped to his feet, his hand pressed against his ear.

"What the fuck's wrong with you?" Gus asked as the giant man staggered down the steps. The answer came as Craddock lurched upright and twisted to face the group. He smiled wide, baring bloodied teeth.

"I thought you said he was dead!" Razor demanded, turning on the Polish inmate.

"He was!" Zielinski said. "His heart had stopped. He wasn't breathing."

"Well, he's tickety-boo now, isn't he?" Razor snapped. He turned to McAllister. "Are you going to shoot him or what?"

The guard aimed the shotgun as Craddock got to his feet. Blood oozed out of the gaping wounds on his face, rolling over his beard as he staggered down the steps. His mad eyes roamed over the group. He let out a shriek as he ran towards them. McAllister fired, striking him square in the head. Craddock stumbled and rolled onto the ground, only to be met by a barrage of kicks from the other inmates. Frank joined the assault, aiming at Craddock's head, stomping viciously until his corpse lay motionless.

"I still can't believe you've only got that little pea-shooter," Gus sneered, wiping his soles on Craddock's trousers. "You'd be better off using your baton."

An eerie silence descended over the wing, a stark contrast to the cries of pain and terror. Frank made to walk down the rest of the stairs, but was stopped by Razor's grasp on his elbow. He turned as Razor subtly pulled him closer.

"Follow my lead, Frankie," he mumbled. His lips barely moved, reminding Frank of a ventriloquist. He watched as Gus and the others convened around McAllister.

"Right lads, are you ready?" The guard looked from face to face. "What are you doing?"

Before he could react, the prisoners attacked. Frank stared open-mouthed as the guard was dragged to the ground. Gus pried the shotgun from his hands as Tony and Zielinski rained a series of kicks into McAllister's midriff.

"Gus, what the fuck are you doing?" Frank snapped, clearing the remaining steps.

"We're getting out of here, Frankie." Razor beamed. "That's enough, lads. Tony, take his helmet."

The assault ceased as Tony pried McAllister's helmet off. The guard chanced a look up.

"You're gonna regret that, Razor." McAllister coughed as he got to his knees.

"Suck it up, buttercup. You're wearing riot gear. It won't have hurt much." He aimed the shotgun at McAllister's face. "But *this* will."

"What do you want?"

"The keys."

McAllister reached down and unclipped the keychain from his belt. He tossed them towards Zielinski.

"I'll take those," Gus said, snatching the keys from the Polish inmate. "You got shot the last time you tried to open a bloody gate."

Zielinski remained silent, shaking his head as Frank spoke.

"We're just gonna walk out of here?"

"Why not?" Gus grinned. "This place has gone to shit. Now is as good a time as any to spread our wings."

"Where will you go?" McAllister asked from the ground. "If this is happening outside, nowhere is safe. No town, no city. You'd be fucked."

"The army base," Zielinski suggested. "We could go there."

"Don't be a tit all your life, Zielinski," Gus said, turning on the man. "How do you think it would look if a bunch of high-security prisoners came waltzing up to their front door?"

"He's already said it's empty," Zielinski replied.

Gus looked back down at McAllister. "Will there be anybody there?"

The guard shook his head.

"Zielinski, you're a fucking genius." Gus beamed. "We'll all go there."

"No," Frank replied.

"What do you mean, no?"

"I mean, it's a stupid idea. If this thing *is* happening outside, chances are you'll barely make it a mile. And that base borders Doxley. If the folk there are being eaten as we speak, what's stopping them from venturing out of town looking for more people to eat?"

The men looked at each other as Frank continued.

"And, suppose the base *is* empty. It's a *military* base. How are you going to get in?"

Gus eyed him angrily. "You're pissing on my parade, Frankie. Do you have any better ideas?"

Frank slowly shook his head.

"I didn't think so. We do it *my* way. Besides, it's been a long time since we've had any fresh air. A brisk twenty-mile walk in the countryside will do us good."

"You can walk, but I wouldn't advise it," Frank said. "It'd be best to look for a prison van." He watched Gus as he contemplated the option.

"Well, I suppose driving with the windows down is enough fresh air for me." Gus snorted. "Where do we find one?" He aimed the shotgun at McAllister again as he struggled to his feet.

"Down there," McAllister said, pointing down a corridor. "The garages are straight ahead. Go through that door, through the two gates after it, and there should be some vans in the garage."

"Thank god they deprivatised prison transport." Gus chuckled. "The government finally got something right!"

Frank stepped toward the guard.

"How do we know you're telling the truth?"

"You mean after you beat the shit out of me?" McAllister glared at the three men behind Frank. "You don't. I guess you'll have to trust me."

"You're not leaving?"

"Are you kidding? We've got over six hundred men trapped here. I need to evacuate them."

"Leave the nonces, mind," Razor said, pointing a finger at the guard. "They can die in agony."

"Where are the keys to the vans?" Frank asked. McAllister looked away before the barrel of the shotgun pressed against his face.

"Tell us," Razor snarled.

"There's an office in the garage. The keys should be in there. I doubt you're going to get far, though."

"We'll be fine," Gus retorted. "We've got this shooter and we've got Tony."

They all looked at the large inmate who was raking his face with a clawed hand.

"What's the matter with you?" Razor snapped. His query was ignored as Tony continued to scratch at his skin. "Behave, man! You'll give yourself a shaving rash."

A shriek sounded as a distant door was thrown off its hinges.

"We need to go!" Zielinski urged as the sound drew closer.

"Good luck," McAllister said. He turned and ran down the corridor, leaving the quartet behind.

"Let's get the fuck out of here," Razor said. He led the inmates down the corridor and through the door McAllister had recommended. It revealed a long corridor, divided by two gates, one at each end. Frank closed the door behind him and held it in place as Razor tried to unlock the first of the gates that obstructed their route. Frank held an ear to the door, trying to determine how close the crazed inmates were.

A series of wails grew louder. They were closing in. He kept his palms pressed against the door, certain it would be struck, but the crescendo of shrieks began to pass. It seemed they had followed McAllister. An advantage, yet he couldn't help but feel sorry for the guard. He looked back as Gus opened the first of the locked gates.

"Aha," he yelled triumphantly. "That's how you get through a gate, Zielinski."

"Hey," Frank said, still pressed up against the door. "What about these guys?"

Gus turned back. "Sounds to me like they've gone after McAllister. Quit messing about and get over here."

Frank sighed and left his post to join the others. "At least lock this gate behind us." He motioned to the first gate as he walked past.

"Tony, lock it," Gus said.

The giant didn't respond. Instead, he clawed at his arms, scratching feverishly now.

"What's the matter with you? Have you got fleas or something?" Razor snapped. The man didn't hear the remark as his attention turned to his crotch.

"Looks like cock pox to me," Zielinski said as the man raked at his lower body.

"Tony!" Gus yelled, hurling the keys at his bodyguard. The key chain bounced off his chest with no response.

"Tony?" He stepped back as tremors rocked the giant's body.

"Oh, shit, he's turning into one of them," Zielinski cried, swiping the keys off the ground and rushing over to the last gate.

"Shut up, Zielinski! He's right as rain, aren't you, Tony?"

The man stopped shuddering and looked up, fixing the gangland boss with a crazed stare.

"Oh fucking hell, he isn't!" Gus stammered, whirling around to where Zielinski was trying in vain to find the correct key. Frank watched from the rear of the group as Tony threw his head back and emitted an ear-splitting roar. The two men yelped in fear, dropping the keys through the bars.

"Zielinski, you tit. Get this gate open!"

Tony stared at the two men, a delighted grin spreading across his face. Frank watched them struggle with the keys. They were cornered and about to die. He had to act fast. Propping the shotgun against his shoulder, he fired. The rubber bullet bounced off Tony's back. He stepped forward, oblivious to the bullet's impact. Zielinski cried out in terror as the deranged prisoner drew close.

Frank exhaled as he dropped the weapon and sprinted forward. He leapt high, landing on Tony's back and wrapping an arm around his trunk of a neck. He roared, bucking and spinning.

"Keep it up, Frankie, you can do it!" Gus cheered.

Frank held on as Tony's bucking and jerking threatened to throw him off. Frank wrapped his arm tighter around his neck. After what felt like an eternity, Gus and Zielinski got through the barred gate and locked it behind them.

"Gus!" Frank yelled, barely audible over the roars of the undead giant.

"Don't worry, Frankie, this is just a safety precaution," Razor replied. "We'll let you in once you've got rid of Tony."

"And as long as you haven't been bitten," Zielinski added.

"Yeah. A bite off one of these things looks nasty. Try to avoid his gnashers."

"Shut up and do something!"

The giant slammed Frank into the wall, the impact forcing the air from his lungs. He held on, gasping for breath and tightening his grip until Tony could no longer shout out.

"Break his neck," Gus called as Frank was slammed into the wall for a second time. He felt his strength wane as the raging man continued whirling around the small corridor. Using all his weight, he lunged to his right, snapping Tony's head sideways. There was a clicking sound, but the zombie's frenzy continued. He tried again, forcing all of his weight on the other side. This time, Tony crumpled to the floor with a sickening crack.

"Good boy, Frankie."

Gus unlocked the gate as Frank rose to his feet. His body ached, protesting as he stooped to pick up the shotgun. With a groan, he turned and walked towards the pair. Once within reach, he grabbed Razor by the throat.

"Easy, Frankie!" Gus raged, trying to push him away. Frank shoved him against the wall.

"You left me to die, Gus. Give me one reason I shouldn't kill you."

"Touch me and you're dead."

Frank dragged him closer. "Yeah? Well, it seems like your bodyguard won't be much help to you now."

He looked over at Tony's corpse. His body was motionless, yet he watched the pair with longing eyes. Frank released the gangland boss and took a step back.

"Fuck me, he's still alive." Razor gasped, following Frank's gaze. "I thought you snapped his neck?"

"I did. He isn't moving."

"No, but he's still alive."

"Maybe you need to destroy the brain," Zielinski offered, peering through the bars at Tony's motionless form. "It's what they do in all the zombie films."

"Oh, don't you start with all that film cobblers!" Razor spat.

They fell silent, all staring at Tony. His eyes remained fixed on them, his face twisting into a snarl.

"Go and put him out of his misery," Razor said, nudging Frank's arm.

"Fuck you. As far as I'm concerned, my debt is paid."

"Fine, we'll leave him."

They made to turn, but stopped as a noise reached them.

"Do you hear something?"

The trio listened as the sound grew louder. The door at the rear of the corridor swung open, smashing against the wall.

"Lee!" Henderson bellowed, sprinting down the corridor towards them.

Zielinski swung the gate shut, hurriedly looking for the correct key attached to the ring.

"No, keep it open," said Frank.

"What? Are you crazy?"

"Do it!"

Zielinski opened the gate as Henderson jumped over Tony's corpse.

"They're behind me," he said.

"Good."

Frank aimed the weapon and fired as Henderson reached the doorway. The bullet struck his thigh, snapping his legs from under him. He screamed in agony as he hit the ground. Frank handed the shotgun to Zielinski and stepped forward.

"I'll get you for this, Lee," Henderson stammered as Frank crouched down beside him.

"No, Henderson. This is one thing you're not gonna get out of."

He unclipped the guard's baton from his belt and kicked him in the ribs. Henderson wheezed as Frank returned to the two men.

"Ready to go?"

"Not yet." Razor approached the downed guard as a high-pitched shriek came from the next room.

"Well, well, Henderson, it seems we have a bit of a situation here," he chided, as he reached into the guard's pocket. "You must have what? Ten? Twenty grand on your person? You can't walk around with that amount of money; you might get hurt!"

He took the wad of bills and rose to his feet triumphantly.

"Gus," Henderson pleaded, "help me out of here and I'll make you a deal."

"Sorry, Henderson, no more deals."

Razor turned and jogged back through the last gate as a horde of undead cons and guards spilled through the door at the end of the corridor. Frank locked the gate as Henderson began to crawl.

"No!" the guard cried out.

He staggered to his feet, limping back to the first gate. He slammed it shut before collapsing in a heap on the floor. Frank watched as the horde of zombies reached through the gaps, their snarling faces pressed against the solid bars.

"Lee," Henderson cried, desperately trying to rise to his feet. "Open the door, please! Be the bigger man."

"Oh, I am, Henderson! I'm being the bigger man. I'm letting *you* choose how you die. Do you want to be eaten alive? Or do you want to starve to death? The choice is yours."

"You can't do this!"

"Sorry, Barry. But like you said: karma's a bitch."

Frank turned and made his way into the garage. The guard's pleas became muffled as he closed the door behind him.

13

The murmuring zombies wandering beneath Amy unsettled her. She could see from her perch some of the disfigured men and women passing underneath the gap in the ceiling. Their expressions were blank as they shuffled about the ward, gently bumping into desks and chairs as if they were not there. They had been that way for the last five minutes, almost as if they had forgotten about their potential meal behind the lift doors. Terry had been silent for the same length of time. Amy longed to shout out to him, to ensure he was still conscious, but doing so would alert the zombies to their presence. Tearing her gaze away, she concentrated on Ben as he tried to manipulate some of the pipes.

"Any luck?" she whispered.

"No, we're gonna have to squeeze through."

Amy watched as he carefully shuffled back along the pipe.

"You wanna go first?"

"Not really," she said, looking back down at the wandering corpses. "Do you think I can fit through that gap?"

"You've got more of a chance than me. Just take it slow and you'll be fine."

She was not convinced, but accepted they had no other choice. She nodded, and wormed her way past him towards the intersecting pipes. The first gap wasn't a problem, and she shuffled through easily. It was the second gap she found troublesome. A thick pipe ran straight across her path, giving her the option of climbing over or crawling beneath it. She chose the latter, assessing it to be the bigger opening.

"Be careful," Ben whispered as she wriggled onto her front, wrapping her legs around the pipe. She looked down at the foam tiles below her. One wrong move and she would fall straight through them. She shuffled slowly along the pipe until she reached the gap. Her head fit through the space fine, but her shoulders hindered her progress. She wriggled as much as she could until she finally squeezed her upper body through. With a sigh of relief, she wormed her way over to the last obstacle and shimmied past.

"I'm through."

"Can you see the vent?"

She looked ahead to the metal grating.

"Yeah, but it looks pretty sturdy. I don't know whether I'll be able to open it."

"For fuck's sake, it isn't locked!"

Terry's outburst echoed up the lift shaft. As soon as the words had left his mouth, the zombies were at the lift door once again.

"Shit," he snapped, as the pounding resumed. "Hurry!"

Amy tried to find Ben, but the darkness and the complex pipeline restricted her view. She looked down at her wristwatch and found they only had three more minutes to escape. Her heart started to race.

"Ben?" she said, scouring the concealing gloom.

"What?"

His voice was close.

"How are you doing?"

"I can't get through this second gap," he said. She had feared as much. It was barely large enough to accommodate her small frame. With Ben's physique, there was no way he could pass.

"What are you going to do?" she asked, straining to hear a response. The pounding and wailing from the crazed zombies below made it difficult. A series of metallic thuds filled the air, diminished by the raging corpses below them. Amy listened as a hissing sound came from the pipe.

"Ben?"

The banging continued until the pipe finally gave way. Ben emerged from the darkness, shuffling under the last pipe. She reached out and guided him the remaining few feet towards her.

"Thanks," he said, easing himself upright.

"They're getting in!" Terry yelled, as an almighty thud reached them. "I'm going down."

"Terry, wait!"

Ben lunged towards the vent, the sound of whirring motors filling the small confines. He ripped the metal grill from the wall and disappeared through the gap. Amy crawled after him, emerging into the dimly-lit shaft. She found him standing on a small ledge, looking down at the descending carriage.

"Oh no," he said, helping her to her feet. "He's going all the way down. Those doors are going to open."

The pair watched the lift's descent until it reached the bottom floor with a prompt ding. Silence. The doors rolled open. The silence persisted for a moment longer before Terry's screams of agony shot up towards them. Amy jammed her fingers in her ears as the sickening sound of evisceration floated up the lift shaft, echoing all around them. Ben held a trembling hand to his face, his jaw clenched.

"There's nothing we could have done," Amy said. She kept her fingers in her ears, muffling the sounds of the grisly feast below. Ben turned to face her.

"We need to get out of here."

"Well, we can't use the lift now," she replied.

"I don't know, we still could." Ben pointed out a metal fuse box attached to the wall on the opposite side of the lift shaft. "I'm guessing the manual override to the lift is in that box. If we can get over there, we can call it up again and proceed with the original plan."

"I don't know, Ben." She crouched down on the ledge, biting her nails as she considered the prospect. "Jumping on top of the lift, then going through the hatch where there could be an endless number of *zombies* to get past. Even if we get out of the hospital, what do we do then? We'd hardly be out of the woods."

She looked up at Ben, hoping to see the same concerns on his face. There was no emotion, at least none she could decipher as he stared hard at the metal box on the other side of the shaft. Eventually, he spoke.

"Okay. Instead of looking at the big picture, why don't we just take each step at a time? Let's get down there. When we survive that, we'll consider the next step. Sound good?"

"It still doesn't explain how we're going to get over there," she said, eyeing the gap in front of them.

"The ledge goes all the way around, look."

The small ridge covered the perimeter of the tunnel. The ledge was less than ten inches wide, half the size of the one they were standing on.

"But that's tiny. We'd never get around there."

The look from Ben made her heart sink.

"No way," she said. "You want *me* to go?"

"I hate to say it, but I genuinely can't see another way out of here. I mean, I could try, but I don't think I'll be able to get around. You've got a better chance than me."

"No. There must be another way. How do the maintenance guys use it? They can't all be the same size as me; look at Terry."

"They use pulleys and cables."

Amy laughed nervously. "No. There *has* to be another way."

"Maybe we could go back on the pipes and find a way back?" Ben said.

"The pipes will be boiling now, and the longer we hang around, the more of those things there will be, waiting for us."

"I don't know what else we can do."

Amy looked down at the enormous drop before examining the small ledge again. If she put one foot wrong, she'd fall to her death. If she didn't do it, they'd die anyway.

"Fine." She groaned. "What do I do when I get over there?"

"Open the lid and look for a way to bring the lift up. It shouldn't be locked. Let's just hope it works."

"It'd *better* work. I only plan on making this trip once."

She rose to her feet and eased out onto the ledge, keeping her chest pressed against the wall. Gripping the corner tightly, she took another step. She took a deep breath to calm her frantic breathing, but the smell of oil, metal, and blood only exacerbated her nerves. She released her grip on the corner as she moved along. Resisting the urge to look down, she kept her gaze fixed ahead, her arms stretched either side. The rough texture of the wall scraped her skin as she made her way around.

"Be careful," said Ben.

Amy longed to utter a sarcastic retort, but her fear of imminent death kept her tongue at bay. She reached the first corner without looking at the vast drop below. As she progressed along the second wall, the urge became too much to bear. She looked back at Ben, and, seeing him staring down into the abyss, her eyes automatically followed. The drop seemed even greater now that she was suspended above it. She pictured herself falling, plummeting towards the steel carriage below. Her legs felt weak, almost unable to hold her weight.

"Careful," Ben said as she swayed into the void.

The fuse box was closer than ever. A few more feet and she would be there. But what if the contents of the box didn't control the lift? What if it was locked? What if, in her struggle to open it, she fell to her death? Amy tried hard to suppress the negative thoughts as she resumed her slow progression. Her deep breaths echoed up and down the lift shaft, offering a welcome distraction as she neared the final hurdle.

"You're doing great. Just a little further."

Amy rounded the last corner and made her way over to the box. It was then that she encountered her greatest challenge so far. Her breath caught in her throat as her T-shirt snagged on something jutting out of the wall. With her body pressed tightly against the cool stone, she could not see what she was caught on.

"What's wrong?"

"I'm stuck." She gasped, feeling her heart race. She tried to move back, but the wall refused to release her. "I can't move!"

"Can you reach the switch? If you can get the lift up here, I can help you."

"I don't know."

The control box now seemed way beyond her grasp. She reached out towards the small metal lid. Her fingertips brushed the side, filling her with a flicker of joy as she felt the cool metal. She tried to move closer, but the wall's grip on the fabric was unwavering.

"Can you open it?"

"I'm not sure," Amy stammered, her voice shaking from exertion. She stretched her arm as far as possible until her fingers slipped underneath the latch. With a flick of her wrist, the metal door swung open.

"I knew it!" Ben yelled. "There are two green buttons close to you. Press the top one and it should bring the lift up to us."

"I can't see," she said. "Which is the right one?"

She leaned farther, straining against the hold on her shirt. Eventually, her wandering fingers found a small plastic button.

"Is this it?"

"I can't see. Your hand is in the way. Just press it and see what happens."

Amy pushed the button and waited. The sound of motors whirred into action. Her ordeal was over. In a few seconds, the carriage would reach them and she could simply step onto it. Ben cheered behind her.

"You did it," he said. "It's coming up."

It was then that Amy lost her grip. She stumbled forward, the wall releasing its hold on her T-shirt. She let out a shriek as she fell, clawing to find a hold on the ledge. She heard Ben cry out as she plunged into the darkness.

14

A gnawing sense of regret ate away at Frank as the trio entered the garage. On the one hand, he was glad Henderson was going to die, whether it was at the hands of the zombies or slowly wasting away. But he couldn't help feeling he'd cheated himself out of the killing blow. The guard had put him through so much during his time inside. He felt it only right that he should have been the one to kill him.

"Right then, where's this office?" Gus said, making his way through the gloom. The windowless room offered no light to aid the prisoners. Frank squinted, trying to penetrate the darkness with his gaze. The wailing of the corpses seemed distant, yet he knew the room might not be as empty as it appeared. With this in mind, he remained still, listening to the fumbling of the others as they blindly made their way around.

"Haven't they paid their leccy bill?" Gus continued. "Zielinski, go and find a light switch."

Frank stayed in the doorway, twirling Henderson's baton as he listened to the two men, one on either side of him, as they groped their way through the garage. A metallic crash came from the right-hand side.

"For fuck's sake!" Gus cried out in pain. "Zielinski, you twat, where's the light?"

"I'm looking for it."

"Well, hurry up."

Frank looked around the room. He could make out two great shapes in the centre of the garage and an office to the right. He looked around and found a light switch on the wall next to him. He flicked the switch, protecting his eyes from the harsh glare.

"It's about fucking time," Gus said as light burst from the fluorescent tubes. He squinted at Frank. "Well done, Frankie. All we need now is sunglasses."

Frank walked down the small steps and followed Gus towards the office.

"Right then, where the hell are these keys?"

Gus swept a handful of paperwork off the desk before pulling out the first of two drawers. Frank turned to a board on the wall and noticed two sets of keys hanging from a row of hooks. Leaving Gus to his search, he took one set and made his way back.

"Are we off then?" Zielinski asked.

"I am," Frank said. "Gus is still looking for the other set of keys."

"We're not going together?"

"I'm not going to the army base, if that's what you mean."

"Then where are you going?"

"I don't know yet." Frank unlocked the door to the prison van and jumped behind the wheel.

"How the bloody hell did you get in there?" Gus garbled from the office.

"Check the wall," Frank called as he started the engine.

"Ah-ha. Come on, my little Polak friend, we're off."

Gus left the office and unlocked the second van before jumping behind the wheel. He rolled down the windows and readjusted his seat.

"So where are you headed, Frankie?" Gus shouted as the engine roared to life.

"Far away from here."

"Sounds like a plan. Listen, if you change your mind, our army base will always be open to you."

Frank nodded, rolling his eyes.

"As long as you haven't been bitten," Gus added.

"You're too kind."

Gus turned to the Polish man as he jumped in the passenger side. "And what do you think you're doing, Zielinski?"

"What?"

"We can't go until you've opened the shutters, son. Go on, on your bike."

Zielinski jumped from the vehicle, mumbling to himself as he made his way over to the chain pulleys in the corner. The way the vehicles were positioned, Frank would have to wait for Gus to leave before he was clear to exit the building. He sat back as Zielinski began opening the shutters.

"C'mon, put your back into it," Gus bellowed, beeping the van's horn. The Polish man obeyed, heaving on the chains and sending the shutters soaring high. Sunlight filled the room, blinding the three men and illuminating the hoard of undead as they spilled into the garage.

"Fuck me!" Gus roared. He put the van in gear and lurched forward. "C'mon, you soppy twat, shake a leg."

He sped past Zielinski, mowing down the crowd. The van bounced and jolted over the road of corpses, with Zielinski in pursuit. Eventually, he jumped onto the back step of the van, holding on tight as Gus made a sharp turn.

Frank put his vehicle into gear as the crushed corpses began to rise. He sped forward, cutting them down for a second time. The van rocked as he made his way over bone and flesh until the road of bodies was displaced by smooth asphalt. He followed Gus Razor's route and soon caught up to the fleeing prisoners.

"Took your time, Frankie," Gus yelled through his open window. "Where the hell's Zielinski?"

"He's on the back of your van."

"Cheeky fucker. I suppose I'd better let him in."

The two vans slowed, allowing Frank to take in the route ahead. It seemed to lead out onto the main road, which stretched far out into the countryside. The only obstacle between the prisoners and their freedom was a tall chain-link gate.

"What the fuck are you playing at?" Zielinski snapped as he jumped in beside Gus.

"What? I didn't fancy becoming zombie-chow."

"So you left me?"

"Hey, I'd rather give them some scraps of Polish dog meat than a slab of fine British beef."

Gus patted his stomach with glee. Ignoring the glare from his passenger, he leaned over towards Frank's van. "So where to now?"

"Through those gates towards freedom, I guess," Frank replied, his eyes fixed on the chain-link blockade ahead.

"Good. Zielinski, go and open those gates."

A cacophony of shrieks sounded from behind them. The zombies with intact legs rounded the corner and ran towards the vehicles.

"Or not," Gus muttered. He sped towards the gate. Frank followed, driving beside the van.

"Gus," he yelled. "You're not seriously going to—"

Frank's question was answered as the prison van smashed through the gates, hurling them aside. He sped after them, noticing the strips of tyre killers strategically placed along the road. For a moment, he feared driving over them. But as Razor's van bounded over the top, he realised they were a measure to prevent intruders, not escapees.

Before long, they were driving side-by-side down the country road.

"Do you know what that smell is, Frankie?" Gus yelled through his open window.

"Smells like you're pushing that van too hard. Ease off a bit."

They both slowed as they approached a bend in the road.

"No, it's the smell of freedom," Gus said.

"Smells like cow shit to me."

"Can you believe we're out of that place?"

"Keep your eyes on the road or you won't be getting much further."

"C'mon, there's nobody about."

"That doesn't mean the rest of the world is infected," Frank retorted. "I don't care what McAllister said. For all we know, it could just be the prison. A car could speed round that bend any minute."

They looked ahead at the turn in the road. The sheer silence made it unlikely that any vehicle was in the vicinity. Yet Razor sped forward and cut in front of Frank.

They approached the bend single-file with no other vehicles coming in to view. Frank listened, only hearing the growl of their engines, noting the distinct lack of sound. No other vehicles, no planes, no birdsong. Nothing. He scanned the fields on either side. The area was deserted. He looked ahead in time to see Razor's van brake sharply. He followed suit, slamming on the brakes and lurching forward as the van squealed to a halt.

"What's going on?" he shouted.

He looked out of the window and saw the pair jump out, walking around the front of the vehicle.

"Gus!"

With a growl of dismay, Frank shut off the engine and jumped out. He approached the van when he heard Razor's voice.

"She's dead."

"Are you sure?" Zielinski asked.

"Of course I'm sure; her tits are missing."

The two men stood over the corpse of a young woman. Her pale legs were smeared with blood, which had formed a small pool around her torso. The top half of her dress had been ripped open, leaving a mass of bloody pulp. There was a palpable trail leading from the woodland bordering the lane. Frank saw it as an obvious sign that she had either fled or been dragged through the forest and onto the road.

"I think this answers your question, Frankie," Gus said. "The crazy fuckers are out here as well."

He turned to walk back to his van when Frank grabbed him.

"If this thing has spread, then chances are Doxley has been hit as well."

"And?"

"And if that's the case, don't you think you should reconsider your army base idea?"

Gus shoved Frank's arm aside and made his way back to the van.

"Frankie." He chuckled as he jumped into the driver's seat. "That place will be fortified. Nobody can get in."

"Including you."

"We'll find a way, won't we, Zielinski?"

The Polish man shrugged as he got in the passenger side.

"If you're sure," Frank said.

"Of course we're sure," Razor yelled. "We've got this far, haven't we?"

Frank got back into his van. The engine roared to life as Razor made his way forward. His van bucked and swayed as he drove over the mangled corpse.

"You sick bastard," Frank muttered, giving the body a wide berth as he drove past. He looked back in his side mirrors and was sure he saw the woman start to rise before he drove out of view. Shaking the unsettling image from his head, he followed Razor around a bend and down another country lane. The trees on either side of the road blocked most of the sun, casting a shadow over the two vehicles as they drove on. The drive, although tedious, allowed Frank to consider the extent of the chaos. If the nearby towns were infected, what chance would he have of finding a safe refuge? He switched on the radio. The harsh sound of static hissed through the van's speakers.

"Shit!"

The pitch of the noise intensified as he tried to tune to a station, but he was unable to pick up anything else. Pounding the dashboard in a rage, he switched off the radio. Perhaps it was the trees interfering with the signal. He looked ahead as Razor slowed to a halt. He veered around the van and pulled up alongside them.

"What're you doing?" he asked, eyeing the junction ahead.

"This is where we part, Frankie," Gus hollered. "We're going right. The army base should be less than twenty miles from here."

Frank nodded, looking at the road sign ahead of them. Doxley was twenty miles to the right, and the town of Sunnymoor was fifteen miles left.

"You can still come with us."

Frank shook his head.

"So you're heading for Sunnymoor, then?"

"Nope."

"Then where?"

Frank fixed his gaze straight ahead towards the open fields bordered by a brick wall. He began to rev his engine. He could see Razor in the corner of his eye, regarding him curiously.

"You're not going cross-country?"

"There won't be any people on the moors," Frank said. "At least not as many as the towns."

He revved louder.

"That's hardly a Land Rover you're driving," Razor yelled. "Where are you going to go? A couple of miles in and set up camp?"

"The moors are filled with isolated farms, Gus. I figure it's less likely they've been affected."

"You're crazy. I bet you a score you don't make it through that field."

"And I bet you the same you don't make it through the night."

A smile slowly spread across Razor's face.

"You're on." He laughed, extending his arm out of the window. Frank slid onto the passenger seat and shook his outstretched hand.

"We've got a deal, then," Gus said.

"See you on the other side."

Frank revved the engine one last time and sped forward. He smashed through the crumbling wall with ease, bouncing over the uneven field. He looked in his side mirrors and watched Gus pull away towards Doxley. Unsure who had made the right decision, Frank drove on.

He was sure he would eventually reach a farm or some other refuge. One thing he was certain of was that his route would steer clear of the infected.

He drove on, unaware that the roar of his engine was attracting the attention of a flock of sheep nearby. They looked up as the van drew near, blood oozing from their mouths, their eyes wide with hunger.

15

Amy looked around, trying to focus her vision on anything other than the darkness. White flashes danced in front of her eyes. Her head throbbed, aching with every beat of her heart. She tried to sit up, but doing so caused her world to spin. Suddenly everything came back to her: the blood, the panic, the zombies. She lurched upright when she realised where she was.

"Hey, hey, it's okay," Ben said.

"I fell," she murmured, quickly checking herself for any injuries. She flinched when her fingers roamed over the lump on the side of her head.

"Yeah. You're lucky the lift was already halfway up."

Amy glanced around the lift shaft. "We're on top of the lift?"

"Yup. Between floors two and three."

"So how did you get down here?"

"I dropped down," Ben said, moving aside and pointing to the ledge above them. "It wasn't that far."

He placed a comforting hand on her shoulder as she rose to her feet.

"I'm fine." She brushed herself down, noticing the long rip in her T-shirt.

"Are you sure?"

"Yeah, I'm okay."

The swelling on her head throbbed, sending waves of agony through her temples. Her entire body ached, the pain worsening as she stretched her muscles. She let out a weak gasp.

"C'mon, we need to get you into a chair or something," Ben said, putting an arm around her back.

"Where are we going to find a chair on top of a lift?" Amy eased out of his embrace and bent down next to the hatch at their feet. "Look, I'll be fine. I don't need to sit down. I need to get out of here."

She opened the hatch and peered inside the lift carriage. The small compartment had been coated in arterial paint, all emanating from Terry's maimed corpse in the wheelchair. She looked away from the grisly scene.

"I know," Ben said, closing the hatch as the smell of death crept up towards them. "But you were right, there was nothing we could've done."

"So, what are we going to do now?"

"We go ahead with our original plan. We ride the lift to the ground floor, see how many zombies we have to face and whether we can get out."

"And if we can't?"

"Then we move on to Plan B."

"Which is?"

"We don't have one yet."

"Oh, well, that's great," she muttered, rolling her eyes.

"Hey, we're taking this one step at a time, remember? With any luck, we won't have to think of another plan."

"But what are the chances there'll be *no* zombies down there?"

"I have no idea. If we're lucky, they'll have left to find more people."

"And if we're unlucky?"

"Then we resort to Plan B."

Amy groaned as Ben opened the lift hatch once again.

"What are you doing?" she hissed as he dropped through the gap. His boots hit the floor with a sickening squelch. He reached over Terry's corpse and pressed the ground floor button. The motors whirred into action and the carriage started to descend.

"Get back up!"

Ben leapt and grabbed the sides of the hatch as the lift reached the ground floor. The sliding doors spread wide as he heaved himself through the gap. Amy grabbed his shoulder, half expecting him to disappear under a wave of eager hands. She helped hoist him up, before looking back into the carriage. Nobody entered. They waited, watching for any signs of movement.

"You idiot," Amy whispered, clapping Ben on the shoulder. "What if Terry comes back as one of those things?"

"Relax, he hasn't been dead long enough."

"And how long *does* it take?"

Ben didn't answer. He stared into the carriage, watching Terry's corpse.

"Do you think there are any down there?" Amy whispered.

"I don't know. I can't see from here."

He crouched down, leaning into the carriage head-first. Amy grabbed his waist as he slid his shoulders through the gap.

"It looks deserted. Help me back up."

"What do you think?" she asked, heaving him back through.

"It looks like nobody's there."

"Do you think we should go for it?"

"I think whatever we decide, we have to do it quick. We don't know how long it's going to be empty."

"Okay, suppose we make a run for it, where do we go?"

"Straight out the front doors."

"No, I mean after we get out of the building."

"Looks like someone isn't taking little steps anymore." Ben smiled. "Okay, we'll see how we go. If we find a bunch of them outside, we run in the direction that looks the clearest."

"But what if they surround us when we get outside?"

"Then we run for the ambulance that's parked out front. If the doors are open, we climb in. If not, we climb on top."

"But they'll surround the ambulance, then what?"

"Then we think of another plan. Look, we'll deal with it when we come to it. For now, we'll just focus on getting out of here, okay?"

Amy nodded. She felt adrenaline coursing through her body as the magnitude of their plan began to sink in.

"Okay. But lower me down first," she said. "If there's anything down there, you can pull me up quicker."

"Fine."

With a deep breath, Amy slid towards the open hatch. She glanced down, determining that no eager mouths were waiting for her, and dangled her legs over the side. That's when a sense of vulnerability hit her. She could almost feel the phantom hands grabbing her feet.

"Okay, lower me down."

She grabbed Ben's hands and slid off the edge of the hatch. More of the lift came into view as she was lowered. Her heart beat hard against her chest. She felt like a hooked worm, dangling in a sea of monstrosity. She held Ben's hands tight as he guided her shoulders through the gap, closely followed by her head. At once, the reception area came into view. It was empty. She looked down at the lift carriage. The floor was carpeted in entrails, organs, and bone fragments.

"Do you want me to let go?"

Amy looked up at Ben through the gloom of the lift shaft. She gave him a single nod and he released her. She dropped into the carriage, landing with a splat amongst Terry's insides. The blood seeped into her trainers, drenching her socks. With a groan of disgust, she cast a glance towards his corpse. His head was bowed against his chest, his eyes staring blankly at the gaping hole in his abdomen. Amy looked away and turned her attention to the deserted hall.

"Are we still clear?" Ben asked. Amy didn't answer. She approached the open doors, peering into the empty reception. There was nobody there. She turned as Ben dropped behind her.

"I think it's empty," she whispered.

"Good, let's get the hell out of here."

She took a cautious step out, silently treading through the pool of blood, eyes fixed on the doors at the far end of the reception. She held her breath, desperate not to make any sounds that would disturb the still atmosphere. She cleared the lift carriage and stepped out into the open reception area. Her shoes squelched on the tiled floor, but it was the eager shriek from behind her that echoed around the hallway. Amy spun around as Terry's corpse leapt from its seat, diving towards Ben. The ambush caught him off guard and he stumbled to the ground.

"Ben!"

She rushed to his aid as the creature tried to grab his legs. Ben kicked it in the face, sending it reeling. The corpse staggered to its knees, only to receive another kick to the head. The impact pushed it back into the lift carriage and Ben rushed in after it. He kicked again, pushing the corpse into the corner. Before the creature could move, he pressed a button on the control panel and jumped out. Terry's corpse screeched as it got to its knees. Its mouth frothed as it let out an anguished cry, which became muffled as the doors slid closed. The lift began to rise.

"Are you okay?" Amy asked.

"Yeah, are you?"

"I will be when we get the hell out of here."

The sun shone into the main foyer as they tiptoed towards the exit, all the time scanning the area for any signs of movement. Amy glanced back as they passed the reception desk. The computer monitor was still turned on, along with the table-top fan, whirring silently.

A mass of corpses lay strewn across the floor. Most were horribly mutilated, but there were some Amy recognised. The porter she had spoken to earlier that day was amongst them, his empty gaze directed towards the ceiling. Huge amounts of flesh were missing from his arms. His legs had been skinned to the bone. Lying next to him was one of the doctors she had seen trying to resuscitate a patient that morning.

She was reluctant to approach the grisly carpet of bodies, but as Ben stepped forward, she realised she was even more reluctant to be left on her own. She followed, glancing at each of the faces as she drew near. She half-expected them to open their eyes and attack, but they remained still.

"We're almost there," Ben whispered. Amy hadn't realised. She was more concerned with her foot positioning as they made their way through the dead. She trod on her tiptoes, looking for gaps in the sea of corpses. It was as they drew close to the exit that the sea began to surge.

Amy shrieked as the bodies rose, bumping into each other as they staggered to their feet.

"Run!"

She pushed Ben forward through the crowd, glancing at the wild, hungry stare of the undead creatures around her.

Within seconds, she felt the warm caress of the sun as they emerged from the building.

She followed Ben closely, fleeing towards the car park as the army of zombies ran out of the hospital in pursuit.

“Where are we going?” she gasped as they sprinted past the few remaining vehicles.

“My car’s up ahead,” he said.

Amy chanced a look behind them as they ran.

“They’re catching up!”

Ben dug into his pocket and produced a key fob. He pressed the button, unlocking a distant Vauxhall Vectra. The cheerful beep from the car attracted the attention of a nearby vagrant. Hearing the sound, he looked up from his bench, blood dripping from his half-eaten face.

“Ben!”

She tugged on his shirt as the tramp darted towards them. She knew straight away that he would beat them to the car. Ben handed the keys to her and split off, running to intercept the zombie. Amy tried to object, but her lungs were burning from exertion. She continued sprinting as the two collided. Ben held the tramp at bay with an outstretched hand. The shrieks from behind became louder and louder as their pursuers closed in.

Amy jumped into the driver’s seat of the Vectra. She started the engine, looking over at the grappling pair. She could see Ben had gained the upper hand and was atop the flailing corpse. Putting the car into gear, she spun the steering wheel and raced to help.

“Move!”

She blasted the horn. She saw Ben look back as she raced toward him. In an instant, he leapt aside as she ploughed over his attacker. She braked hard as the car bucked over the corpse.

"Nice one," Ben said as he jumped into the passenger seat. "Let's get out of here."

Amy looked out at the swarm bounding towards them. She nodded and sped towards the road. She veered left onto the main junction and took off around the side leading to the rear of the hospital.

"Where are you going?"

"Seeing if the other car park is empty. If it is, I can get my car."

"Don't you think we should stick together?"

Amy turned to him. "Don't you have any family you want to check on?"

"My sister is all I have. I was certain she'd be here. I'm gonna have to think of something else."

"We'll find her."

"What about you? You have any family?"

"Yeah, I've got my mum and my grandparents. I need to make sure they're okay."

She fell silent as they neared the rear entrance to the hospital. Her stomach knotted at the thought of losing her family. She had to know they were alive. She slowed as the entrance to the underground car park drew near. Two zombies emerged from the gloomy confinement, eyeing the car with excitement.

"Shit."

Amy looked on as more emerged into the daylight. She put the car into gear and drove away, watching the milling figures in the rear-view mirror. Some gave chase, others lost interest and shambled back into the darkness.

"Now what am I going to do?"

"Let's go and check on your family."

She looked at Ben quizzically. "Are you sure?"

"Yeah, you need to know they're okay."

"But what about your sister?"

"I'm out of options at the minute. I need to think of something else. Let's just check on your family. We can come back here later."

"Deal."

Amy smiled, turning the car towards Cranston. Although unsettled at the prospect of returning to Sunnymoor, she had to help Ben look.

Yet, his sister was closer than they thought. Watching from the gloom beneath the hospital, she cried out longingly, her eyes wide with desire, her mouth dripping with crimson saliva.

16

The van bucked as it sped over the uneven ground. Frank kept his seat belt off, preferring a quick escape should anything happen to the vehicle. Although this meant his head hit the roof every time he drove over a clump of soil. Before long, he'd had enough. Seeing a lengthy stretch of road to the side, he veered away from the moors and was back on the even surface.

Frank sat back in his seat. He massaged his temples as he sped towards his unknown destination. Although he had passed three farmhouses within the last fifteen minutes, he still wasn't deep enough into the moors to garner a sense of safety. He glanced around, trying to assess any threats. The fields were empty. He didn't know whether to feel comforted or apprehensive. With no signs of life, it was unlikely he would have to face any of the undead. Yet, there had to be a reason there were no animals grazing amongst the lush grass. He had a feeling it was a sinister one.

He looked ahead, just in time to see a cow walk into his path. He didn't have time to react, ploughing straight through it with an almighty crash. The impact caused him to lurch forward, striking the wheel hard. He slammed on the brakes, screeching to a halt farther down the road. He sat gasping for air, winded by the collision. The exploding carcass had showered his windscreen in blood. Through sections of clear glass, he could see there were no vehicles approaching. Once he had filled his lungs, he staggered out of the van.

The cow's remains lay scattered across the road, with the bulk of its carcass lying dormant in the bordering field. Frank examined the damage to the reinforced vehicle.

The front bumper hung loose. There was clear damage to one headlight and a large indentation in the centre. Lumps of flesh mottled the warped grill. Lowering himself to the ground, he checked underneath. There were no signs of obstruction, with most of the cow scattered halfway down the road. He got back to his feet and looked down his intended route. The road stretched on for as far as he could see, deep into the vast moors. It seemed his only option was to keep going until he found a suitable farm. He made for the driver's seat, but a distant scream stopped him in his tracks.

He turned, trying to pinpoint the person in distress. The fields were empty. He listened again. Silence. He shook his head as he opened the driver's door, certain his sanity was wavering.

When he heard the scream again, he confirmed he wasn't going crazy. He dashed to the back of the van. In the distance, he saw movement: a trio of people being chased by another three across the fields. He had to act fast. Sprinting back to the van, he restarted the engine and swung the vehicle into a nearby wire fence. The barrier gave way without resistance, and once again Frank found himself leap-frogging over mounds of cultivated earth. The fleeing people came into view as he neared. Two women and a bearded man were out front. The three pursuing them were closing in. Frank floored the accelerator, unsure whether he would catch up before the creatures claimed their first victim.

With a shriek of delight, one pursuer lurched forward and dragged the bearded man to the ground. A pang of guilt swept through Frank as two of the creatures tore into their prey. He didn't slow as he neared. The man was a lost cause. He focused on the two women ahead of him with the remaining zombie in pursuit.

He pounded the horn, beeping intermittently as he approached. The creature was unfazed, its eager eyes fixed on the nearest woman. She shot a glance behind her and screamed for help when she saw the prison van.

Not willing to damage the van any more than it already was, Frank veered left until he was side-by-side with the zombie. The creature regarded him with a glare before reaching towards the woman. Frank swung his door open, smashing the zombie on the back. It stumbled and fell, missing the woman by inches. Frank accelerated until he was level with her.

"Get in!"

The woman ran around to the passenger side as he pulled to a stop. He moved the baton off the passenger seat before she jumped in.

"Did you save the guy?" She wheezed as she jumped into the seat.

"He's dead."

The woman nodded, not a sign of empathy shrouding her flawless features. She ran fingers through her long blonde hair, tying it back into a ponytail. Her steely blue eyes fixed ahead as Frank took off once again.

"Let's catch up to her before any more of those things come," she said.

Frank looked ahead at the figure in the distance. He pushed the accelerator harder, decreasing the gap between them and the fleeing woman.

"You know these people?" he asked, casting a curious look towards his passenger. She shook her head. "Do you know what the hell's going on?" he pressed.

"Let's just pick her up first and we'll share stories when we're safe."

Frank scoffed and looked ahead to the fleeing woman.

He beeped his horn as they approached, waiting for her to turn around. She kept running, oblivious to their presence.

"Hey, lady!" Frank bellowed as they drew level, but she still didn't respond. He frowned at his passenger. "What's wrong with her?"

"She's deaf."

With a scowl, Frank pushed the van until they were within the woman's line of sight.

"Hey!"

He waved an arm through the window until her eyes locked on the van. She stopped and hurried over as they slowed to a halt.

"She hasn't been bitten, has she?" Frank murmured.

"I don't know. I don't think so."

Frank leaned out of the window as she drew near. "Are you okay?"

The woman looked at him with a frown before launching into a tirade he couldn't understand.

"Are you sure she hasn't been bitten?" Frank asked.

"She communicates through sign language."

Frank observed the woman's actions, trying to understand what she was saying. When she brushed a hand under her chin, he realised what she meant.

"The guy with the beard? He's back there."

The woman glanced in the direction and stared at him with wide eyes.

"He's dead."

Frank dragged a finger across his neck to ensure she understood. She put a hand to her mouth and began to bawl.

"Oh, shit."

He swung the door wide and jumped from the van. But as soon as he walked towards her, the woman whirled around and bolted towards the peak of an embankment.

"Wait!"

He ran after her. The passenger door slammed behind him and he heard his companion join the pursuit.

"We need to get out of here," she said as she caught up to him. "There could be more of them."

Frank scanned the area as they ran after the woman. There didn't seem to be anyone else around. The woman reached the peak of the embankment. She tried to slow, but her feet slipped from under her. Frank watched in horror as she tried to turn. In an instant, she had vanished over the side. The pair dashed forward until they reached the peak.

They peered over the top, assessing the steepness of the other side. It was a huge drop. It was then that they observed the scene beneath them. A mangled sheep's carcass lay at the bottom, with the deaf woman sprawled nearby. Atop her was a second sheep. It had finished eating its own kind and was now feasting on her. Its white fleece was red with congealing blood, its ravenous moans audible as it devoured its prey.

His new companion put a hand to her mouth and turned away, heading back to the van. Frank followed her, the image of the sheep tearing through the woman's stomach lingering in his mind. He'd had no idea the virus could spread to animals. He still didn't know if it *was* a virus. He jogged to meet his passenger as she approached the vehicle.

"Okay, I need to know what's happening. What do you know?"

"I told you, we'll talk about it later."

"No, we'll talk about it now."

He grabbed the woman. She turned to face him, ripping her arm from his grasp. "What are you—" She stopped when she noticed the wounds on his face. "What happened to you?"

"Nothing. Now tell me what's going on."

"Can we just get moving again? I'll tell you everything I know once we're safe."

"There's nobody here."

"There's a fucking flesh-hungry sheep down that hill! Not to mention those guys back there." The woman pointed down the field. "They've probably finished eating that bloke and are looking for us."

Frank stared back down the field. Sure enough, the silhouettes of four people, the fourth he assumed was the bearded man, drew closer. The woman turned back towards the van.

"At least tell me your name," he said.

"It's Lisa," she replied, jumping into the passenger seat. "What about you?"

"Frank."

He climbed behind the wheel and veered across the field towards the main road. With no signs of the living or the dead, the only threat to them was the quartet in the distance. Frank glanced in the side mirror, watching as they faded to minuscule specks.

"So, Frank." The woman looked at him as they began driving on the long stretch of road. "How is that you're driving a prison van through the middle of the Yorkshire Moors wearing blood-soaked prison scrubs?"

"Prison scrubs?" He frowned, looking down at his stained tracksuit bottoms and jumper.

"Well, you're hardly a prison *officer,* are you? Where did you come from? Harrodale?"

"Sure did, Sherlock."

"That's a high-security prison."

"Yep."

"You must be a nasty piece of work."

"Not as bad as what's out here." He motioned towards a hollowed-out sheep's carcass at the side of the road.

"So where are you heading?" Lisa asked.

"I have no idea. Somewhere safe."

"Good. You can take me with you."

"Are you sure? No one you need to look for? No family or friends you want to get killed over?"

"No, why do you ask?"

Frank shrugged. "It's what ordinary people do during a crisis, isn't it? Emotions get in the way of logic and they get killed looking for their gran."

"Yeah, except I'm not ordinary. I've got me, myself and I, and that's the way I like it."

Frank grinned; he was warming to the woman already.

"So what do you think is causing all this?" she asked.

"I've been banged up for five years. The only time I knew something was wrong was when they tore up the prison."

"So you don't know anything?"

"I know they don't die when you break their neck. I know they have a taste for human flesh and I know if you get bitten, you'll become one of them within the minute."

"Within the minute?"

"Yeah."

"That's weird," she muttered, more to herself than to Frank.

"What do you mean?"

"My friend and I were in a car crash. Some guy jumped into the road and we ended up crashing into a telegraph pole."

"A zombie?"

"If that's what you want to call them."

"Did you run over him?"

"Yeah, but he got straight back up and ended up biting my friend."

"How did you get away?"

"That guy with the beard was driving past and he picked us up."

Frank slowed and veered around another corpse in the middle of the road. For a deserted stretch of land, the moors were becoming more and more populated by the minute.

"When we got back to his house, my friend started to shake. I thought she was cold at first, but then she began having a seizure."

"Is that why you ran?"

"No. We ran because the guy's sons came bursting into the room and attacked us."

"Were they the ones chasing you?"

She nodded, turning to look out the window as they veered onto another road.

"What do you mean it's *weird*?"

"Huh?" Lisa asked.

"I said they turn within a minute and you said that's weird. Why?"

"Well, that didn't happen with us. When the guy saw my friend's arm, he told us that his two sons had been hurt, too."

"And?"

"And the drive alone took fifteen minutes before we reached his house."

"So it took fifteen minutes for your friend to change?"

"At least, and it was probably longer for the two guys that were there."

Frank contemplated this briefly until Lisa spoke again.

"Maybe it depends on the person? My friend was quite big, so it might not have affected her as fast. And you saw how big those other guys were."

"No. One of the blokes inside changed within a minute or two."

"Was he a big guy?"

"The biggest guy I've ever seen. It has to be something else."

"Maybe it's becoming more advanced?" Lisa offered, as they avoided another corpse in the road. "Whatever *it* is, might be growing stronger and turning people faster."

"Ever the optimist, huh?"

"I can't think of any other reason. Can you?"

"I don't know. All the lads I saw go mental were bitten around the face. Maybe it's however long it takes to get to your brain?"

Frank looked around at their surroundings until he picked out a distant house. It was far off the main road, surrounded by miles of open field. A balcony was fixed to the right-hand side of the upper floor, allowing a perfect vantage point should they encounter an attack. He grinned.

"What?" Lisa asked.

"I finally know where we're heading."

"Where?"

Frank pointed towards the farmhouse, noticing the Land Rover that was parked outside. It dawned on him that the house may contain survivors; or worse, zombies. Despite the danger, he knew they would be safer in a barricaded house than out on the road.

"You can't be serious."

"Why not?"

"Because there are loads of those things out here. Not to mention the ones chasing us."

"So where do you suggest?"

"I don't know."

"Well, towns and cities will be *crawling* with those things. We wouldn't even get a chance to hide. We can fortify this place, it probably has food and water, and if he's a decent farmer, he'll probably have a shotgun lying around as well."

"But what if the people inside are already infected?"

"Chances are we'll encounter two or three at the most. I'd rather take my chances with them than an entire city."

They fell silent as they drove the rest of the way. As they pulled onto the dirt road leading to the farm, Lisa finally spoke.

"Suppose we can't get in? Then where do we go?"

"We'll deal with that if we have to."

Frank gripped the steering wheel tighter as the van shuddered over the uneven ground. He observed a sign as they approached.

"Cobton Farm. Can't say I've heard of it."

"Let me guess, you used to be a farmer?" His passenger smirked.

"Nope." Frank eased off the accelerator, slowing the van to a crawl next to the Land Rover. "But I did grow up on a farm."

He eyed the house with a frown. Every window, both top and bottom, had been boarded up with planks of wood. The front door appeared to be the only untouched aspect of the house.

"Interesting."

"What?"

"We might be in luck."

He grabbed the baton as he jumped from the van. He approached the house with Lisa in tow.

"Why?" she asked.

"Because this house is already barricaded. There are probably survivors in there."

He pounded on the door and took a step back, scanning the acres of farmland.

"What if they don't want us here?" Lisa asked.

"Then we don't give them a choice."

Frank stepped forward, pounding the door a second time. There was still no sound from within. He approached a window and peered through a gap in the boards. The curtains were drawn, but a small opening gave him a glimpse inside. He could see at least two candles contributing to the trifling light in what appeared to be a living room. Turning back, he approached the door.

"Well?" Lisa asked.

He pressed an ear against the wooden frame. A quiet shuffling from within the house met his ears. He scowled and stepped away, handing the baton to Lisa. "There's definitely somebody in there."

He kicked the door, striking it three times. He stopped and listened for a further sound. It came, but not from the house.

A high-pitched shriek caused them both to whirl around. In the next field, a topless woman was sprinting towards them. Her tattered hair sailed back as she ran, her disfigured breasts swinging wildly, connected only by strands of flesh. She was close when the sound of opening locks met their ears. Frank turned as the door burst open. He didn't see the owner, but he did see the firearm aimed at his face.

17

The town was filled with chaos. Everywhere Amy looked, fires raged, corpses walked, and the people she vaguely recognised were scattered around the road like discarded trash. She fought to keep her composure as the extent of the infection became clear. If Cranston had been destroyed in such a short time, what did that mean for the rest of the country?

"Are you okay?" Ben asked as they drove through the desecrated streets.

"I just can't believe it. I know some of these people."

Her eyes fixed on the blood-stained corpse of Mrs Carmichael as it tore a chunk from a severed leg. It regarded the car as they passed, ligaments and tendons dangling from its mouth.

"I don't think we'll be able to stay put for long," Ben said, glancing around at the corpses littering the floor. "It might not be safe."

Amy nodded, determined only to get home and retrieve her phone. She had to know her loved ones were safe. She turned a corner onto the street that led to her house. The area seemed a lot less populated, with only two dead bodies lying in the road. She manoeuvred around them before pulling up outside her home.

"We here?" Ben asked.

"Yeah."

Amy led the way to her front door. She instinctively reached for her bag; the same bag she had left in her car.

"Oh, no. I left my keys at the hospital."

Ben let out an exasperated groan, pressing his back against the wall. "Wanna break in?"

"What?"

"If you really wanna get in, we can break a window."

"I'm not breaking a window."

"Why not?"

"Because then my house will be unsecure."

"And? Are you planning on staying?"

"No. But what if I get burgled or something?"

Ben laughed. "Burgled? There are zombies on every corner. If any burglars are left, I doubt they're thinking about your silverware."

Amy matched his gaze, succumbing to his infectious laugh. "I suppose. But at least break a back window."

"Why? So the *burglars* don't see?"

"No, so the *zombies* don't, smart arse."

She led the way around the side of her house towards the back garden. It was there she met Norman Collins. Her neighbour was standing with his back to the pair, swaying as he observed her withered flower bed. Amy gasped, staring at the man with wide eyes. The noise caught his attention. He turned, revealing a grotesque, disfigured face. A gooey crimson mess had replaced his tanned skin. His left eyebrow had been ripped away, giving him a peculiar stare. His lips had been torn off, exposing grotesque teeth that gnashed as he darted towards them.

Ben rushed forward, tackling the corpse to the ground. Amy followed. Jumping over them, she stood on Norman's head, pushing his face to the side.

"Ben, there's a hand fork by your side," she said, motioning to the garden tool in the flowerbed.

He nodded. Keeping his bulk pressed on the man, he felt blindly for the fork. Norman fought hard against his oppressors. He arched his back, with muffled growls sounding beneath Amy's foot.

"Got it," Ben said, bringing the tool into view. He rose to his feet, placing a boot on the man's chest. Amy twisted Norman's head, exposing his right ear. In an instant, Ben drove the pointed tips into his temple. He applied force, pushing the metal prongs deeper. Amy looked away as a startled cry came from Norman. Ben stomped on the handle, plunging the fork down to the hilt. She could feel the corpse shudder beneath her foot, its muscles twitching until it finally lay still.

"Are you okay?" Ben asked.

Amy nodded, swallowing hard before responding. "He was my neighbour."

"I'm sorry."

"It's okay." She looked away, fighting to keep the tremors out of her voice. "Shall we go back to playing Billy Burglar?"

She motioned towards the kitchen window, casting a glance at Norman. She couldn't help but wonder whether her family had succumbed to the same fate. What if they were already dead? What if she was too late?

"We need something to smash it," Ben said, tearing Amy away from her morbid thoughts. "Any ideas?"

"Try Norman's garden." She led Ben over to the wall. "How about something on that barbecue?" She pointed towards the fixed appliance near the conservatory doors. A series of cooking utensils hung from the grill, shimmering under the caressing breeze.

"Yeah, maybe. I'll go and see what's there."

Amy stepped back as Ben hoisted himself over the wall. He landed with a soft thud on the other side before stealthily moving over the lawn. She looked back towards Norman's corpse, ensuring he hadn't moved. The body remained still, the trowel handle jutting skyward.

Ben examined the contents of the barbecue. A frown creased his face as he spotted something next to the glass doors.

"I've got something even better," he hollered. He stooped down next to the conservatory windows. Before he could grab the item, a heavy thud sent him staggering aside.

"Fuck!"

Amy moved along the side of the wall, searching for the cause of Ben's outburst. When the glass panels came into view, she saw the decrepit form of Norman's father slamming the door in a rage. His muffled roar showered the glass in crimson spittle.

"I think you should get out of there," she said.

"Yep."

Ben stooped down and retrieved the hammer he had spotted, before rushing back to her. She stepped aside as he vaulted the wall, keeping her eyes on the conservatory. Ben raised the hammer before her.

"Good call."

She followed him as he approached her kitchen window. Without hesitating, he swung the hammer towards the glass. The metal head collided with the top corner of the window, creating a web-like crack. He swung again, connecting with the centre of the glass, causing it to shatter. The pair jumped back as the diamond shards scattered across the floor. Ben stepped forward. Taking off his jacket and wrapping it around his palm, he brushed the remaining shards aside.

"You live alone, right?" He unwrapped his hand and spread the jacket over the window ledge.

"Yeah."

"Are there keys in the back door?"

Amy nodded.

"Okay, wait here, I'll open the door for you." With that, Ben vaulted the windowsill and disappeared inside.

Amy waited, looking back at Norman's motionless corpse. Then she heard the rattle of keys. The door swung wide, with Ben stepping back to allow her entry.

"Nice place." He smiled.

"Thanks."

The kitchen was as she had left it, discounting the particles of glass scattered everywhere. She carefully walked over the broken shards, cringing as the crunch beneath her shoes filled the silent house. Eventually, the hallway came into view. Amy continued to step cautiously as she left the kitchen behind. Her mobile phone was on the table near the front door, but to reach it, she had to walk past the living room.

"What are you waiting for?" Ben asked. "The house was secure when we got here."

"You've got me spooked now," she hissed, keeping her eyes fixed on the open door as she passed. With a deep breath, she rushed the last few steps and grabbed the phone. The list of missed calls brought tears to her eyes. She quickly scanned through them all. Her mother and grandparents had tried to ring many times. Not waiting a second longer, she dialled the first number.

18

"What do you want?"

The demand came from within the house. Frank looked past the barrel of the shotgun, trying to see through the gap in the door. A wrinkled eye topped with a furrowed brow was the gunman's only visible feature.

"What do you think we want? Let us in!"

Frank could hear the zombie drawing near. He felt a tug on his shirt as Lisa tried to get his attention.

"C'mon," she urged.

Frank shrugged her away, maintaining his locked stare with the elderly farmer.

"Are you hurt?"

"What?"

"Are you *hurt*?"

"We fucking will be if you don't open this door!"

An enthusiastic shriek came from behind. Tearing his eyes away from the farmer, he watched the undead woman as she neared. Drool spilled from her mouth. She fixed the pair with wide, crazed eyes. Frank turned back to the man.

"We're gonna die out here. Let us inside!"

The farmer considered the option as the undead woman reached the end of the field. She raced over to the pair with arms outstretched. With a growl, the farmer swung the door wide and turned the shotgun on her. A deafening blast caused Frank and Lisa to recoil as the woman's head exploded into fragments. They watched the twitching body fall to the ground, before turning back to the farmer.

"Look, we're not injured and we don't mean any harm; all we want is a safe place."

The elderly man regarded the pair with a frown.

"Okay," he said after a moment of deliberation. "But there's not much food here and I've already got a house full."

He stepped aside to allow the pair entry, closing the door behind them. The hallway was dark and humid. A slit of light shone through a gap in one of the boards. Motes of dust danced in the fleeting light, disturbed by the arrival of the pair. Frank scanned the narrow confines, trying to take in his surroundings. He listened to the snap of bolts and the rattle of a chain behind him. Once finished, the farmer motioned for them to follow him.

"We've got two more joining us," he announced as he led them into the lounge.

Frank looked around at the four faces in the room. He counted two women, and a man seated on the couch, with a lone woman on a rug near the empty fireplace.

"Make your own introductions. I'll be back in a minute."

They all watched the farmer hobble out of the room.

"I'm Louise." The woman on the floor smiled. She was painfully thin, with sharp features. Her hazel eyes danced between the pair, staring at them expectantly.

"I'm Frank," he muttered.

"And I'm Lisa." She grinned forcefully, digging Frank in the ribs.

"I'm Simon." The chubby man on the couch raised his hand. His swollen face encompassed his tired eyes. *Like pissholes in the snow,* Frank thought. Simon placed an arm around his equally obese spouse. "And this is my wife, Elaine."

Lisa nodded, smiling warmly as she turned her attention to the last unidentified female. Sensing the gaze of the group, the teenager looked up. Streaks of purple ran through her long black hair. The flickering candlelight was reflected in the various piercings adorning her face. She stared at Lisa with cold blue eyes.

"Tina," she uttered.

"Nice to meet you, Tina. So, who's the old codger?" Lisa motioned to the door.

"His name is Ronald Carter," Elaine said. "He's a lovely man."

"Yeah, he seems quite the charmer," Frank scoffed, rolling his eyes as he approached the window. Peering through the gap, he saw no sign of the infected. He sighed indignantly as he turned back to the room. "So what the hell is going on here?"

Simon shrugged. "You know just as much as us."

"No, I don't. All I've seen is a bunch of guys eating people. Then they get up with their guts hanging out and go after others. That's it."

"Well, you must have been living under a rock." Simon chortled. "Don't you own a TV?"

"They don't allow them in Harrodale."

The smile slid off Simon's face. The group regarded Frank in horror. Even the teenager's interest had been captured by the abrupt announcement.

"So he was a prisoner." Lisa shrugged. "Who gives a shit?"

"I do!" Simon snapped. "Harrodale is a high-security prison. Only the worst criminals are kept there."

"That's true," Elaine said, gripping her husband's arm. "He could be a killer or a rapist."

"Don't be stupid," Frank said. "Sex offenders don't last five minutes in there."

"So you're a killer, then?"

Frank didn't respond.

The group regarded him with a horrified expression as Ronald returned to the room.

"What's up with you lot?"

"Ask him," Simon answered, pointing an accusing finger at Frank.

"What's the matter, have you been bitten? Are you one of them?"

Frank made to answer, but was stopped by an outburst from Elaine, her curly dark hair bouncing as she jumped to her feet.

"He might as well be. He's a serial killer from Harrodale."

"Serial killer?" Frank scoffed. "Serial killer implies I've killed loads of people. I only killed one." He looked around at the horrified faces. "Disregarding the zombies I've killed today, of course."

"I'm not having a serial killer in my house," Ronald said.

"I told you, I'm *not* a serial killer. I've gotta kill someone else before I get that title."

"Get out!"

Frank stood his ground, glaring at the farmer. After a brief silence, the old man shrugged.

"Fine."

He approached the shotgun propped up against the wall.

In an instant, Frank darted forward, grabbing Ronald before he could seize the weapon.

"Don't even think about it, old man."

"Let go of me!"

"I don't want to hurt you, but if you're a threat to me, I won't think twice about *becoming* a serial killer."

"You don't frighten me. And I'm not having the likes of you in my house."

"What if those things get in here? How many bullets do you have?"

Ronald looked pleadingly at the others, but nobody came to his aid. "Enough."

"And will you have time to reload? Who's going to back you up? This guy?" Frank pointed to the obese man standing next to the couch.

Ronald's eyes flicked to Simon before returning to Frank. "They—they won't get in here," he stammered.

"How do you know that? You're gonna have to leave, eventually. What if those things are still outside?"

He released his grip as the farmer sighed dejectedly.

"You need me," Frank said. "I'm not going to harm any of you. If everyone keeps cool, we might survive this."

"Oh, please." The teenager rolled her eyes. "We're not going to survive this. Nobody will."

"Why not?" Lisa asked.

"Because this is the end of the world. The virus isn't just here. It's everywhere."

"Worldwide?"

"I dunno. I just know that it's spread throughout Britain."

"Are you sure?" Frank asked.

"That's the last thing they said on TV before it all went off."

"What about the rest of Europe?"

"I don't know. They just said it's constantly spreading."

"Do they know what's caused it?"

"If they do, they're not telling."

"Then let's hope they closed the Channel Tunnel. If those things get through there, you can say goodbye to the rest of the world."

"Not necessarily," Simon retorted. "What about all the islands? And America, for God's sake. They'll help us."

"Oh, fuck off." Frank laughed. "America will either lock themselves in their own little bubble or press the big red button and nuke us all. We're on our own here, but that doesn't mean we won't survive."

"Unless they *do* press the big red button," Lisa said.

Frank shrugged.

"What do you have in mind?" asked Ronald.

Frank glanced around at the expectant faces. They were looking for a leader. A role he sure as hell didn't want to take on.

"I don't know yet. What I *do* know is I'm not putting all my hopes on another country coming to save us."

He made his way back over to Lisa.

"Okay, so we keep referring to this thing as a virus, but we don't know that for sure. It could be chemical warfare, or anything."

Some of the group nodded.

"How long has it been going on?"

"A few days," Louise said. "There were loads of cases yesterday on the news, but it really took off early this morning. By that time, it was everywhere."

Frank nodded, taking the baton from Lisa.

"So let's talk weapons. What do we have to fight these things?"

"I've got this shotgun." Ronald motioned to the weapon. "And there's a rifle in the cupboard under the stairs."

"What about ammo?"

"There are two shells there." He pointed to the pair of cylindrical red bullets on the table. "But I'd say twenty shotgun rounds and twenty rifle bullets in total."

"Good stuff. All we've got is this." Frank raised the baton into view.

"And this," Lisa added, producing a knuckleduster from her pocket.

"I didn't know you were packing that."

"There's a lot you don't about me." The woman smiled mischievously. Frank laughed, turning to the rest of the group. Simon and Elaine had returned to the couch, with Tina perched on the edge.

"What about you guys?"

He looked at each of them as they all raised empty hands. His eyes rested on the teenager.

"What about you?"

Tina looked up, staring at him briefly before rising to her feet. "I've got this."

She pulled up her trouser leg, revealing a combat knife in a sheath. She placed it on the coffee table in front of them.

"Where the hell did you get that?" Lisa gasped.

"My old man left me it in his will. He was a crazy motherfucker."

"Okay, so we've got three guns, a baton, an iron fist, and a knife. We need more."

"I've got some tools out back," Ronald said. "Hammers, spades, and that kind of stuff."

"That's great, but in case you're forgetting, those things are out there."

"It won't matter if—"

Ronald was cut off by a loud thud above them. Frank stared at the man, who started rubbing his eyes.

"It's my wife," he said. "She's not well. I'd better see if she's okay."

Without waiting for a response, he left the room and made for the stairs. Once he was out of earshot, Frank turned to the group.

"Is she infected?"

"No," Elaine whispered. "We've heard him talking to her."

"But has she been bitten?"

"No, I don't think so. Ronald said she's had the flu for the past few days."

"But what if she *is* infected?" Simon asked, adopting the same hushed tone as his wife.

"Then we kill her," Frank said. "I'm not putting my life at risk just because this guy is clinging to a corpse."

"She's not dead," Louise said. "He's been going up to see to her since we arrived."

"When was that?"

"About four hours ago."

The group flinched as the shrill ringing of a telephone filled the room. All eyes fixed on the device.

"Should we answer it?" Elaine asked. She looked at her husband, who put a hand on her knee.

"This isn't our house, Elaine."

"But it could be the police."

"Oh, yeah." The teenager snorted. "The entire country is falling to pieces, and the law decides to ring this old guy for a natter?"

The ringing continued, causing some of the group to fidget nervously.

"It might be someone in trouble," Elaine said. "We should answer it."

"If it's someone in trouble, we'll know soon enough," Frank said.

"What do you mean?"

"I mean, he's got an answering machine. Whoever's ringing can leave a message."

As if to verify his statement, the recording device clicked to life. An automated voice requested that the caller leave a message, before concluding with a shrill beep.

"Grandpa? Are you there? Grandma? It's Amy."

The voice was that of a tearful woman. Frank stared at the machine as she continued.

"I've rung everybody and nobody's picking up. I just want to know if you're safe. Please pick up the phone."

Elaine let out a sob as the pleading continued.

"If you want to call me back, I've got my mobile. I'm with a guy from work. We're at my house now, but we'll be moving on soon. It's not safe here. If you get this message, please call me. I love you both."

The machine clicked as the woman ended the call. The group remained silent, all staring at the device which had returned to its dormant state. The farmer's arrival broke their trance.

"Ronald, your granddaughter just called," Elaine screeched, jumping from her seat.

"What?"

"She just rang. Look. Look." She ushered him over to the machine and pressed the playback button. The heartfelt message floated around the room once more, all eyes focused on the farmer.

"Amy. She's alive."

As the message concluded, Ronald wiped tears from his eyes. He sniffed hard as he picked up the phone.

"I have to let her know I'm okay," he said, more to himself than to the others. He retrieved a leather-bound book from a nearby drawer and skimmed through the pages. The group watched as he punched in a phone number.

"Damn it. It's saying it can't connect." He slammed the receiver down and turned to the group. "What does that mean?"

"Maybe she hasn't got a signal," Lisa offered. "Try again in a bit, you might have more luck."

"Don't wait too long," the teenager said. "All communication will stop shortly."

"What?"

"Have you guys never seen a zombie movie?" She laughed. "First, communication goes. Then you say goodbye to electricity, running water, and before you know it, you're living like a Neanderthal, rubbing sticks together to make fire."

"She's right," Lisa said. "Give it a few minutes, then try ringing again."

Ronald gnawed at his fingernails as he paced back and forth. The group watched, all except Frank, who had taken to the window again.

"Where are your animals?" he asked after a while.

"What?"

"Your animals, where are they?"

"I only have a dozen sheep. They're in the next field across, and I've got chickens in a coop outside. Why do you ask?"

"Because the animals are turning as well. We saw a woman get ripped apart by a sheep earlier. It might have been one of yours."

"Jesus Christ." The farmer groaned, running a hand through his wavy hair.

Frank read the troubled look on the old man's face. "What is it?"

"I'm just thinking. Gordon Chesterfield's slaughterhouse is only ten miles away. He's one of the biggest distributors of meat in the country."

"So that means he has animals there?" Lisa asked.

"Hundreds. Farmers send him their stock to be slaughtered. Hell, I used to send my cattle there."

"Shit, let's just hope they don't head this way."

Ronald tried the phone again. After a few seconds, he growled and slammed the handset back down.

Minutes passed, with the farmer becoming more and more agitated. Eventually, the silence was broken as Louise got to her feet.

"Erm, Ronald?" she began, slowly approaching him.

He looked up at her, chewing another fingernail. "What?"

"Is it okay if I use your bathroom?"

He stared at her, as if deliberating how best to answer. Finally, he nodded.

"Thanks."

"Top of the stairs, *first* door on your left," he said. "My wife is asleep, so make sure you go up quietly and come straight back. Don't go in any of the other rooms."

"Got it."

Louise stepped out of the living room and into the hallway. The area was dark, something she wasn't accustomed to during the early hours of the afternoon. Her eyes slowly adjusted to the gloom as she made her way up the stairs. The candlelight was enough to illuminate the living room, but darkness blanketed the rest of the house. A shuffling sound greeted her as she reached the top of the staircase. She turned, startled by the noise. She located the source behind a closed door.

"Mrs Carter?" she uttered softly. She stared at the door. Through the gloom, she could see it had been barricaded shut. Four heavy planks adorned its wooden frame. Deciding to question Ronald when she returned, she made for the bathroom. That was until a small opening in the door caught her eye. She had to look twice, but sure enough, towards the bottom of the barricade, was a small rectangular hole. It had been crudely cut, leaving a hole the size of a letterbox. She stooped down and tried to look through. Her eyes could not penetrate the darkness, but she picked up a faint whisper coming from within.

"Mrs Carter?" she repeated, "Are you okay?"

The whispers grew louder as she neared, but were indecipherable.

"What are you saying?" Louise turned her ear towards the gap. A sudden, delighted shriek came from the room.

"Mrs Carter, are you—"

Her sentence was cut short as a pair of hands sprung through the hole and grabbed her by the head, pulling her toward the darkness. Louise yelped as her face was pressed up against the door. When she felt teeth clamp around her nose, she let out a muffled scream. With a vicious yank, her nose was ripped off, leaving her sprawled on the floor, blood gushing from her face. As the zombie chewed hungrily, Louise screamed again.

The first shriek caused every member of the group to flinch. While the rest of them exchanged alarmed glances, Frank grabbed a candle and made for the stairs. He bounded up, reaching the top as another scream sounded. The yellow glow illuminated Louise. She lay cowering on the floor in a crimson puddle, holding her hands to her face. The sound of eager chomping came from a boarded-up room.

"What the fuck happened?"

Louise continued to howl as the rest of the group reached the top of the stairs. Each held a candle, contributing to the flickering light. Hearing their arrival, Frank turned and rounded on the farmer.

"Your wife's a fucking zombie!"

He shot Ronald a glare.

"Have you been *feeding* her?"

"She's… my wife," he whimpered. "I couldn't kill her."

"Well, that's a shame, because now I'm going to kill *both* of you."

Frank grabbed him by the neck, pinning him helplessly against the wall.

"Stop it!" Elaine whimpered.

Frank ignored her. He pressed his arm against the farmer's throat, crushing his airway.

"Frank."

The voice was Lisa's. He pushed harder, watching as Ronald turned a dark shade of purple. Lisa jerked his shoulder.

"Frank!"

"What?"

He snapped his gaze toward her, but saw that her wide eyes were fixed behind him.

"I think we'd better run."

"Why?"

He followed her line of sight to the injured, shuddering woman on the floor, whose crying had subsided, replaced with a raspy, guttural moan. He released his grip on the farmer as Louise arched her back, emitting a frantic squeal. He heard most of the group flee down the stairs, crying out for him to follow. He ignored them, keeping his eyes fixed on the shuddering figure. Slowly, she started to rise. She got to her hands and knees, her head drooped. Blood dripped from her face.

"Frank! What are you doing?"

He looked back to see Lisa, the only other person on the landing.

"We have to kill her. I'm not going back outside. I'd rather take my chances with one, than hundreds."

With that, he turned back as a low growl rumbled from the corpse's mangled face. The bloody pulp dripped down, running into her crooked grin. Frank stood still as she let out a squeal of delight. She lunged forward but was met by his open hand. He grabbed her neck as her gnashing teeth tried to reach his flesh. She clawed at his face, raking at his skin as he slammed her into the wall. Her snapping teeth went for his arm, but he kept her at bay.

"Get something!"

Frank gasped as a flailing leg struck his stomach, but he maintained his grip.

"Like what?"

"Anything," he wheezed.

He felt Louise's nails break the skin of his cheek as she clawed at him again. He hissed in pain before slamming the corpse into the ground.

"Ronald, get that shotgun up here, now!"

Lisa looked from the struggling pair to the staircase, waiting for the farmer to appear. Frank did not wait for a weapon, choosing instead to stomp on Louise's head. After five strikes, she fell silent. Yet he continued. After a few seconds, a crunching sound split through the hallway as his foot sank into the caved skull. The corpse juddered and twitched as he retracted his foot, wiping blood and brain matter onto its sodden blouse.

"I'm sorry," Lisa said. "I wanted the gun, but—"

Frank brushed past her. She followed him as he descended the stairs.

"Ronald?" Frank's voice was calm as he looked around the empty living room. He listened for a response before heading into the kitchen. There was nobody in sight, but a muffled noise was coming from behind a closed door. He could feel blood trickling down his face. He rubbed it away as he approached. The muffled sounds increased before the door flew open.

"Get off me," Tina growled, forcing her way out of the pantry. She strolled into the kitchen, leaving the rest of the group cowering.

"They dragged me in there. They say you've gone mad."

Frank sneered at the cowering trio.

"Where's your gun, Ronald?"

"Why? So you can kill us all?" The old man wheezed, massaging his neck, which had turned a deep red.

"No, so I can kill *myself*."

"What?" Lisa gasped, entering the kitchen behind them.

He turned to face her. "I've been injured. And I am *not* turning into one of them."

The group emerged, eyeing him cautiously.

"You've been bitten?" Simon asked.

"No, but she tore hell out of my face."

"That doesn't mean you'll turn," Lisa said.

"C'mon. We've seen it happen!"

"From a *bite*. There's nothing to suggest you'll turn into one if you get scratched."

"And I'm not going to risk it."

"But what about us? What will we do?"

"I don't give a shit about any of you." He pushed past Lisa into the living room, looking for the shotgun.

"We need you alive," she protested. "You're no good to us dead."

"I'm no good to you anyway. It won't be long before I turn into one of those things."

"Just wait and see."

"Where's the fucking gun?" He turned to the farmer.

"It's next to the armchair."

Frank spotted the weapon. He snatched it up and pressed the muzzle beneath his chin. He felt blindly for the trigger until a sharp tug pulled it away from him. He turned to face Lisa, who held the barrel in a vice-like grip.

"What have you got to lose?"

They locked eyes. Her query danced around his mind as he considered a response. After a brief silence, he could find no answer. He growled indignantly and pried the shotgun out of her hands. With a slight nod, he turned back to the group.

"Ronald. I'm not going to hurt you, even though you almost got us killed."

The farmer looked at the floor.

"I think you know what to do."

He placed the weapon in the old man's withered hands. Ronald stared at the gun. With his head down, he quietly left the room.

"Right, you lot, get over here. I think we've had enough excitement for one day."

Frank motioned for the others to follow him into the living room. He slumped into the armchair and watched as the group cautiously entered after him. They took up their previous positions around the room, listening to the farmer prising boards from the bedroom door. It dawned on Frank that the woman might escape her confines and kill her husband first. But before he could voice his concerns, a loud blast contradicted this thought. Muffled sobs from the farmer reached them. Frank eased back in the chair.

"Should we go to him?" Elaine whispered.

"No. Leave him for a while, he'll come down when he's ready."

They waited several minutes before Frank was proven wrong again. This time, by the sound of a second gunshot ringing throughout the house.

19

Her grandparents had been the last family members Amy had tried to contact. After leaving the message on their answering machine, she hung up the phone.

"Maybe they've fled?" Ben suggested, joining her in the passageway. "Everyone else has."

"No, my grandparents are frail, and my mum broke her leg a few weeks ago. She can't really get around."

"Okay, we need to make a plan. If you want to go and check on them, we'd better leave sooner rather than later."

"You'll come with me?"

"Of course. We need to stick together."

"What about your sister?"

"The only other place I can think of is back at her house. Where do your mum and grandparents live?"

"My grandparents live on a farm in the middle of nowhere. I just hope none of those things have reached them yet."

"Hopefully not."

"But my mum lives five minutes away. I need to make sure she's okay."

"Okay then. How about we go there first and then drop by my sister's place to see if she's there?"

"Sounds like a good idea."

Amy grabbed her spare keys from the sideboard and headed for the door. She pressed her eye to the spyhole for any sign of danger. Apart from a tiny figure swaying in the distance, there was no sign of movement. Giving a quick nod to Ben, she fumbled with her keys and swung the door wide.

The warm air hit her once more, but this time it was tinged with the smell of burning flesh and debris. She glanced around at the countless fires raging in the distance. Smoke billowed high into the air, casting a dark cloud over the town. The screaming had been replaced by an eerie silence. She glanced over at the car, wishing they had parked closer to the house. With a deep intake of breath, she made her way down the steps and back towards the road.

She heard the zombie before she saw it. With an eager roar, the corpse of Mrs Carmichael lunged at her from the side. Amy shrieked as she was tackled to the ground.

"Amy!"

She could hear Ben rushing forward, as the withered hands of her neighbour grasped her arms in a crushing grip. The corpse grunted, fighting to sink her teeth into flesh.

"Run!"

Ben leapt onto the elderly creature's back, forcing its teeth away. Amy shoved herself free and jumped to her feet. Her mobile phone lay a few feet away, but she kept her eyes glued to Ben as he smashed the woman's head into the ground again and again. Within seconds, the zombie stopped resisting. Rolling away from the body, he jumped to his feet and grabbed Amy by the arm.

"I said run!"

He pulled hard, dragging her towards the car. Mrs Carmichael was no longer a threat, yet something had spooked him. The answer came as soon as they jumped in and slammed the doors. Amy flinched as a series of blows rained down on the car. She spun around in horror as countless hands pounded the windows at the rear of the vehicle.

"Where the hell did they come from?"

"I told you to run."

He turned the key, revving the car to life. The roar of the engine was barely audible over the thunderous roll of fists-on-metal. He forced the car into reverse and promptly drove through the undead crowd behind them. Bodies bounced off the car, with those still standing continuing their assault. Quickly changing gear, he sped away from the group, pursued by those still able to use their legs.

Ben lifted his hand from the wheel, examining a wound on his knuckles.

"Did she bite you?" Amy asked, watching as a trickle of blood crept down to his wrist.

Ben wiped the blood on his knee. "No, I grazed it when we hit the ground." He looked ahead as they approached a junction. "So, where are we heading?"

"Elliot Street," Amy said, watching their dwindling pursuers.

She turned her attention to the rest of the town, aghast at the scenes of carnage. When they veered around an overturned bus, she had to look away from the mangled bodies inside, many of them children.

"Why is this happening?" she whispered, closing her eyes as one of the undead infants watched them pass.

"I have no idea. Terrorism, maybe? It was bound to happen."

"You're starting to sound like Terry."

The reminiscence of the dead man created a flicker of sorrow deep within. Amy felt a knot form in her stomach at the thought of a similar fate befalling her family. She longed to get to her mother's house.

"Elliot Street? That's the new housing estate, right?" Ben asked after a while.

"Yeah."

"Where did your mum live before that?"

"She moved when I transferred here. She wanted to be with me so I knew somebody."

"Nice of her."

"Yeah, she hasn't got anyone else. When I left, she wanted to stay close, so she came with me."

"That's very considerate. So how did she break her leg?"

"Tripped down the stairs while she was viewing the house." Amy chuckled. "I told her it was a bad omen, but she went ahead and bought it anyway."

"That's parents for you."

"So, what about yours?" She watched the smile fade from his face.

"My mum died of cancer last year, and my dad… we don't really see eye to eye."

"Oh, I'm sorry."

"No, it's okay. My sister is the only person I have. Not knowing whether she's safe is killing me."

"We'll find her."

Amy placed a comforting hand on top of his. He took his eyes off the road and stared at her briefly before the smile crept back onto his face.

"I know."

They turned onto the housing estate. Neither uttered a word as the car slowed to a crawl, allowing them to take in the scene. The street was silent. Some doors stood ajar, others were swung wide. When Amy saw a bloody handprint on one of the doors, she let out a quiet gasp.

"Which one is it?" Ben asked.

"It's the house towards the end of the road. There, that one, on the right."

They pulled up outside the house, staring at the front door. It stood open, like so many others, but there was no obvious sign of damage. As soon as he stopped the car, Amy bolted.

"Wait!"

Amy paid him no heed as she raced towards the house. She shouldered the door aside, breaking the silent atmosphere.

"Mum?"

Ben followed her as she darted inside the house. He cast an eye over the surrounding gardens before peering into the doorway. The hallway was empty. Amy was gone.

"Shit."

He made his way down the hall, scanning each of the open rooms. When he reached the kitchen, he peered inside. There, Amy sat in a heap on the floor. Next to her was an upturned wheelchair spattered in blood. She sobbed into her hands, allowing Ben to survey the rest of the room unnoticed. The absence of a body concerned him. If Amy's mother had fallen victim to the horde of zombies, where was she now?

"Amy," he whispered, as she continued to cry. He approached slowly and placed a hand on her shoulder.

"Amy."

This time she turned, looking up at him with tear-filled eyes.

"I'm sorry," he said.

"We have to find her." She snivelled. "I have to know if she's alive."

She tried to stand, but Ben held her at bay.

"Listen, Amy, if your mum couldn't walk, there's little chance she would've escaped."

"You don't know that."

She tried to rise again, but Ben's grasp kept her in place. "Look at the blood."

"Get off me!"

She lashed out, causing Ben to step back. She jumped to her feet and made for the sliding patio doors at the back of the conservatory, which were already open. Ben turned away, deciding to leave her to calm down. He ran an appraising eye over the kitchen. Despite the bloodied wheelchair, the rest of the contents seemed untouched. A pair of wine glasses stood beside two plates in the sink. Ben glanced at the kitchen table, noticing that two of the four chairs had been pulled out. Amy's mother hadn't been alone—but she'd never mentioned her father.

"Shit." Ben approached the sliding doors as an outburst from Amy came from the garden.

"Mum!"

He looked around, noticing the majority of the back yard veered to the left. A lone woman swayed at the bottom of the garden, turning as Amy drew near. The cast on her foot caused her to stumble.

"Mum?"

"Amy, get away from her!"

Ben ran over as the woman lunged for her daughter. They fell to the ground in a tight clinch.

"Mum, get off me!"

Amy fought hard to escape her mother, but her grip was fierce. Finally, Ben wrenched the woman away.

"No, don't!" Amy cried.

She struggled to her feet as Ben glanced around the garden at the array of ornaments. Choosing a long, colourful wind spinner, he pulled it from the ground and impaled the woman through the eye.

"No!"

Amy screamed as her mother bucked and jerked beneath the pole. Ben applied more pressure. Eventually, the sound of breaking skull signalled its exit through the back of her head.

"You killed her," Amy stammered. Ben turned, wiping a stream of sweat from his brow.

"That wasn't your mother."

Amy whirled away and ran back into the house. Ben glanced down at the bloody ornament still clutched in his hand. A slight breeze disturbed the fan, causing it to spin in a colourful blur. He dropped it to the floor and ran after her.

"Amy?"

The house was quiet.

He strolled into the hallway and continued down the passage to the foot of the stairs. He went to call her again, but stopped when a hand grabbed his shoulder. He whirled around, meeting Amy's tear-stained face.

"Where's my phone?" she stammered.

"What?"

"My mobile phone. Where is it?"

"I don't know. Look, is there somebody else here, your dad, perhaps?"

"I need my phone," she repeated, eyes glazed over, staring at the wall. *She's in shock,* he thought.

"Amy!" Ben grabbed her by the shoulders, stepping into her line of sight. "Does your dad live here?"

Amy blinked before a frown creased her face. "No, my dad died when I was five. Why?"

A floorboard creaked somewhere in the house. They both looked towards the stairs, instinctively.

"I think somebody else is here," he whispered. "We have to go."

"Wait, I can't find my phone."

"You had it back at your place."

"Oh god, I must've dropped it when Mrs Carmichael attacked me. We have to go back."

"Have you forgotten my sister?"

"No, but I need to see if anybody has tried to ring me. Please, Ben. I need it."

"Okay. Let's just get out of here."

With a parting look at the stairs, he stepped out of the house and followed her down the garden path. The street was still empty, with the exception of a lone kestrel perched atop a telegraph pole. It stared at the pair as they walked towards the car, ruffling its blood-stained feathers. As they neared, it turned its head in order to get a better look. A trickle of blood dripped silently from its beak. Its body trembled. The temptation became too much to bear. With an ecstatic screech, it leapt from the pole and swooped down.

"Get down!" Ben managed as he ducked the bird's attack. It sped past him, soaring high into the air before curling back for a second strike. Ben ducked again, only this time, the bird's claw tore into his shoulder. He grimaced as it rose once more, preparing for a third assault. He fumbled with his keys, pressing whatever buttons he could. A prompt beep signalled the car was unlocked and the pair scrambled inside as the bird swooped again.

"Are you okay?" Amy asked as Ben examined his wound.

"Yeah, I'll be fine."

The pair flinched as the kestrel struck the roof of the car. It bounced onto the bonnet, where it lay motionless.

"Jesus," Ben whispered, unable to take his eyes off it. "It's not just humans this thing is affecting."

"We have to watch out for birds as well?"

"Maybe. But I doubt many can fly. If it's a bite that's turned them, then chances are they'll be too injured."

"You think?"

Ben nodded.

"But what if it's not just a bite that can turn them?"

"What else could infect them?"

Amy shrugged, her eyes fixed on Ben's shoulder. He looked down, noticing that blood had started to seep through the fabric. He hissed in pain as she pulled back his shirt. A fresh trickle of blood ran from the narrow graze.

"It's not deep, you're lucky," Amy said.

"Yeah, I feel it. Most people get shit on by birds. I'm the one who gets attacked by one."

He looked for a smile on Amy's face, but there was none. Her raw eyes were blank as he started the car.

They drove in silence back to her home, Amy staring out of the window, numb, for the entire journey. With a newfound indifference, she glanced at the deceased men and women littering the streets. Now that her mother was gone, the turmoil of the rest of humanity seemed trivial. The thought of the rest of her family succumbing to the virus had less impact now that her mother, the most important person in her life, was dead.

"I can't do this anymore," she said, as they arrived back on her street.

"What?"

"This. Constantly running from these things. One mistake and it's over." A fresh wave of tears rolled down her cheeks.

"Which is why we need to stick together."

"For what? What good will it do?"

She spotted her phone on the road as Ben pulled up. After a cursory glance to make sure they were alone, Amy got out of the car, the unsettling silence causing her heart to beat more urgently. She wiped her tears away and strode over to her phone, conscious of how loud her footsteps seemed. She sighed in dismay when she saw a long crack spider-webbed across the screen. With another quick glance around, she picked it up and returned to the car. To her surprise, a white light glared from the screen as it resumed its normal start-up process.

"Huh, it still works."

"Why wouldn't it?"

"I dropped it when I fell. I'm surprised it didn't break."

A notification on the screen made her heart race.

"Oh my God."

"What?"

"It's my grandparents. They tried to call me back!"

"Seriously?"

"Yeah, I've got two missed calls."

She dialled the number again, waiting anxiously for one of them to pick up. Her heart sank; the call went through to the answering machine again.

"Hey, it's me, Amy. Are you there? If you're there, please pick up."

She waited patiently, hoping to hear one of her grandparents on the other line. After a brief pause, she let out a sigh.

"Okay, well, ring me back as soon as you can. I've got my phone with me now. I'm just going to Sunnymoor with a friend from work and then we'll come for you, okay?"

She looked at Ben, who was nodding.

"Hope to see you soon, bye."

She hung up the phone. "Is that okay?"

"Sure." Ben grinned. "Where do they live?"

"On a farm about ten miles north of here."

"North?"

"Yeah, why?"

"Just don't tell Fran. Our dad has a place a few miles north. She might insist on checking up on him." He laughed as he started the car and turned back onto the street.

"Really? What's his name? I might know him."

Amy tried to recall the countless farmers she had met through her grandfather. In such a small community, everyone knew each other.

"Gordon Chesterfield."

Amy gasped. "Your dad's Gordon Chesterfield?"

"Yup."

"He owns the slaughterhouse?"

"Yup."

"Oh, I'm glad you're not fond of him. I could never go there. That's one of the reasons I'm a vegetarian."

"Yeah, I've got to admit I can't touch beef either. Chicken I'm okay with, but not cows."

They veered onto the main road and proceeded back towards Sunnymoor. Amy still felt the crippling grief of losing her mother. But the notion of her grandparents still being alive helped to ease the pain. The prospect of losing them as well was too much to bear.

20

The first thing that hit them was the smell. The bedroom door was wide open, releasing the putrid odour from within. Already aware of what they would find, Frank and Lisa entered cautiously, eyeing the blood-spattered walls and vomit-soaked carpet. Minimal light shone through the boarded windows, just enough for them to make out the dead couple on the bed, hand-in-hand, each with half their head missing.

"Oh God," Lisa muttered, putting a hand to her mouth.

Frank stooped down beside the bed and retrieved the shotgun, covering his nose to dispel the gagging stench.

"Let's go."

"We can't just leave them."

"Do you fancy sleeping in here? Because I sure as hell don't."

"I mean, we can't leave them in the house. They'll start to rot."

"One night won't make a difference," he said, making his way back downstairs.

"You never know."

"You can move them tomorrow. I'll help you—if I'm still alive."

"Ever the optimist." Lisa sighed as they returned to the living room.

"Is he—"

"Dead? What do you think?" Frank interrupted Elaine as he slumped back into the armchair.

"So now what?" Simon asked.

"We need to establish a plan."

"Oh, so now Ronald's dead, that makes you the leader?"

"No. As far as I'm concerned, you lot are on your own."

"Really? Then, in that case, I'm the leader, and I say get out of this house."

Simon rose to his feet, glaring at Frank in a display of simulated bravado.

"Yeah?" Frank sneered, rising to meet his opposition. "Well, I'm the one with the gun, and I say go fuck yourself!"

He levelled the shotgun at Simon, watching as all the aggression disappeared from his face.

"So tell me, fat boy, who's leaving the house?"

"Nobody," Simon stammered.

"Wrong. You are."

With that, he grabbed the man by his shirt and dragged him towards the door.

"No!" Elaine screamed, running over to his side.

"Get off me," Simon shouted.

Frank ignored his pleas as he pushed him into the hallway.

"Open the door," he ordered. Sobbing, Elaine didn't move. Frank aimed the shotgun at her husband's head.

"Do it, or I redecorate Ronald's hallway."

Elaine let out a whimper before rushing to the door. Lisa and Tina joined them in the passageway, watching as she frantically released the locks.

"Frank, this isn't right," Lisa said.

"Open it!" he bellowed as the final guard chain was released. Elaine hesitated, but the shotgun pressed against her husband's head spurred her into action. With trembling hands, she pulled the door wide and jumped back.

Frank was surprised to see no zombies as he shoved the man outside.

"You can't do this," Simon protested, stumbling to the ground.

"Watch me."

Frank returned to the house, facing Elaine, standing in the doorway.

"Choose a side: in or out?"

After a moment, she begrudgingly stepped outside. As she turned to protest, Frank slammed the door in her face.

"Frank, that's not right," Lisa said. "They might be a pain in the arse, but they don't deserve to die."

"I'm not killing them. They have loads of options, but being here isn't one of them."

He pushed past the remaining pair and into the living room. The screams of the couple outside were muffled by the boarded windows.

"Frank, there're zombies out there! They're gonna be killed."

"If those fat bastards just lie down and die, then tough. They would have been a burden to us anyway."

"Whoa, they sure ain't lying down." Tina chuckled, staring through a gap in the window.

"What's happening?"

"They've jumped on top of your van."

"How many are out there?" Lisa gasped, rushing to another gap in the window.

"Two, I think. Look, he's hitting them with his belt."

Frank sat in the armchair, watching the flickering flame of a nearby candle. His gaze fell onto the pair of shotgun shells. He reached over and reloaded the gun, silently clicking the rounds into place. He sat back once finished, gliding his finger along the barrel while he listened to the muffled screams.

"We can't leave them out there," Lisa said, turning to face him.

"Why the hell not?"

"Because they're attracting attention. In a few minutes, every zombie within earshot will be here."

Frank shot Lisa a look. They stared at each other for some time as the screams intensified. Eventually, it was the phone that disrupted them. It rang through the house, diminishing the noise from outside. They watched as it vibrated with each ring. Even Tina tore her eyes away from the scene outside to stare at the device.

"Shall we answer it?" Lisa asked.

"No."

"But it might be his granddaughter again."

"And if it is, what do we tell her? That her grandparents are dead and we're house guests?"

They fell silent as the machine beeped. Sure enough, the voice belonged to the woman they had heard earlier.

"Hey, it's me, Amy. Are you there? If you're there, please pick up."

The woman fell silent.

"Okay, well, ring me back as soon as you can. I've got my phone with me now. I'm just going to Sunnymoor with a friend from work and then we'll come for you, okay? Hope to see you soon, bye."

The click of the machine signalled the end of the message.

Frank groaned. "Oh great, more company."

"We have to let them stay, just like we have to let Simon and Elaine back in."

"How is that going to help us? There's not enough food here as it is, bring in more people and it's going to get worse."

"Sooner or later, we're going to have to go back out there. Now do you want to do it alone, or do you want someone backing you up?"

"That fat bastard is only good for a shield. What other use does he have?"

"He can fly," Tina muttered.

Frank turned towards the teenager with a scowl. "He can fly? What is he, a superhero?"

"No, he can fly a plane! He told me earlier. It's a hobby or something."

Lisa gave him a smug grin.

"We can use these people."

With a snarl, Frank cocked the shotgun and strode out of the room. He released the locks and swung the door wide. Atop the prison van stood the distraught couple, trying to maintain their balance as the two zombies below slammed against the vehicle. The creature closest to him reminded Frank of a young Ronnie Corbett. He was a small, pudgy man, wearing a stained waistcoat and trousers. He turned as Frank levelled the shotgun.

The blast sounded like a clap of thunder, splattering the man's head into tiny pieces. The body fell, giving him a clearer view of the second zombie as it charged closer. Frank squeezed the trigger, reducing its head to a pulp.

"Get in, now!"

The pair jumped down and darted into the house, closely followed by Frank. He slammed the door and applied the locks before joining the group in the living room.

"Thank you," Simon wheezed, his hands on his knees.

"Don't thank me yet. I still don't know how useful you're gonna be. Tina says you know how to fly?"

"I do."

"Okay, that's one point. Do you own a plane?"

"No."

"And you're back to zero."

Frank hurled the empty shotgun aside and flopped into the armchair.

"So what're we gonna do?" Lisa asked.

"We're going to have to make some kind of plan."

"What do you have in mind?"

"I don't know. But we're going to need supplies soon. We're also going to need to reinforce this place until we come up with a *better* plan."

The group nodded in agreement.

"Now I don't know any of you, and to be honest, I don't give a shit about any of you. But now is the time to learn a bit more about each other and identify any skills we can bring to the group. Agreed?"

They all nodded.

"Okay, then let's start with you, Tubs."

"Me?" Simon asked.

"Yeah, you. What skills have you got?"

"I can fly?"

"Yeah, but what use is that if we don't have a plane? I can't even think where the nearest airfield is."

"That old army base up north," Lisa said.

"Will there be any planes left?"

"I doubt it."

"Exactly."

"What about Teesside Airport?"

"It's too far to travel." Frank turned back to Simon. "So what can you do apart from flying?"

"I don't know," he stammered.

"Well, what are you good at?" Frank persisted. "What do you do for a living? Are you a joiner? Electrician?"

"I'm a solicitor."

Frank let out an exasperated groan while Lisa winced, as if the man had just struck her.

"So you have no use at all."

"I wouldn't say that. I am good at some things."

"Alright then, you're a solicitor, so you're a good liar. Next up, we have Mrs Tubs." He turned towards Elaine.

"I can cook?" she said hopefully.

"Not great when we've got no food."

"I can knit and sew."

"Great. Except it isn't winter and I don't need a jumper."

"I can clean."

"Finally, you have a use!" Frank beamed, giving her an over-dramatic round of applause. "Can you clean, too, Simon?"

"Yes."

"Good. Then your first job is to go upstairs and get rid of the Carters and that other woman."

The pair looked horrified.

"Then when you're done, you can clean the bedroom. That's where you two will sleep tonight, so I'd do a good job if I were you."

Simon gasped. "We can't sleep in there."

"And there's me thinking I was being nice. Why the hell not?"

"Because Ronald and his wife are in there," Elaine said. "There'll be blood everywhere."

"Hence the cleaning."

"But they *died* in there. I can't sleep in that room."

"Okay then, you can either sleep in there or you can sleep outside. Make a choice." He turned to the teenager. "What can you do?"

"I can put my legs behind my head."

"Not something I was looking for."

"Really? I thought most men love that." She glanced over at Simon, who observed her with a curious stare.

"Hey!" Frank snapped, turning on the pair. "Those corpses aren't gonna move themselves, at least not with their heads blown off. Get to it."

They rose slowly from the couch. Once they had left the room, he turned back to Tina. "So what can you do?"

"I told you."

"And I said I'm not interested. You're half my age and very, very strange."

"Your loss."

"So give me a reason not to throw your arse outside."

"I'm good with a blade. I've got good eyesight, good hearing. I'd be a good lookout. Oh, and I hate Roly and Poly as much as you."

Frank snorted.

"You've won my vote. Why don't you go and put that eyesight to good use and find Ronald's stash of ammo?"

Tina nodded and went on her way, leaving Lisa, who stood with her arms folded, glaring at Frank. "Well?" he asked.

"Well what?"

"Why should I let you stay?"

A splintering thud came from upstairs, but Frank paid no heed as he watched Lisa approach. He raised a brow as she drew close, bending down until her lips were brushing his ear.

"Because I'm the finest piece of arse in this hellhole."

Words failed him. All Frank could do was stare after her as she walked into the kitchen. He looked up at the ceiling as another thud came, followed by an angry exchange. With a long growl, he jumped to his feet, snatching the shotgun and storming upstairs.

"Just grab her arms, Elaine!"

Simon was holding the legs of Louise's corpse, eyeing his wife angrily.

Frank stormed over. "What the fuck are you two shouting about?"

"She won't help me."

"You won't let me get the legs," Elaine retorted.

"What's the difference?"

"I'm not going at the head end! It's disgusting!"

"Oh, give over—"

"Hey, children!" Frank snapped. "You'll be back out there if you don't shut up."

They fell silent, glowering at each other.

"Now, who cares how you lift her? You can *kick* the fucker downstairs for all I care."

"Downstairs? We were just going to throw her out the window."

"Fucking hell, I thought it'd got lighter in here." The boards on the outside had been removed, leaving a sizeable gap.

"What the hell did you do that for?"

Simon shrugged.

"Where are they?"

"Who?"

"The boards, dickhead. Where are the boards?"

"They fell outside. I don't know why they were up here in the first place. Those things can't exactly fly."

"No, they can't, but what if the *birds* fly in here?"

"Why would they?"

"Because it's not just humans that can turn, you prick! The animals are infected as well."

Simon's dumbfounded look mirrored his wife's.

"You think birds might come after us?"

"I don't know!" said Frank. "We don't know what can get infected. But I'm not gonna take any chances."

"What do you want us to do?"

"You can go out there and nail them back on."

"What?" Simon gasped.

"You heard me."

"What about her?" He pointed at the dead woman at their feet.

Frank grabbed the corpse by the legs and dragged it over to the window. In one fell swoop, he picked it up and hurled it through the gap. The body hit the ground with a thud.

"Problem solved. Now get outside and fix that window."

"But what if there are zombies out there?" Simon protested.

"Frank!" Tina called from the bottom of the stairs.

"What?"

"I've found the rifle. There's a box of bullets here, as well."

"There you have it." He smirked, turning back to the couple. "I'll cover you."

He made his way downstairs, begrudgingly followed by Simon and Elaine.

"Let's see it, then."

The teenager handed him the hunting rifle and a box of bullets, and he motioned for the couple to head towards the door.

"I thought you said you were covering us?" said Simon.

"I am. There's a balcony in Ronald's bedroom that will give me a good vantage point. Anything comes near you, I'll kill it."

"Oh great, we're putting our lives in the hands of a serial killer."

Frank aimed the rifle at Simon's head. "You did that the second you walked back into this house. Now move."

"We don't have a hammer or nails."

"Ronald said he had some out back. Go and check it out."

Lisa's arrival prevented further protests from Simon.

"No need, Frank," she said. "I've already been out."

"You went outside?"

"Yeah, the back door isn't barricaded, either. I went into the tool shed and got us some supplies." She pointed over her shoulder at the assembled tools at the end of the hallway. A shovel, crowbar, and hammer were amongst the things she had collected.

"And I got these," she said, retrieving a handful of nails from her pocket.

"That was a stupid move. You could have got us all killed."

"Relax, I had this." She pulled the baton from her back pocket.

"And you're a thief?" Frank laughed. "I guess I'm not the only criminal in here."

"Is that it?" Simon gasped. "You're going to let her off? Why does she get preferential treatment?"

Frank looked back at Lisa and winked.

"Because she's the finest piece of arse in this hellhole," he said. "You've got your hammer, you've got your nails, and I'm pretty sure I saw a ladder out there, so you're good to go. Lock the door behind them, Lisa. I'm going to get into position on the balcony."

"What's happening?"

"Just a bit of DIY."

With that, he made his way upstairs, listening to the protests of the couple below.

"We're not going back out there," Simon raged.

"He's got you covered," Lisa said.

"I don't give a shit. You can't make us go back outside."

Frank yelled down from the top of the stairs. "If I have to come back down there, I'm going to shoot you both in the fucking face. Now go!"

He listened for a response from the couple, but heard nothing. Satisfied his message had sunk in, he made his way over to the bedroom. The smell struck him once more. He strode towards the balcony, wrinkling his nose as he went, the carpet squelching under his shoes as he stepped through puddles of blood and vomit. He pulled back the curtains, exposing the balcony doors. He expected a wave of sunlight to embrace him. What he got was more boards barricading the exit.

"Ronald, you prick."

He heard the door slam downstairs.

"Okay, they're outside, it's all on you!" Lisa shouted.

"Not yet, I'm not ready."

He grabbed a handful of bullets and fed them into the rifle. The rattle of locks sounded downstairs before he heard the front door swing open again. Seconds passed before it slammed shut.

"I can't see them!" Lisa called. "They must be round near you."

Frank growled in dismay as the sound of screaming came from outside. In an instant, he kicked at the boards. Gradually, the wooden planks came away as the shrieks intensified.

"Frank!"

Simon's cry was accompanied by a loud screech. Sensing he was running out of time, Frank tucked the rifle under his arm and hurled himself at the barrier. The boards gave way, and he landed in a heap on the balcony.

"Help!"

Composing himself, Frank jumped to his feet and observed the scene below. The pair were cowering against the side of the house as a trio of zombies sprinted towards them. He aimed the rifle at the nearest creature and fired. The bullet struck the man's shoulder, sending him whirling to the ground.

"Frank!" Simon shrieked.

Frank turned away from the downed creature and aimed at the second. Positioning the rifle against his shoulder, he stared down the sights until the crossbar lingered on the creature's head. He pulled the trigger, dropping the monster in seconds. He looked back towards the first zombie, which shambled along on a broken foot. The bone had snapped through the dead man's boot and was clearly visible as he shuffled towards the couple.

"They're coming!" Elaine squealed.

Frank aimed again, bringing down his original target with a single shot. The zombie fell to the ground, showering the grass with brain matter. He turned back to the final creature. It had almost closed in on the pair when they retreated around the front of the house. It let out an agonised cry as it reached for them. Its loss was short-lived as Frank put a bullet in its head.

"They want to come back in!" Lisa called. "Shall I open the door?"

"No, they're safe. Tell them to get the job done."

He leaned against the bar encircling the balcony and looked down at the bodies below. The men all seemed to have been from a farming background, judging by their clothing. He glanced around at the rest of the landscape and found there were no more threats in sight. Eventually, the couple trudged around the side of the house. They looked at him with malice.

"What's up with you two?"

"You almost got us killed!" Simon snapped.

"Oh, you're exaggerating. Now c'mon, the sooner you get those boards on, the sooner you can come back in."

"Oh yeah, so we can move more bodies, I'm ecstatic."

"Hold on."

Frank disappeared from sight.

Simon frowned at his wife. Without their marksman, they were vulnerable. He glanced around the field, looking for any sign of moving corpses. He found one. With a cry of terror, he jumped back as the dead body landed at his feet. His wife shrieked as a second body came hurtling down from the balcony. Ronald's corpse hit the grass with a dull thud. The remains of his head spilled over the green blades as the couple looked up in terror. Frank wiped his bloody hands on his trousers before leaning on the balcony rail.

"There you go. Now all you gotta do is clean up."

The pair looked at each other incredulously.

"C'mon then, we haven't got all day. There's a ladder over there. Get a move on."

"So you want us to barricade the windows, but you're gonna leave the balcony unsecure?"

"We can lock these doors, genius. You left a fucking hole in the side of the house."

When he saw Simon was about to protest further, he aimed the rifle at the pair. "Don't make me shoot you."

He watched as they walked away, approaching the ladder in the grass. They had a brief dispute before they each grabbed a side and dragged it towards the house. Frank looked away from them and studied the field. There was no sign of the undead, but that didn't mean they weren't close. The sky was void of any birds, planes or insects. The sun shone brightly over the farm as it began its downward arc towards the rest of the world. He estimated they had four hours until darkness; more than enough time to reinforce the barricades.

He gingerly touched his cheek, grimacing from the sting of his wound. While it was all well and good trying to keep zombies out, what would the rest of the group do if one was already in the house?

21

The sight that greeted them upon their return made Amy wish they'd stayed at her house. The previously empty streets were now inundated with corpses. Mutilated remains and half-eaten organs were scattered around the area like discarded waste. She stared as they drove past a procession of entrails that wound along the road, like inside-out snakes.

"Where did all these people come from?"

"I have no idea."

The harsh truth unravelled as she glanced down at the bodies. Whilst she'd assumed Sunnymoor had been wiped out, it had never occurred to her that others could be fighting for survival. The succession of fresh corpses was evidence enough that people had tried to escape.

"They weren't here before," she said.

"I know."

"How many people do you think are still alive?"

"Who knows? It depends how many have found somewhere to hide."

"We can't be the only people with loved ones."

"No, but we might be the only people brave enough to go looking for them."

"Brave? Or stupid?"

Amy checked out houses as they sped past, considering the possibility. Each building could house a range of survivors, people barricaded inside for protection. The option started to appeal to her.

"Do you think we should do the same?"

She looked on as an elderly man stepped out into the road. At least she guessed it was a man. It was hard to tell the thing's gender as the front of its torso was missing, along with most of its face. Only the soiled trousers and the short wispy hair offered any insight.

"Do what?" Ben asked, veering around the decrepit pensioner.

"Barricade ourselves in somewhere."

"When we've found my sister, we can go wherever you want."

Once again, they faced a path of destruction. Amy looked out of the side window, noticing that every storefront had been broken into. Shattered glass littered the pavement and the store's products lay strewn across the road.

"Jesus."

"Looters," said Ben.

"You think?"

"Oh yeah, when the world ends, there's always going to be arseholes who go on a looting spree."

His words played on Amy's mind as they passed another procession of undead creatures. The end of the world was something she had never even considered. But if the disease was spreading to neighbouring countries, what hope did they have? A young boy broke her reverie as he sprinted towards the car. He was barely ten years old. Yet, as Ben sped past him, the little boy's ferocious eyes and foaming mouth gave her goosebumps.

"So when we find your sister, what then?"

"We'll have to find somewhere to lie low."

"Where?"

"I don't know. There doesn't seem to be anywhere that's safe."

They turned onto a side street and faced more of the undead.

"Can't we go another way?" Amy asked as they drove toward the crowd.

"No." Ben started to accelerate. "Fran lives at the bottom of this street."

Amy braced herself as the first body hit the car. The impact sent the corpse hurtling aside before they struck another. Soon, the dull thuds became constant as Ben ploughed through the gathering.

"Hold on!" he yelled, over the barrage of bangs and clatters.

Amy gripped the door handle as blood spattered the windshield. The car slowed as the bodies piled up.

"Get us out of here!" Amy cried.

The undead banged on the rear of the car.

"I'm trying."

The road ahead of them was almost clear, but the imminent obstructions were becoming too much of a hindrance. Amy watched in horror as the car came to a stop.

"What are you doing?"

The crowd swarmed the car. Everywhere they looked, eager hands pounded the windows. The undead bodies blocked out most of the light as they climbed on top of the vehicle. Amy stared at Ben, whose gaze was fixed firmly ahead.

"What are you doing?"

"Waiting."

Zombies were scaling the bonnet. They initially slid back off, but soon gained their footing. Once the last zombie had climbed aboard, Ben put the car in gear and lurched forward. As they sped ahead, those that were on top of the vehicle flew back to the ground. With no more obstructions blocking its path, they raced away, leaving the crowd behind.

"Thank god." Amy sighed as she looked back at the crazed corpses. Ben slowed once more.

"Her car's not here."

The house in question was a small detached building with its own drive. Like her mother's, the front door was ajar.

"Are you planning on going inside?" Amy was unable to mask the concern in her voice. They had only travelled a few hundred yards from the group of zombies. If they waited too long, they would catch up.

"I'll be right back."

"Ben!"

He jumped out of the car and sprinted into the house as the undead shambled closer. None of them seemed capable of running; some had legs so mangled they could only crawl. Yet, they still shuffled quickly. Amy's heart hammered.

"C'mon," she whispered.

As the agonising seconds continued to pass, she began to suspect the worst. *How long does it take to check a house?* Within seconds, they would reach the car. She considered getting into the driving seat until the door swung open. Amy gasped in alarm as Ben jumped behind the wheel.

"She's not there," he said.

He put the car in gear and drove to the end of the road.

"So where are we going now?"

"I don't know. There's one more place we can try, but I'm not sure if it's wise."

"Where?"

"The hospital."

Amy shot him a look.

"Are you serious?"

"Yeah."

"But we've already been to the hospital and she wasn't there."

"Yeah, but her car might be. If it's there, then it'll give me a better idea of where she might be."

Amy sensed Ben's eyes on her. Pressed for a response, she shrugged. "Okay, let's go."

They drove in silence the rest of the way. A few of the more athletic creatures pursued them, but they soon gave up as the car sped on. The vast majority of the buildings they passed had been broken into and destroyed, but there were some that were barricaded. One house had a car backed up against the front door, with the windows blocked by furniture. Another had barbed wire circling the garden wall.

Before long, they arrived back at the hospital. Once again, Amy looked around at the fresh, mangled corpses and felt a wave of guilt. The corpses littering the road were not part of the initial outbreak. They had survived the first wave, only to be killed during the second. She couldn't help but feel partly responsible for their deaths. If they had stayed close by, rather than returning to her home, they could have helped some of the survivors. Ben cast an appraising eye over the carpet of corpses.

"We'll have to drive over them to get to the car park."

Amy nodded, closing her eyes as the car trudged over the strewn bodies. A sickness rose deep within her stomach with each jolt. All she could imagine was the wheels crushing the corpses beneath. She longed for the grisly path to smooth over, to be out of the field of cadavers and back onto regular asphalt.

It was a nearby scream that caused Amy to open her eyes.

"What was that?"

"I think it came from behind the hospital," said Ben.

They drove around the side of the building, both scouring the area as the scream came again.

"There!"

A woman sprinted around the corner. They sped after her, veering around the side until she came into view again and ran into the underground car park. They stopped as another scream echoed from beneath the structure.

Amy felt her heart lurch. She dared not imagine how many zombies dwelled in the dark confines of the car park. The woman was running towards certain death. Before she could voice her concerns, she flinched at Ben's outburst.

"I think that was Fran!"

He pushed the car forward, the headlights dancing around the walls as they rolled down into the gloomy parking lot. Amy scanned the dark confines, looking for Ben's sister. If she was screaming, she had to be fleeing from someone. Yet, there had been nobody behind her when she had run beneath the hospital.

The tyres squealed as Ben ushered the vehicle around the tight car park. The reach of the headlight's beam was limited, but the woman was nowhere in sight.

"Where is she?"

Ben made to reply, but stopped, his eyes wide. The car lurched to a halt as the headlights revealed a grisly spectacle. The hunched backs of the undead were evident first. The squelching sound of their feast merged with the rumbling engine. Ben looked on in horror as his sister joined the morbid banquet. She dropped to her hands and knees and reached into the bloody carcass of a shuddering woman. Fran was not the one who had screamed, nor was she the one fleeing.

“No,” Ben stammered.

“Ben, I’m so sorry.”

The pair remained frozen, watching the morbid feast in a trance. Amy didn’t want to look, but the grotesque scene ensnared her. The spell was finally broken when an open palm smacked the rear window. The pair twisted in their seats as the zombie emitted an ear-splitting screech.

“Shit,” Ben snapped, as more hands joined the assault on the car.

“Let’s get out of here!”

Fran’s corpse rose to its feet. It fixed the car with a glare before sprinting towards them. In one swift motion, Ben reversed in a cloud of smoke and squealing tyres. The undead figures behind were sent reeling as the car made its way towards the exit. Amy gripped her seat as they swerved around a pillar, their pursuers roaring in anger. The car struck the ramp and sailed out into the open once more.

“Thank God.”

Amy sighed as Ben spun the car around and drove away from the hospital. She glanced at his stony face, unsure whether to continue speaking, or allow silence to envelop them. Before long, it was Ben who spoke.

“Where are we going now?”

Amy watched his unblinking eyes.

“Ben, I’m sorry.”

“I know.”

“I don’t know what to say.”

"Then don't say anything. Just tell me where you want to go." He held the steering wheel in a firm grip, his eyes still fixed ahead.

"Do you still want to check on my grandparents with me?"

The unyielding look on his face slackened. "Of course. Just lead the way and we'll go there."

"You don't mind?"

"Not at all. I suppose I ought to visit my old man while we're out there. It's what Fran would have wanted."

They left Sunnymoor behind. Although it was only fair to visit his father, Amy couldn't quash the feeling of dread that had formed in the pit of her stomach. She didn't know why, but going to the slaughterhouse seemed like the worst idea imaginable.

22

"That wasn't so hard, was it?" Frank looked at the weary couple as they stood in the doorway. "Care to join us?"

"Not if you're going to make us do more work," Simon muttered.

"If you want to stay here, you have to pull your weight. And let's face it, there's enough of *that*." He eyed the man's midriff with disgust.

"And what have *you* done?"

"I saved your arse while you were out there," Frank said. He stood aside to allow the pair entry then locked the door. "And you're welcome."

"What do you want us to do now?" asked Elaine.

"I told you, you'll be sleeping upstairs. Unless you want to sleep in a pool of blood, I'd advise you get a mop and bucket."

"And what will everyone else be doing?" Simon demanded, as they moved to the living room.

"Whatever they want."

"So why do we have to clean?"

"Look, do what the hell you like. If you want to sleep in a pile of shit and blood, be my guest."

He slumped in the chair.

"Well, perhaps we don't want to sleep in there," Simon continued.

"Oh?"

"Maybe we want to sleep in here."

"Not while I'm here, Tubs. I've already called this room."

"There was another bedroom up there," Elaine said. "We could stay in there."

"Tina has claimed that room," Lisa said.

"She's just a kid." Simon stared incredulously. "We'll kick her out."

"Good luck," Frank said. "She's got a mean-looking blade up there, and I doubt she'd have any qualms using it on you."

"Well, where else can we sleep?"

"I told you. You have a choice: the big bedroom, or outside."

"What about the kitchen?"

"Ha. You think I'd trust you fat bastards next to our food supply? Keep dreaming, Tubs."

"There's a mop and bucket in there." Lisa motioned to the kitchen. "Use it if you wish."

"C'mon, Elaine, it might not be that bad," Simon offered. The couple trudged back upstairs.

Once they were out of earshot, Frank turned to Lisa. "So how much food do we have?"

"Not a lot," she said. "A couple of tins and jars, but not enough to keep us going."

Frank rubbed his forehead, emitting a hefty sigh.

"I think we've got three days' worth," she said.

"That's if the granddaughter doesn't turn up with her boyfriend." He cast a distasteful glare towards the answering machine.

"What do you think we should do?"

"Kill Blob and Blubber upstairs. We could live off them for a good few weeks."

"I meant seriously."

"Seriously? I think we're fucked."

"I was hoping for some kind of plan."

"Why am I the one who needs to think of a plan? Ever since I got here, all you people want me to do is be the leader."

"You're the one with the gun. That makes you Alpha Male, Top Dog, Billy Big Bollocks, or whatever you want to call yourself. And I know you've got a plan."

"We're going to have to go into town, aren't we?" Frank said, sitting forward in his chair. "The only problem is, who do we send?"

"*That's* the only problem? If that's all you're worried about, we'll be fine. How is that a problem?"

"We'll have to send at least two people, right?"

"Right."

"So who do we send? The two whales wouldn't survive two seconds out there, Tina will probably leave us behind the minute she finds somewhere better, and *we* can't go."

"Why not?"

"Because if Mr Sensitive is left to run things, he won't let us back in."

"But we need food."

"I know. Let's just wait and see how we go. Three days is more than enough time for something to go wrong."

"Oh, stop being so pessimistic."

"Pessimistic? We're in the middle of a fucking zombie apocalypse. What's there to be *optimistic* about?" He watched the woman rise to her feet.

"And I've got a feeling that sneaky bastard upstairs is going to try something," he continued as Lisa left the room. "He's not gonna stand in line."

She returned with both hands behind her back.

"Maybe this will make you feel better?" She produced a large, unopened bottle of rum.

A smile crept across Frank's face. "Now you're talking. Where did you find that?"

"Stashed away under the sink. Care to drown your sorrows?"

"Definitely."

He reached out for the bottle, but stopped when he heard footsteps on the stairs. Lisa quickly retreated to the kitchen as Tina entered the room.

"Those two have finally started cleaning," she said.

"Cleaning? But they didn't take the mop or bucket."

"Well, they're doing something up there."

Frank watched as Tina stepped over to the window. She stooped down, peering through a gap in the boards.

"It's getting dark," she said. "And it looks like we've got more company."

"What?" Frank leapt out of his chair and joined the teenager at the window. "Where?"

"Over there next to that barn."

Frank saw four zombies staggering towards the house.

"Let's not draw their attention." He turned away as Lisa re-emerged from the kitchen.

"Dinner's on."

"What we having?"

"Tuna and spaghetti."

Tina scrunched up her face as she left the room. "Not for me thanks, I'm vegan."

Lisa sighed, looking at Frank for approval.

"It's better than what we got in prison."

She smiled, turning on her heel and striding back into the kitchen.

Frank looked back outside. The zombies had stumbled closer but were still too far away to be a threat. What worried him were the shambling figures in the distance. All faced the house. All were approaching. Somehow, they knew where to go. It was as if they knew the farmhouse was occupied. He rubbed his face as the pain in his cheek worsened. The touch of the scathed flesh brought back all his fears. He tried to dismiss the sweat on his brow as being down to the heat. He fought hard to convince himself that the tremors in his hands were down to nerves. He strived to suppress the notion that he was becoming one of the undead.

***

Gordon Chesterfield strode through the slaughterhouse amidst a backdrop of metallic thuds and shot a glance at the loading bay as the steel support started to buckle. An exasperated roar merged with the crescendo of blows as the animals fought to break free.

"Go fuck yourself."

Turning on his heel, he marched away, the puddles of blood erupting around his boots as he went. Whether it was the life fluid of his livestock or his employees, Gordon couldn't tell. Everywhere he looked he saw death and decay, a sight he was accustomed to seeing, but not on such a grisly scale. Body parts of humans and animals alike littered the area, all from the original breach. Trying to disregard the grotesque sight, he made for the stairway.

An almighty crash echoed around the room, causing him to flinch. He whirled in the direction of the noise and watched as the metal support gave way. The cows on the other side spilled out of the enclosure, skidding clumsily on the blood-soaked floor. Regaining their footing, they caught sight of the abattoir owner.

Gordon darted up the stairs leading to the raised walkway. He bounded across the metal grating, stopping short when he noticed the machinery below, and realising the crazed heifers had followed and had almost reached the top.

"I'm going to make leather jackets out of you cunts!"

The first animal stumbled around the corner. The others followed, causing the gangway to sway under their bulk. Gordon scaled the metal barrier and dropped back down to ground level, straight into a pool of blood. He darted forward and turned on the meat-separation grinder. At once, the blades burst to life, drowning out the noise of the undead cows.

"Go back to hell!"

The animals tried to scale the barrier. As the whirring blades reached maximum velocity, Gordon retrieved his handgun from a holster beneath his jacket. He aimed the Smith & Wesson revolver and, with precision accuracy, fired a single shot. The bullet struck the connecting bolt beneath the strained metal gangplank. On impact, the walkway buckled, sending the cows hurtling into the grinding machine.

A screech displaced the droning blades as they chewed the carcasses. The machine devoured most of the animals in a haze of bloody mist. Gordon fired at those that missed the contraption, killing them all as he strode away, the machine rumbling on as he made his way up a different flight of stairs leading to his office.

He replaced his handgun as he entered the well-lit room, sweat trickling down his chubby face. He glanced out of the large round window which occupied the wall behind his desk. The view of the vast landscape, once so calming, now only served as another stressor. Distant figures roamed the farmland, searching for their next meal. Gordon turned his back on the countryside. The window opposite him looked out over the factory floor. Once the source of his multi-million-pound empire, it was now a tomb for his fallen employees.

He slumped in the chair and ran a hand through his mottled-grey hair. He had learned a long time ago that money couldn't buy happiness, but now he realised it couldn't save him from the end of the world, either. He reached into the cupboard beneath his desk and produced an unopened bottle of whisky.

Leaning back in his chair, he gulped down the honey-coloured liquid as the sun disappeared beyond the hills.

***

Frank dragged on the cigarette clasped between his lips. He leaned against the balcony, looking out at the darkening sky. He had always planned to spend his first night of freedom out in the open, taking in the cool night air, looking up at the stars with a cigar in one hand and a bottle of the finest whisky in another. True, he'd almost got what he wanted: a cheap brand of cigarette and a bottle of rum. But the fact it was during a zombie apocalypse was a bit of a downer.

He blew a cloud of smoke into the air as he heard somebody enter the room behind him.

"Wow, what have they done in here?" Lisa asked, from the previously blood-soaked bedroom.

"They threw the sheets out of the window, flipped the mattress, and laid towels over the blood on the carpet."

"Home sweet home," she said, and joined him outside on the balcony. "So what's wrong?"

"Wrong?"

"Yeah, you didn't say a word while we were eating."

"I did."

"What?"

"I told those fat bastards to do the dishes when we finished."

"Fine." She sniggered. "You said one thing."

The pair fell silent as he took another drag of the cigarette and flicked the ash over the balcony. The glowing embers drifted down, landing on the horde of zombies below. They grappled furiously, reaching towards the elevated couple.

"You still think you're going to turn into one?" Lisa asked, her eyes fixed on the eager crowd below.

"Who knows? We'll just have to wait and see."

"Do you feel different at all? Dizzy? Headache?"

"I feel sick, but that might be down to your cooking."

Lisa shoved him playfully as he took a final drag of the cigarette.

"Ready to go back downstairs?" she asked.

"Might as well. There's not much of a view out here now."

He flicked the remains of the cigarette onto the onlookers before following Lisa inside. The door leading to Tina's room was closed.

"Where's our gothic princess?" he asked.

"Locked herself in the tower."

Frank smirked as they entered the living room, a smile that quickly faded when he eyed the robust couple occupying the couch.

"What are you two doing?"

"You kicked us out of our room, remember?".

"I was trying to be courteous by smoking outside, you ungrateful prick. I won't bother next time."

Frank sat in the armchair, watching Simon expectantly. "Well, off you go."

"What?"

"I want to get my head down. I'm not sleeping while you're in here."

He glared at the couple as they got to their feet and marched out of the room, muttering obscenities as they left.

"Man, you really don't like them," Lisa said.

"I hold a grudge for life."

"But what did they do?"

"Oh, I don't know, how about wanting to kick me out because I'm a criminal? Or how about leaving me to fight that crazy woman upstairs on my own? Or better yet, because they're a bunch of pompous twats who would sooner see me dead than in the same vicinity as them."

"Okay, I see your point."

"Good. Now, why don't you get that bottle of rum?"

"Get it yourself." Lisa stood beside him, arms crossed.

Frank raised an eyebrow. With a snort, he jumped to his feet and strode into the kitchen as she settled into his chair. The dimly lit room provided little insight as to where she had hidden the bottle.

Frank searched the cupboards, dismayed. "Where did you stash it?"

"You're not going to find it in there." Lisa laughed, joining Frank as he looked in the bin.

"Then where is it?"

"Where it should be." She walked over to the fridge and pulled out one of the vegetable trays. She reached into the green foliage and retrieved the bottle. "You can't drink rum if it isn't chilled."

"Chilled rum? First I've heard of it."

"Now all we need is to find some glasses."

"We don't need glasses." Frank took the bottle and entered the living room.

"You criminals are so vulgar." Lisa watched as he took a swig.

"You not joining me?"

"Of course, I'm not letting you get pissed on your own."

She sat beside him on the worn sofa, prising the bottle out of his hands. Frank watched as she gulped the liquid, holding the bottle high.

"Hey, leave some for the fishes."

"The fish will probably be dead."

"Fine, well, leave some for me." He took the bottle back and took a hefty swig.

"You want to be careful, that might go straight to your head."

"Trust me, darling, you'll be seeing stars way before me."

"Really? When was the last time you had a drink?"

"The night I was arrested."

"And how long ago was that?"

"Five years."

"Well, if it's been five years since you had a drink, I think you oughta slow down. Your body won't be used to it."

"Yeah, right."

Frank laughed at the prospect, but as he tipped the bottle for another swig, he knew she was right. The weightless feeling of euphoria was slowly creeping up on him.

"So how did you end up in Harrodale?"

Frank looked at her curiously as he passed the bottle back. "You really want to know?"

"Absolutely."

He wiped his mouth with the back of his hand, waiting for the words to come to him. "I murdered my wife with a hammer."

The statement didn't seem to faze Lisa. "Really? What made you do that?"

"I found her fucking another guy."

This time, Lisa almost choked on the rum. "You're kidding?" she spluttered.

"Nope, I came home early one night and they were going at it like rabbits. So I picked up a hammer and beat them to death. Or at least that's what I thought. Turned out the guy survived."

"Did you plead guilty?"

"Their blood was all over my clothes when they arrested me. I could hardly play dumb."

"No, but you could have pleaded diminished responsibility. People do that all the time."

Frank laughed. "You mean the whole 'I lost my mind' or 'it was the heat of the moment' bullshit? No. I knew exactly what I was doing."

"Do you regret it?"

Frank considered the question. "Kind of, yeah. She was dead after the second or third blow. It was too quick. If she was alive now, I'd happily watch her get ripped apart by those things."

"Wow, you're really fucked up, huh?"

"I did warn you."

"Well, just think: the guy might've survived back then, but he's probably dead now."

"There's no 'probably' about it, I *know* he's dead." He took the bottle from Lisa. "When I found out he was alive, I arranged a hit. A guy inside had connections. He agreed to organise it, providing I paid him back. He did, and I did."

"How did you repay him?"

"By fighting for him."

He took another swig from the bottle, noticing how much they had got through in such a small space of time. A silence enveloped them.

"I bet it feels good to be able to taste alcohol again," she said after a while.

Frank nodded.

"In a way, this whole zombie thing has worked out well for you."

"How so?"

"Well, you've got your freedom again. And in a world without laws. It must be a criminal's paradise."

"I admit it has its perks. I just wish those fucking zombies would give it a rest."

"They won't bother us in here. We're all alone."

"Locked in a house with a murderer? No wonder that lot are shitting themselves. You guys have it rough."

"Yeah, I'd be completely at your mercy. After all, there are other things you haven't had for five years."

Frank sneered. "I'm not going to *rape* you if that's what you think."

"Hey, it's not rape if you've got consent."

He saw the mischievous glint in her eyes. Before he had time to react, she was straddling him, pushing the bottle aside and mashing her lips against his.

"Whoa, hang on."

"What?"

"Let's slow it down a bit. I wanna enjoy this."

She sat back on his lap. "Okay then, I'll give you it slower."

Frank watched as she rocked on his legs, moving her hips seductively as she slowly unbuttoned her shirt.

"Now you're talking. This is turning into a good apocalypse."

"Let's make the most of it."

He looked on as she spread her shirt wide. A floral tattoo adorned her side, rising up her ribs and under the cup of her black bra. She dangled the shirt above his face before releasing it, concealing his view. Frank closed his eyes, inhaling the lingering notes of perfume. He pulled the garment aside, noticing that she had unclasped her bra and was now holding it loosely over her breasts. She pushed her chest into his face as she pulled the bra free.

"These are great tits."

Frank groaned as she leaned back, allowing him to massage the smooth flesh of her breasts. Slowly, she slipped to her knees, massaging his crotch.

A flurry of hurried footsteps caused his eyes to snap open. Lisa jumped to her feet as Tina burst into the room. Her face, at first shrouded in a cloak of alarm, quickly lightened as she looked at the pair.

"Well, well, what's going on here? You two? I never would've guessed."

"What do you want?" Lisa demanded, placing her arms across her chest.

"Just to let you know that we've got company; *living* company."

"What?!" Frank jumped to his feet and dashed to the window.

"There's a car in the distance," Tina continued. "You'll be able to see the headlights in a minute. They're coming this way."

"The granddaughter," Lisa said, putting on her shirt. "What are we gonna do? Food is scarce enough as it is."

"It's not that which worries me," Frank said. "If they've come from town, they could have the entire population behind them."

23

The sun had started to sink ahead of them, with the promise of darkness at its back. Despite it disappearing from view, the heat inside the car was suffocating. Amy wound the window down as warm beads of sweat formed on her brow.

"I was just thinking the same thing," Ben said, winding down his own window and resting his arm on the outside of the car.

Amy leaned closer to the cold air. It cooled the film of sweat on her face, soothing her with its medicating touch. She inhaled deeply, savouring the aroma of the countryside.

"Brings back some fond memories," Ben said, looking around at the fields as they passed.

"Did you grow up around here?"

"Yeah. I moved to the town when I was eighteen and haven't been back since."

"How come?"

"Nothing really to come back for. Fran had gone off to university and my old man was always preoccupied with work. I just fancied something different."

Amy nodded, casting her eyes back outside.

"It's good to be back," Ben continued.

"Just a shame it's under these circumstances."

"Yeah," he muttered as they rounded the remains of a cow in the middle of the road. "I wonder what turns them."

Amy shrugged, as another dead cow came into view. "If it's a virus, it could be spread by airborne droplets: coughing, sneezing, and that sort of thing."

"I haven't seen any of them cough or sneeze. They just bite."

"Spread in their saliva, perhaps?"

"Maybe."

They came to a halt and veered onto another road. Amy closed her eyes as they accelerated once more. The wind whipped her hair back as she leaned closer to the window. She let out a sigh of relief, inhaling the fresh countryside air. Her eyes snapped open when she detected a hint of smoke. Looking around, she scoured the endless fields, trying to find the source.

"Do you smell that?"

"What?"

"Smoke."

Ben inhaled deeply, his brow furrowed. "Yeah, what is that?"

"It's not the car, is it?"

"I hope not." Ben slowed down as the pungent smell grew worse. "It smells like rubber."

"Where's it coming from?"

They both looked ahead as they reached the pinnacle of a bank. At once, the source of the smell became apparent: a lone car ahead, burning ferociously, a dark plume of smoke hanging high above it.

"There!"

Ben stepped on the accelerator, pushing the vehicle harder as they sped down the bank.

Amy sank back in her seat as the car tipped a hundred miles per hour. She kept her eyes glued to the burning remains as they drew near.

"There's someone there," she said. The pair stared at the lone figure that motioned to them frantically.

"Do you think it's one of them?" she asked, straining her eyes. The dwindling light offered no support, but she could see the figure jumping up and down, arms waving.

"I've never seen them do that before."

Ben slammed on the brakes as the man ran into the middle of the road. His clothes hung loose from his skinny frame. He readjusted them as the car drew near.

"Let's pick him up," Amy said.

"Are you crazy? He might've been bitten. What if he becomes one of them?"

"We can't leave him out there."

The man ran to the window as they slowed to a stop.

"Thank god," he panted. "Please, help me. I crashed my car and—"

"Are you hurt?" Ben interrupted.

"What?"

"Have you been bitten?"

"Oh, no." He raised his arms and turned around to support his statement.

"Okay, get in."

"Thank you."

The man jumped into the back of the car. As soon as the door slammed shut, they took off once more.

"Thank you so much," he said, wiping sweat from his brow.

"No problem." Amy smiled, turning in her seat. "What's your name?"

"Glen. Glen Reeves."

"Nice to meet you, Glen, I'm Amy and this is Ben."

Ben eyed the dishevelled man in the rear-view mirror. The smell of cannabis quickly became apparent, and Amy was glad they had their windows down.

"So what happened?" she asked, eyeing the man's oversized clothes.

"I was trying to get away from all those *freaks*. I didn't think there would be any out here, but I was wrong."

"How did you crash?"

"I hit a bloody farmer in the middle of the road."

Amy looked back at the distant wreckage. "I didn't see a farmer."

"That's because he was stuck to my bumper. Once I hit him, I veered off the road and smashed into a frigging rock. Next thing I know, there's smoke coming out of the bonnet and I got out before it went up in flames."

"What about the guy you hit?"

"What about him?"

"Was he alive? Or was he one of them?"

"After I hit him and crashed into the rock, I could hear him snarling underneath the car. Even when it caught fire, he was still growling."

Amy looked at him wide-eyed.

"So where did you come from?" Ben asked, breaking the silence that had formed.

"Bealsdon."

"How bad is it there?"

"Really bad."

"Where were you heading?"

"Anywhere. I just want to find out what the hell's going on."

"Don't we all? How much do you know?"

"Nothing! The only time I realised there was anything wrong was when Mrs Cropley burst in while I was in the bath!"

"Who's Mrs Cropley?" Amy asked.

"The old dear who lives next door to me. She kept trying to bite me. Luckily, she didn't have her false teeth in."

Ben snorted, shaking his head as he drove.

"Anyway, I got past her and saw two blokes coming up the stairs. So I got out the window and ran down the road completely starkers!"

Amy tried hard to suppress her amusement, but as soon as Ben started laughing, she couldn't help but join in.

"It wasn't funny," Glen said. "I had to steal these clothes off somebody's washing line."

He tugged at his shirt in disgust. At that point, Amy felt the laughter cripple her. Her chest felt tight as tears streamed down her face.

"Oh, I'm glad you find it so funny." He pouted, looking out of the window.

"Sorry," Amy said. "But it's laugh or cry in this situation."

"Looks like you're doing both."

She nodded, wiping her eyes as she composed herself. "So how did you end up in your car?"

"I made my way back home so I could get my own clothes. But as soon as I got through the front door, Mrs Cropley came racing down the stairs! So I grabbed my keys and jumped in my car. Now here I am."

"Well, it's good to have you with us, Glen. I just wish we could have saved more people."

"Me too. I don't know how many times I drove past people getting eaten. I should've stopped to help."

"It wouldn't have done any good," Ben said. "Once you're bitten, you're dead."

"Really?"

"Yeah, we think so. Then you turn into one of those things."

"Is there no way to cure it?"

"None that we know of."

"Shit."

They fell silent briefly before Glen spoke once more. "I don't suppose either of you have a light?" He raised a rolled cigarette into view.

"Sorry," Amy said. Ben shook his head.

Glen sighed and sat back in the chair, placing the cigarette behind his ear. "So where are we going?"

"My grandparents have a farm near here. They've tried ringing me, so I'm hoping it's safe there."

"And what if it isn't?"

Amy didn't answer. She had experienced enough grief for one day.

"Take a left here," she said, noticing they were nearing the farm.

The car turned onto the track, creating a plume of dust as it went. Amy strained her neck to catch a glimpse of the building. On an ordinary summer's day, she could see the small house in the distance. But with the last light far behind them, all she could see were dark fields. She sat back in her chair, winding up the window as a chill swept over her arms.

"Doesn't look bad," Glen said.

"I'm not sure," Ben replied. He pointed to a broken wall as they passed. Tyre tracks were present on the field encased within the brick wall, with mud spatter clear on the road. Whoever had been driving had come off the field and onto the road they were now travelling on.

"Is it much further?" Ben asked. "We can't travel in the dark. I can't see a thing out here."

"Take your next right and it's a straight road up to the house."

"But what are we gonna do if there's any trouble?" Glen asked.

"They'll be there. They called from their house phone."

"That's not what I meant."

Amy ignored the comment.

"We'll sort out any issues when we get there," Ben said. "Either way, we'll have to spend the night."

He slowed the car as the right turn neared. Amy looked across at her grandparents' farm, just as an almighty thud struck the roof.

"Jesus!" Glen cried.

The car swerved as another impact came from the side. Amy spun around and saw a large man disappear from view. She gripped onto the door handle as they swerved onto the lane leading up to the house.

"How many are out there?" Glen whimpered as a hand smacked the window. Ben ignored him. The narrow beam of the headlights danced over the uneven ground. Amy gasped as a snarling man appeared, blocking their path. Ben floored the accelerator, sending the zombie reeling high into the air. The impact caused a headlight to shatter, plunging the left side of the track into darkness.

"Shit!" Ben spat.

They flinched as another loud bang came from the roof.

"It's on top of the car!" Glen shrieked, cowering on the back seat.

With that, a body landed on the windshield. The man's wide eyes stared at them as he clung to the bonnet.

"I can't see!" Ben raged. Amy looked around helplessly as more snarling faces flashed past. She tried hard to think of a way out, but with so many zombies surrounding them, they would be dead for sure if they stopped. She stared at the man on their windscreen as a loud crack obliterated his head. Blood spattered over the glass as the body slid from the car. Moments later, a second gunshot came from the house.

"It's my grandpa!" Amy cried as the zombies running alongside them began to fall.

"I still can't see." Ben turned the wipers on, but the blades smeared the blood across the windscreen.

"There's still some left!" Glen shouted as another gunshot filled the air.

Ben sprayed soapy water onto the screen. The red liquid started to become transparent as the wipers dashed over the window. Their view ahead was clear, and the remaining headlight lit up a vehicle right in front of them. Amy shrieked, bracing herself for impact as the car smashed into the stationary Land Rover. The collision threw her forward and she hit the dashboard hard, sending a wave of pain sweeping through her body.

She groaned, clutching her head as the gunshots continued to ring out. She glanced across at Ben, who was slumped over the steering wheel.

"Ben?"

He didn't respond. She reached across to him, searching for a pulse. Another gunshot resonated.

"Ben!"

She heard movement behind her. Turning, she saw Glen looking out the windows, his quick head movements resembling those of a meerkat.

"They're gone," he said. "Let's get the hell outta here."

He threw open the door and jumped outside. Amy turned back to Ben and placed a hand on his chest. It rose steadily in time with his breathing.

"Thank god," she said.

The driver's door swung open.

"C'mon, we need to go," Glen urged.

"Ben's unconscious. We can't leave him."

Glen turned back to the house. "We need help to get this guy in!"

Amy's eyes narrowed as a female voice sounded from the farmhouse.

"Frank, we need you."

The voice seemed unfamiliar, but she could not get a look at the woman. Amy stepped out of the car, her head throbbing. She stared at the rugged gunman as he approached the car, muttering under his breath.

"Who are you?" she demanded.

The man paid her no heed as he leaned into the car. He came back up moments later, dragging Ben across the ground.

"Who are you?" she repeated, following them towards the house.

"Shut up and get inside! I can't shoot those fuckers with this prick in my arms." With that, he dragged Ben over the threshold and vanished from sight.

"Come on," Glen said, pulling on her sleeve as he made for the house.

Amy followed, noticing another unfamiliar person in the doorway.

"You must be Amy," the woman said.

"Yeah, who the hell are you? Where are my grandparents?"

"Let's go inside, there could be more out here."

Reluctantly, Amy stepped into the house. She watched the young woman slide all the locks into place.

"Everyone's in the living room," the woman said, sweeping her blonde hair out of her face.

"Where are my grandparents?"

Before she could get an answer, a confrontation sounded in the next room.

"*Three* people! What are we running, a hotel?"

Amy recognised the voice as the gunman's. She walked into the living room as he rounded on Glen.

"So which one of you is the boyfriend?" he raged, looking between the trembling man and the unconscious guard on the floor.

"What do you mean, *boyfriend?*" Amy snapped, crouching down to Ben's aid. His pulse felt normal, and the rise and fall of his chest comforted her. She pinched his arm, but he didn't respond.

"Is he dead?" Glen asked.

"One of you get me a light."

The unknown woman disappeared into the kitchen. She returned seconds later with a torch. Amy took it without words and lifted Ben's eyelids, shining the beam over his pupils.

"What are you, a nurse?" the rugged man asked.

"Yes," Amy replied as Ben started to move. She looked up at the gunman. "Where are my grandparents?"

The rage in his eyes depleted, and at once Amy knew their fate. She looked back at Ben as he raised a hand to his head. He blinked hard, wincing as his fingers roamed over a gash in his hair.

"More company?" The query came from a dark-haired teenager who had appeared in the doorway.

"Yeah," the gunman replied. "The granddaughter and her boyfriends."

Amy ignored the remark and helped Ben sit up.

"What happened?" he groaned.

"We crashed into a car."

"Whoa, have they trashed the fat twat's Land Rover?" the teenager asked excitedly as she made her way to the window.

"Yeah, it's completely written off." The gunman sneered.

The teenager snorted as Ben got to his feet.

"Who are you lot?" he asked, eyeing the people in a daze.

"We're the ones who saved you," the blonde woman said. "I'm Lisa, this is Frank, and that's Tina."

Amy looked around at the familiar surroundings from her childhood. Everything was the way she remembered it. Framed photographs were fixed around the fireplace. Many of the beaming faces belonged to her. The old oak coffee table stood proudly in the middle of the room, the centrepiece surrounded by the rest of the furniture. The worn sofa that had been there longer than her years was still pointed towards the aged TV set. Then her gaze fell on the lone armchair, her grandfather's 'throne,' as he so often called it. A pang of grief gripped her stomach. She tried to dismiss it, focusing instead on the continuing conversation.

"That was some pretty reckless driving," Frank said, eyeing Ben with distaste. "I'm guessing you're a taxi driver?"

"Security," Ben retorted. "What about you? Gunslinger? Cowboy?"

"Serial killer, actually."

The remark came from an obese man as he and a chubby woman joined them in the living room. Amy looked from the couple back to Frank.

"You're a serial killer?"

"Aren't we all? You must've killed your fair share of zombies by now?"

"None."

"Somehow I'm not surprised. I'm guessing you've had your bodyguard here doing all the dirty work."

Ben lunged forward but stopped short when the man forced his shotgun beneath his chin.

"Play nice doggie, or you'll be put down," Frank said.

Amy grabbed Ben's arm, willing him to back off. After a tense silence, he tipped his head back and returned to her side.

"Good boy. Now if you want to stay here, you have to help out."

"With what?" Amy asked.

"Put it this way, your grandparents were hardly stocking up when this zombie epidemic hit. We need supplies. First thing tomorrow, we're heading to the nearest town and ransacking it. If you want to stay here, you'll help."

"Not likely," Ben replied. "At first light, we're leaving."

Frank glared at the man. After a few seconds, he raised the shotgun again.

"If you're not going to help us, then I see no use for you."

"What are you gonna do? Kill us?"

"No. I'll give you five seconds to leave. After that, yes, I'll kill you."

"You wouldn't."

"Really? What if I tell you this fat cunt wasn't lying when he said I was a killer?" He motioned towards the chubby man standing by the kitchen.

"I wasn't," the man urged, shaking his head rapidly. "He's from Harrodale."

"Make no mistake: I'll blow your head off without thinking twice."

Before Ben could answer, Amy butted in.

"Okay, we might help you. But first, answer me this: did *you* kill my grandparents?"

Frank scoffed, lowering the shotgun once more.

"Your grandmother was already dead when we got here. Soon after, your grandfather killed himself."

The news hurt. But Amy had experienced far too much grief for the shock to sink in.

"Where are they?"

She watched as he nodded towards the window. "With the rest of the dead."

Amy closed her eyes. She exhaled slowly as she turned back to the two men.

"Okay, we'll stay the night, and we'll help them," she whispered, trying to stop the tears from flooding her eyes.

"What?" Ben spat. "I'm not risking our lives going into town when it doesn't benefit us."

"Shh! It *does* benefit us."

"How?"

"We can't get very far without transport, can we?"

Ben looked towards the window, realisation showing on his face.

"Your car is in no fit state to drive," she continued. "I say we go to town, help them out, get a few things for ourselves, and take a car while we're there."

Ben nodded. Amy turned to face the rest of the room.

"Okay, we'll help you," she said. "But can we please stop all this negativity? We're in this together, right?"

"Right." Lisa smiled. "We're not bad people. Even Frank here has a pleasant side."

The man twisted his face into a sickly grin before rolling his eyes.

"Let's just be civil to each other from now on."

"That's fair enough," Amy said. "So where can we sleep?"

"Wherever you want." Frank shrugged, sitting down in the armchair.

"Can I take my grandparents' room?"

"Sure."

"What?" the obese man snapped. "After everything we went through to clean that damn room?"

"What can I say?" Frank said. "It was her grandparents' house. If she wants to sleep there, she can."

"This is ridiculous!"

"Okay, we're gonna turn in," Amy announced over the man's indignant grumblings. "We'll see you guys tomorrow." She motioned for her two companions to follow her.

"Go on, I'll be up in a sec," Ben said.

Amy looked back at him with a frown. "Fair enough. Are you coming, Glen?"

He nodded, following her to the doorway, but Amy didn't leave. She turned, watching as Ben stepped forward.

"Got a problem, *friend?*" Frank asked from the armchair.

"I don't know yet." Ben sat on the edge of the coffee table to face Frank. "If we help you, you have to help us."

"Are we not doing that by letting you stay here?"

"No, this house belongs to Amy's family. We're letting *you* stay here."

"The rules have changed, pal. It's survival of the fittest now. We hold all the weapons, which makes it *our* house. So don't try anything funny."

"Don't worry, I won't," Ben said. "But weapons or not, if you go into that bedroom at any point, I'll kill you."

"Why the fuck would I wanna go in there? I admit it's been a while since I've seen a threesome, but two fellas popping a lass does nothing for me."

Ben squeezed his hand into a fist and leaned forward.

"It's not like that," he said. "But since we're helping you tomorrow, I want you to help us."

"What do you want?"

"One of those guns and some ammo."

"There'll be a gun shop in town, Rambo. You can take whatever you want."

"I meant *before* we go."

Frank's eyes narrowed. "Why?"

"Because if we get attacked, we'll need more than a few gardening tools to fight them off."

"I'll think about it," he said, after a moment of deliberation. "We'll discuss it before we leave."

Ben nodded as he rose to his feet.

"Give her one from me." Frank winked.

Ben inhaled slowly, his fists clenched. He ignored the remark as he walked towards Amy. She led the way up the stairs.

"What?" she heard Frank exclaim. "Someone ought to be having sex tonight."

24

Frank lurched awake as a shriek filled the farmhouse. He grabbed the shotgun by his side and leapt from the armchair. The room was lighter now, with the sun starting to creep through the boarded windows. He scanned the area, noticing that Lisa was no longer sleeping on the couch. He made for the doorway, tripping over a shadowy bulk on the floor.

"Wassup?" Simon grumbled from his makeshift bed.

"What the fuck are you doing there, shithead?" Frank spat as he stumbled towards the stairs.

A dull thud shook the ceiling as another high-pitched wail sounded, this time from a man. Frank bounded up the stairs and rounded the corner of the landing. As he turned, one of the doors opened. Tina emerged, rubbing her eyes.

"What's going on?" She yawned.

The answer came as Lisa and Glen came crashing out of the bathroom. Frank looked on as Lisa pinned the whimpering man to the ground. She held his arm tight behind his back, pushing his face into the floor.

"What happened?"

"This little perv was spying on me!" she snapped, kneeing Glen in the lower back.

"I wasn't, I swear."

"What happened?" Frank repeated.

"I had to pee. So I went into the bathroom, sat down, and who did I see? Old peeping Tom here, ogling me from the bath."

"It was the only place left to sleep. Ben and Amy wouldn't let me sleep in there."

"I wonder why." Frank snorted. He stepped over Lisa and her captive before rapping on the bedroom door. "C'mon, lovers, rise and shine!"

He stepped back as the door swung wide. Ben entered the hallway, closely followed by Amy.

"What's going on?"

"Lisa found this guy in the bathroom because you two wanted to be *alone*."

"Yeah, because we don't know him. I didn't want to spend the night watching the door as well as *him*."

"Sure," Frank said.

Lisa dragged Glen to his feet. "Look at me again and I'm taking your balls."

With that, she shoved the man back into the bathroom.

"C'mon," Frank ordered. "I want you all down here now. We need to make a plan." He eyed Simon and Elaine as he strode into the living room. "Nice of you to join us."

"What happened?"

"Nothing, just sit down and shut up."

He sat in the single chair, with Lisa perched on the arm, waiting for the rest of the congregation. Once everyone had assembled in the room, Frank relayed his strategy.

"Okay, I've been thinking about this all night, so if anyone disagrees, I'll shoot you in the face. Understand?"

Some of the group nodded, others stared at him with expressionless masks.

"We're going to split into three groups."

"Why three?" Ben asked.

"Did you not hear me say I'd kill you?"

"Yeah, if we *disagree*, I'm merely asking why."

"Because there are three different things we need: food, equipment, and weapons."

"What do you mean by equipment?" Amy asked.

"Things like wood, torches, batteries, nails. Anything that can help secure this place and help us survive."

"Okay, well, how about me and Ben get the weapons, half of you guys get the food, and the other half get the equipment?"

Frank shook his head, scoffing at the prospect. "You'd love that, wouldn't you? No, I've already decided who's going where. You and G.I. Joe aren't together. Call it an insurance policy."

"So where are we going?" Simon asked.

"Don't get comfortable, Tubs. You and Mrs Tubs aren't sticking together either."

"I'm not leaving my wife!"

"You will, or we'll take you out there and leave you."

"So what are the teams?" Tina asked, before Simon could protest any further.

"You, Lisa, and Fatty can get equipment."

"Which one?" Tina asked.

"The one who's supposed to be a man."

Simon snarled at Frank as he looked around the rest of the room.

"In charge of food will be Amy, Mrs Tubs, and whatshisface." He pointed towards Glen, sitting sheepishly in the corner.

"Which leaves me and you?" Ben asked.

"Precisely, Rambo. And if there aren't any more questions, let's get moving."

He made to rise, but stopped when Amy spoke.

"But how are we all going to get there?"

"We're going in the van."

"The *prison* van?"

"Yeah."

"Can we all fit in?"

"There are two seats up front, and five cells in the back. One of you will have to stand." He looked around at the anxious faces as he got to his feet. "Shall we?"

He passed the rifle to Lisa before loading cartridges into the shotgun.

"I thought we could have a gun?" Ben objected.

"We? There's no *we* anymore. I've told you the groups."

"Okay, but *we'll* be getting guns at the shop. The others won't have anything to protect themselves."

Frank sighed. “Fine. The other group can have this gun when we get there. Now let’s go before I change my mind.”

He made his way over to the door, closely followed by the rest of the group. Lisa stayed behind, approaching the gap in the window once everyone had left.

“How we looking, Lise?” Frank yelled from the door.

“Looks clear to me.”

“Okay, let’s go.”

He removed the bolts and chains and swung the door open. He noted a trio of zombies near the barn, but there were no more in sight.

“Let’s go.”

He led the group over to the prison van, watching the three zombies nearby. They appeared not to notice the procession as they rushed to the vehicle. Their quiet footsteps and bated breath aided their silent escape.

“Oh, fuck me!” Simon gasped.

Frank whirled around. Simon stood beside his wrecked Land Rover with a hand to his mouth.

“Look at the state of this!” he said.

“You idiot,” Lisa snapped as the trio of zombies let out a yearning screech.

Frank levelled his shotgun, waiting for them to come into range. “In the van, now!”

The rest of the group made for the vehicle as Lisa stood by his side, aiming the rifle at their targets.

“You any good with that thing?” he asked.

A thunderous clap reduced one attacker’s head to fragments. “Yeah.”

Lisa aimed again, dropping another zombie in seconds. The final creature was within a few metres of the pair when Frank obliterated his head with the shotgun.

"Two out of three ain't bad," he sang, opening the driver's door and jumping in. The air was warm, with a faint smell of death, no doubt emanating from the fragments of cow stuck in the grill. He looked to the seat beside him, staring at his passenger in wonderment.

"What the hell are you doing?" he asked Glen, sitting rigid in the front seat.

"What?"

"That seat's reserved. Get in the back."

Lisa opened the door wide. Not waiting for Glen to respond, she grabbed his shirt and dragged him outside.

"Thanks, Perv," she said, climbing in.

Frank started the van as Glen jumped in the back. After performing a quick U-turn, they were racing down the narrow country lane.

"Which town are you planning on ransacking?" Lisa asked.

Frank shrugged, concentrating on the road ahead.

"You do have some idea, though, right?"

"Every town nearby will have what we need: a hunting shop, a hardware store, and some kind of grocery store. We'll visit the closest one and hope for the best."

"Yeah, but a hunting shop might not be good enough. I mean, they might only have pellet guns and air rifles."

"If that's the case, then we can modify them. It's easily done."

"Oh yeah, I forgot I'm sat next to a prisoner."

"*Former* prisoner."

"Yeah, whatever."

"Don't worry. Deer hunts are a big thing around here. Most gun shops should stock more than pellet guns."

"I hope you're right."

They both glanced at a sign showing the distance to the nearest towns.

"Newchurch or Bealsdon?" Frank wondered aloud.

"Both are six miles away, just go left or right."

"Fair enough."

They drove on until the junction loomed ahead. Debating the two routes in his mind, Frank decided on the right turn.

"Bealsdon it is."

After only five minutes, they were at the edge of the ruined town. Fires raged, alarms blared, and the dead wandered the streets aimlessly.

"Excellent choice," Lisa said as she thumbed cartridges into the rifle.

"There's a Transit van over there," Frank said, pointing outside. "Shall we let the first group out here?"

"That'll be me, I'm guessing?"

"Only if there are keys in there. If not, we'll keep looking."

"Keys?" She scoffed. "Who needs keys?"

She leapt outside and approached the side of the van.

"Okay, we're here," she told the group. "Tina and Simon, you're up."

She walked around the front of the van to Frank's window.

"All set?" he asked.

"Yup."

"You sure you can start that thing?"

"Please. I've been wiring cars for years. You're not the only hardened criminal around here."

"The murderer and the thief." He grinned. "Sounds good, huh?"

"Shakespearean, my dear."

Standing on her tiptoes, she leaned in through the window and kissed him lightly on the lips.

"Make sure you come back in one piece," she said.

"You too. Meet you back here in an hour?"

"Any longer and I'll come looking for you."

"You care that much?"

"Hell, yeah. Those guns will come in handy. I'm not leaving them just because you're dead."

She cast Frank a mischievous grin before turning towards the Transit van.

"Looks like *you're* the one who's throwing it about."

"Jesus!" Frank exclaimed. He whirled around to see Ben in the passenger seat. "What the fuck are you doing?"

"I came to find out where the hell we are."

"Bealsdon."

"Huh. That's where Glen's from."

"Great, get him up here and he can tell us where the nearest supermarket is."

He waited for Ben to leave before looking back at Lisa. The van door stood ajar, with her legs visible over the passenger seat. She worked the cover beneath the ignition whilst Tina and Simon served as lookouts. A few seconds passed before the white van rumbled to life.

"What are we doing here?"

"For fuck's sake!" Frank gasped. He spun around to see Glen beside him. "What are you people? Ninjas?"

"Why are we here?"

"Because it was the closest place. Now, where's the nearest shop?"

Glen looked away, trying to find the best answer. "The nearest DIY shop is a few minutes from here."

"Which way?" a voice asked.

Frank flinched. Lisa had approached his window again.

"Could everyone stop sneaking about?"

"Kinda hard when there are zombies everywhere."

"You go straight ahead," Glen said. "Take a right and follow the road to the end. The shop is on the corner."

"A corner shop?" Frank asked. "How is that going to help us?"

"No, it's a depot. It's pretty big."

"Sounds good to me," Lisa said.

Frank turned back to face her. "Remember, pick up anything we can use. But if it's too crowded, don't hang around. You don't have many bullets left."

"I know. See ya soon."

She jogged back to the Transit van. Tina and Simon were already inside waiting for her. With a parting glance, she raced ahead. Frank stared as she cut down some milling zombies before bearing right. Once the vehicle was out of sight, he turned back to Glen.

"Right, now, somewhere for food?"

"A bit more complicated, we're going to have to go quite far into town."

Frank sighed.

"But it's a supermarket. It'll have everything we need," Glen continued.

"Okay. What about a gun shop?"

"There's one a few minutes from the supermarket. It's a good one as well, but you might have trouble getting in."

"Why?"

"It's only open during hunting season. Other than that, it's normally locked tight."

"Let me worry about that. You tell me where to go."

He put the van in gear and drove onward. The remaining zombies had chased Lisa, leaving the rest of the road empty. He took the left turn as instructed and sped along a similarly deserted road.

"So what are we gonna do about cars?" asked Glen.

"We'll get to the supermarket first. After that, we'll worry about the cars." He looked over at Glen. His face was creased with uncertainty. "Don't worry; we won't leave until you've got a way back."

Their journey to the supermarket was relatively uneventful. Apart from a couple of instances when they had to drive past a gathering of the undead, the roads were deserted. Frank pulled up alongside the store and turned to Glen.

"You're in luck." He nodded towards the destroyed shop front. "Looks like somebody's already broken in, saves you the trouble."

Glen jumped out, joining the others who had already convened in the car park.

"What if it's those *freaks* that broke in?" Glen asked.

"Then you'll have this to protect you," Ben replied. He leaned into the van and reached for the shotgun. Begrudgingly, Frank handed over the weapon and the remaining shells.

"Fine. But you'd better hope those things aren't in the gun shop."

Ben passed the shotgun to Glen and walked over to Amy.

"Be careful in there. I don't want anything to happen to you."

"I'll be fine," she replied, placing a comforting hand on his shoulder.

"C'mon, Rambo!" Frank yelled from the van. "Let's get this over with."

"They don't have a car yet."

"We do," Glen said.

He stood next to a parked sports car. He lifted the key triumphantly as he joined his team.

"There, you see?" Frank yelled. "Now get in."

With a parting look at Amy, Ben turned and jumped into the prison van.

"Right then, where's this gun shop?" Frank called from his open window.

"Straight down there," said Glen. "Take a left, and it's halfway down the street. It's called Llewellyn and Bough. You can't miss it."

"Noted. Anything else we need to know?"

"No, but I don't suppose you've got a light?"

"Lay off, Cheech." Frank glared at the man. "Keep your head in the game or you won't be coming back." He looked at the other two. "The same applies to you lot: if there's too many zombies in there, grab what you can and get out. You don't have many bullets, either."

He made to drive off, but stopped as another thought entered his mind.

"Oh, and make sure you get *sensible* things. Tinned food, bottled water, jars. Basically, anything that doesn't expire soon."

"We know," said Amy.

"Alcohol is always good. Don't forget that."

"Okay."

"And for god's sake, don't forget a tin opener. Not everything is a ring-pull!"

"Can we go?" Ben snapped.

"Fine."

They took off, proceeding down the route Glen had suggested.

Ben stared at the side mirror, watching the group fade into the distance.

"Will you relax?" Frank said. "They'll be fine. It's us I'm worried about."

"Why?"

"You gave away our guns! What are we gonna do if we get attacked? Throw our shoes?"

"Let's hope we can get inside and grab the gear before they get us."

They drove down the road, scanning both sides for the gun store.

"There it is."

Ben pointed to a shop ahead of them. A big storefront read 'Llewellyn and Bough Professional Hunting Supplies.' The front of the building had been destroyed, surrounded by glass and debris. Frank felt his heart sink as they pulled up outside.

"Okay, smart arse. How do we get past *them* without guns?"

He glanced back at the shop as one of the armed looters looked up from his plundered goods.

25

Lisa reversed up to the DIY depot. She'd had to circle it twice to draw the gathering of zombies away. Now the area was finally clear, she could pull up outside.

"Right, here's the plan. We try that door. If it's unlocked, we'll reverse as close as we can and leave the rear doors open. That way we can load up the back without the zombies seeing us."

"What if there are any inside?" Simon asked.

"Then we kill them."

"That's it? There might be loads of them in there."

"I've got more than enough bullets."

"But what if they all come at—"

"Will you shut up?" Tina snapped. "The longer we discuss it, the more time they have to catch us. Let's move."

"She's right, let's get inside." Lisa retrieved the rifle and jumped from the van. She strode around to the building, followed by her companions.

"Are you gonna leave the engine running?" Simon asked. "We don't know how long this will take."

"It's hot-wired, genius," Tina said.

They looked on as Lisa tried the side door. The handle met resistance.

"Looks like we're smashing our way in. Let's just ram the shutters and get this done."

"Wait, there's a window there." Tina pointed towards the end of the building.

"It's probably locked as well," said Simon.

"Yeah, but it'll be easier to get through the window than ramming the bloody shutters."

"But the noise will attract attention."

"And ramming the shutters won't?"

"It'll be quicker than climbing through the window."

"Stop," Lisa said, eyeing the pair with a frown. "Tina's way *does* sound like a better option. We'll try that first."

She made her way over to the window, cupped her hands to the glass, and peered inside. The room was empty. After glancing around to ensure they were alone, she struck the window with the butt of the rifle. The pane cracked on one side but remained intact. Lisa swung again, this time striking the centre of the glass. The window shattered, setting off an ear-splitting alarm.

"Great plan, *genius*," Simon shouted. "What do we do now?"

"We get inside and get this done quickly."

"What? But that alarm is going to draw every one of those things here."

"Which is why we need to hurry."

She raised the rifle as the first zombie rounded the corner. Its head darted left and right before spotting the trio. It emitted a screech until a bullet smashed through its brain.

"Go!"

Lisa ushered the pair over to the window, covering them as they climbed inside. She picked off another two creatures as more cries came from nearby. Checking the loading area one last time, she darted toward the rumbling vehicle.

"What are you doing?" Tina cried.

Lisa ignored her as she swung the rear doors wide. Running back to the driver's seat, she fired another shot and jumped inside.

She floored the accelerator, cutting down two more of the undead. She swung the van around until it was facing away from the window. After checking she was perfectly aligned, she dragged the gearstick into reverse. Another manic cry came from beside her as the van flew back. Keeping her foot down, she struck the wall with an almighty bang.

"Lisa!" she heard Tina call from within the building.

She looked ahead as more of the zombies rounded the corner. In one quick motion, she slid out of her open window and clambered onto the roof of the vehicle. She rose unsteadily as the van was rocked by the first body slamming into the side. Lisa staggered as a succession of hands pounded the van.

"I'm coming in!" she shouted, eyeing the window on the second floor.

It was too high to strike with the butt of her rifle, but she knew a bullet would make short work of it. Aiming the weapon high, she fired a single shot, instantly shattering the glass. She looked over her shoulder, feeling her heart sink as more of the monsters came into view.

"Are you okay?"

She barely heard Tina's muffled voice over the longing wails of the zombies and the whining alarm.

"Yeah!"

Lisa took off her jacket and wrapped it around her hands. The monsters below her roared as they stretched up, desperate to reach the top of the van. With a parting glance at the crowd of faces, she took a step back before running towards the wall. She leapt high and gripped the ruined window frame. The jagged edges pressed into her palms, but the bulk of the jacket protected her. She pulled herself up and into what seemed to be a small office. A desk and chair stood in the corner with a coffee table in the middle of the room. A single coat occupied a hook by the door.

A quick scan of the room confirmed that there was nobody present. Back outside, the horde of undead had grown, their indignant roars matching the piercing alarm. Before she even counted the remaining bullets in her pocket, she knew her group were in trouble.

***

"I'd still prefer a different one," Elaine said, regarding the sports car with distaste. "We won't be able to fit much food in there."

"Who cares? Let's grab the stuff and leave."

"No, she's right," Amy said. "We're going to need another car if we hope to get much food."

"I thought you said we weren't staying?" Glen whispered.

"I did, and it'll be easier if we can get a car stocked with food and water for us and one for them. That way we can leave as soon as we meet up with Ben."

"Fine." Glen scanned the area, counting five cars, a lorry, and a van. "Let's check the rest of these."

The trio spread out across the car park, glancing in the windows of the cars and trying the doors. After he had checked the majority, Glen turned his attention to the lorry.

"If we can get in this, we'll be able to fit the entire shop in the back."

He approached the driver's side and pulled the handle. The door swung wide, revealing a wide-eyed trucker on the floor.

"Shit!"

Glen fumbled with the shotgun as the zombie tried to grab him. He pulled the trigger, obliterating the creature's head.

"Are you okay?" Amy gasped, running to his aid.

"I'm fine."

With the blast still fresh in their ears, they fell silent, listening. Seconds passed, with no sound other than Glen's rapid breathing. The shotgun shook in his trembling hands. Amy looked past him into the driver's cab.

"We're in luck."

"What?"

"This one has keys." She pointed to the key chain dangling from the ignition.

"Oh, it has more than that!" Glen reached over and grabbed the lighter from the footwell. He held it into view triumphantly.

"Glen, Frank was right; we need your head in the game. Don't be lighting up a joint when there's work to do. Let's get as much stuff as we can and get out of here."

"Relax," Glen mumbled, the cigarette clasped between his lips.

He lit the end as they congregated around the shattered storefront. Various food products and other goods littered the entrance. They trod carefully around the discarded items as they stepped onto the threshold.

"Look at this place," Glen said. "Why would anyone steal a TV?"

"Some people have no common sense," Amy replied.

They continued, cringing as their footsteps echoed around the silent supermarket.

"So, shall we get trolleys?" Glen suggested.

"May as well. Remember, we need to get *sensible* things. Don't go getting bread and milk. Check the dates on everything. If it expires within six months, we don't want it."

"Alcohol's hardly sensible," Elaine grumbled.

"I know, but I think your life will be a lot easier if you get Frank what he wants."

"Can we get going?" Glen whispered, blowing a cloud of smoke into the air. "I don't like being here."

"Okay. Make sure you don't get any dairy products. Look for tins, jars, cereals, vitamins, biscuits, and sweets."

"Sweets?" Elaine frowned.

"Yes. They're a valuable source of sugar and have a long shelf life. They'll give you energy."

"I doubt Frank will appreciate that."

"Call it nurse's orders. And make sure we raid the medicine supply. Bandages, Paracetamol, Aspirin, Ibuprofen, anything you can get."

"Can we please get moving?" Glen urged. He pitched the trolley forward, wheeling it down the first aisle and out of sight. Amy and Elaine followed, both choosing different aisles.

Amy scanned the trashed shelves, knocking tins aside that littered the floor. She wrinkled her nose at some of the products.

"Pepperoni in spaghetti?" She replaced the item and walked on. She smiled as the rows of baked beans came into view. "Now we're talking."

She held out her arm and scooped every tin into the trolley. She immediately regretted her decision. The metallic clamour echoed around the entire store, ringing in her ears.

Elaine gasped in alarm from the next aisle. "Are you okay?"

"Yeah."

She continued down the aisle, quietly placing the rest of the tins in the trolley one-at-a-time. She reached the end and turned down the next aisle, which stocked a variety of cereals. She filled the trolley with a selection of boxes as Elaine followed her.

"Cereal?"

Amy looked back at her. "Yeah."

"How long do they last?"

"It's dry food. It lasts quite a while."

She turned back as Elaine began filling her trolley with the scattered boxes. Amy continued, zigzagging around the discarded items.

Why did they throw the boxes around? she pondered as she turned into the next aisle. Seeing that it held mostly bakery produce, she moved on to the next, where she saw Glen standing in the middle of the aisle.

"What are you doing?" she hissed.

"What?"

"This is the *frozen* food aisle."

"So?"

"So it won't be frozen anymore. The power's off. We can't eat it."

"We could still take it back."

"Glen, when the power is down, there are no freezers. If it was winter, we could keep it outside, but we're in the middle of summer."

"I suppose you're right."

"Of course I'm right, now hurry. I thought you wanted to get out of here?"

"I do."

"Then let's fill the trolleys and go."

She turned away, leaving Glen behind. He had already filled most of his trolley, but he knew what he still needed to get. He made his way to the savoury aisle.

"C'mon," he whispered, his eyes roaming the shelves.

Finally, he found the empty box of Cheddar Bites. He let out an exasperated sigh as he checked the others.

"Damn."

He made to turn back, but stopped when he spotted the storeroom door at the end of the aisle. It was risky, but the thought of never tasting his go-to munchie snack again made his heart ache. He moved cautiously, looking back to check there was nobody near.

He pushed the door, surprised that it swung inwards. With a final look over his shoulder, he left his trolley and stepped into the dark confines of the storage area.

Floor-to-ceiling metal shelves lined the walls, each filled with boxes. Glen walked on, conscious of the sound of his footsteps. As the endless procession of boxes continued, he began to realise the enormity of his quest. He reached the far end of the row, where more aisles came into view, with another line of unopened products.

"Great."

He begrudgingly turned back to the main store. It was then that he saw the tall zombie blocking his path. An eager grin creased its face as he fumbled with his shotgun.

"Shit, shit, shit."

The creature emitted a guttural roar, causing him to lose his grip. The weapon clattered to the ground, along with his cigarette, as the zombie approached.

"Fuck!" he cried. He clenched his fists and swung a punch at his attacker as it drew near. The blow collided with the creature's jaw, sending it staggering into a pile of boxes. Glen stooped down and grabbed the shotgun.

"Fuck you!" he roared as he pulled the trigger. The blast perforated his eardrums, filling his head with a high-pitched ringing.

The shot removed half of the zombie's head, a pool of blood and brain matter creeping out of its shattered skull. He lowered the weapon, his entire body trembling.

As his senses returned, he became aware of a new sensation. He raised his hand as a single trickle of blood crept down it. He traced the crimson trail to a small gash halfway up his finger. His heart quickened as realisation set in. He had grazed the zombie's teeth.

"Oh shit."

He had no idea how fast the virus would spread, but if Ben was correct, it was transmitted from a bite. He jabbed his finger between his lips and sucked hard. The warm, metallic taste filled his mouth. Turning aside, he spat out the blood and sucked the digit again—

"Glen?" The voice was Amy's. She sounded close. He examined the cut. He had no idea whether he was infected, but hoped he had extracted enough tainted blood to keep him alive. He swept his hand behind his back as she burst into the room.

"Glen?" she gasped, surveying the area. "What happened?"

"What do you think?"

"Are you okay?"

"Not yet." He scanned the floor until he found the cigarette that had fallen from his mouth during the attack, and retrieved it from the ground. "Now I'm good. Shall we get moving?"

He ushered Amy back into the main store where Elaine stood waiting. Her trolley was overflowing with supplies, as was Amy's.

"Is everyone okay?" Elaine asked.

"Yeah," he said. "Let's get all this stuff in the lorry and get going."

"Should we bag everything up?" Elaine asked as they passed the checkout area.

"No."

"I think we should," Amy said. "It'll be easier to get it in and out of the car."

"Look, I want to get out of here," Glen said.

"And we do too, but it will take a couple of minutes at the most."

"Fine."

The two women quickly packed the shopping into plastic bags while Glen kept watch. Once finished, the trio left the store.

"I'll take the lorry, you guys can have the car," he said.

Amy regarded him with a furrowed brow.

"I used to work for a haulage company," he added. "I drove them all the time."

"Okay, I'll come with you. That car can only hold one trolley of food."

She made to follow him, but Glen blocked her path. Elaine was busy loading the shopping into the boot.

"No, it's alright. I'll take your trolley. One of us needs to stay with that car so we can leave in it when we get back."

"Okay," said Amy, "but stay close."

Glen wheeled the two trolleys over to the HGV. He imagined the driver's corpse lying in the footwell, but he no longer felt afraid. He spun the trolleys as he neared, allowing them to roll sideways the rest of the way. They rattled over the uneven asphalt before clattering into the wheels of his vehicle.

After a quick check of his surroundings, he opened the rear doors of the lorry. Rows of packed crates filled the trailer on both sides. Glen snorted as he loaded the contents of their two trolleys. The HGV had enough food to keep them going for months.

He glanced down at his finger. A fresh trickle of blood had started to run down his hand. He wiped it aside, watching as the line of raw flesh turned crimson. The wound throbbed with each beat of his heart, a brutal reminder that the virus could be coursing through his body. Glen sighed dejectedly and slammed the trailer doors. After heading to the front of the cab, he dragged the mutilated body out of the footwell and climbed into the driver's seat.

He tapped the steering wheel as the two women finished loading the sports car in front of him. Blood continued to flow from his finger. If he was infected, he knew it was only a matter of time. Yet, he felt completely fine. He had no reason to believe his fate was sealed, apart from the open wound.

The fresh trickle of blood ran down the side of his hand, settling on the steering wheel, the wound itself having adopted a purple hue. With a hefty sigh, he looked ahead as the women disappeared into the car. He started the ignition, conscious that his finger was beginning to itch.

26

"What the fuck do you want?"

One of the hooded thugs stepped forward as Frank and Ben jumped from the van. They advanced cautiously, holding up their hands, conscious of the four guns aimed at them.

"We're just trying to survive, friend," Frank replied.

"Yeah? Well, go and survive somewhere else."

"We need weapons."

"So do we!" one of the other looters shouted. He was smaller than the rest, his voice tinged with the squeak of adolescence.

"There are enough guns to go around," Ben said. "Let us grab some, and a few boxes of bullets, and we'll be out of your hair."

The first looter strode forward, aiming a semi-automatic shotgun at the two men.

"I told you to go somewhere else. Now leave, or die."

"We're not leaving without those weapons."

"Then you give me no choice."

"You won't pull the trigger," Frank sneered. He stared, unblinking, as the gunman stepped closer.

"Won't I?"

"Nope. One gunshot will bring every zombie within a mile here. And I'd hazard a guess that you lot haven't even held a gun in your life. I mean, look at that kid back there; he's shitting himself."

Frank waited for the thug to look over his shoulder before making his move. He grabbed the barrel of the shotgun and tugged it aside. The startled gunman pulled the trigger, blasting a hole in a nearby bus stop. He tried to regain control of the weapon, but a quick elbow to the face sent him reeling. As soon as the thug was out of their line of sight, the other men opened fire.

"Down!" Frank yelled, dragging Ben to the ground.

The bullets sprayed the side of the prison van as the two men retreated around its sturdy frame.

"Brilliant plan," Ben snapped.

"Hey, it got us a gun, didn't it?"

"Yeah, and three blokes shooting at us."

Frank leaned against the door of the van as the firing stopped.

"You might want to come up with another plan," Ben said. "Guy number four is back on his feet."

Frank dashed to the end of the van. Sure enough, the man was arming himself with another weapon.

"Shit."

Frank checked the chamber of the shotgun before lowering himself to the ground. "Cover me," he ordered.

"With *what?*"

"Your eyes! Keep a look out for zombies."

"What about that lot?"

"I'll take care of them."

Frank shuffled underneath the van, watching the three pairs of legs in the ruined shop. He wondered where the fourth gunman could be until a foot stepped right in front of him. He watched the looter creep alongside the van. As he reached the edge, Frank pulled the trigger. With an agonised scream, the man fell to the ground, as his legs exploded in a crimson haze. His squeals subsided when a second bullet tore open his chest, sending him sprawling backward. His body twitched as the others looked on.

"Cooper!" one of them yelled, firing at the van. Frank quickly shuffled out of sight, waiting for the bullets to stop.

"Ben!" he yelled over the gunfire.

"What?"

"Take this."

He pushed the shotgun down past his legs and kicked it over. He heard Ben retrieve the weapon as the gunfire ceased.

"What do you want me to do?"

"Fire it!"

Ben emerged from his hiding place, firing shot after shot at the startled trio. Using the distraction to his advantage, Frank crawled forward. He reached out and snatched the dead man's rifle.

"I'm out!" Ben yelled as the gunmen returned fire.

The bullets pounded the van's metal frame, shattering the windows and deflating one of the tyres.

Frank hissed as a bullet ricocheted off the ground nearby. He checked the magazine of the rifle. He had four bullets. Squinting down the scope, he saw none of the men in view. He guessed they were all under cover, until his sight picked up another dead body lying prone on the ground.

"You got one?"

"You sound surprised."

"I thought you city boys were all talk?"

He swept his sight back and forth across the store, waiting for one of the men to appear.

"Yeah, well, I'm not a city boy."

"Coulda fooled me."

He grinned when he saw movement in the corner of his eye. The hooded teenager briefly came into view before disappearing behind the counter.

"Gotcha."

He lined his shot over the wooden surface, picturing the lad crouched behind it. Once he was sure of his target, he pulled the trigger. Fragments erupted from the counter as the bullet smashed through, striking the teenager, who cried out as the shot tore through his ribs. Unfazed, Frank swept his view over to the other side of the room as the commotion stirred the final gunman.

As soon as the man's head came into view, Frank fired. His aim was slightly off, but the bullet still removed a sizeable section of the man's face. He fell to the ground, leaving the store vacant.

"I think we'd better go," Ben urged, kicking Frank's legs as he shambled out from beneath the van.

"I know, the zombies might've heard."

"There's no *might* about it."

Frank rose to his feet, staring at the mass of undead at the end of the street. Some sprinted towards them, others shambled slowly on fractured limbs. They were closing in.

"Good job we're at a gun shop, huh?" he said, as they ran through the dilapidated storefront.

"Where are the bullets?" Ben searched the shattered display cases, swiping the glass aside. Frank ignored him as he strode towards the back room. "Where are you going? We need weapons."

"Yeah, but they'll be chewing your arse before you can load them. Get over here."

The first zombie staggered into the store, emitting a gleeful screech. Ben darted into the back room after Frank and slammed the door shut. He propped his shoulder against the frame as Frank scanned their surroundings.

"A little help?" Ben snapped, as the bulk of undead flesh-and-bone crashed into the other side of the door.

Frank looked back as the horde struck again. "I'm thinking."

He turned and made his way around the room. Various boxes of ammo were stacked neatly along the shelves. Frank's eyes widened when he caught sight of a semi-automatic handgun.

"Holy shit, what's going on here?" he mused as he grabbed a box of bullets. "Looks like our gun shop's dabbling in illegal firearms."

He filled the magazine and resumed his search, ignoring the angry wails and thunderous strikes against the door.

"Oh, ho. Look at these!" A mounted display of shotguns adorned the wall.

"What are you doing? We need to barricade the door!" Ben urged.

"We don't need to do shit."

He pulled one of the weapons down and rushed over to a box of bullets. Another thud sounded throughout the room. The zombies struck the door harder, this time almost hurling Ben aside.

"What are you doing?"

"This is a ten-gauge, pump-action shotgun, my friend. I'm surprised to see one of these here. Must be an American import."

"How's that gonna help us block the door?"

Frank dismissed him and scanned the array of boxes on the shelf, reading aloud. "Twelve, twelve, twelve, ten!"

He grabbed a box and dug inside, feeding the shells into the chamber. He cocked the shotgun as the door emitted a snapping sound.

"They're getting in!"

Frank propped the shotgun against his shoulder and aimed the weapon at Ben.

"Move."

Before Ben could say anything, the final assault caused the wood to give way. He jumped aside as the door swung open and the bodies stumbled forward.

Frank fired, striking the first woman in the chest. The impact caused her to crash back into the others, sending many of them staggering aside. Taking a step forward, he fired again. The boom of the shotgun thundered around the room as the blast devastated everything in its path. With each shot, the wave of zombies fell back farther and farther. Frank followed, directing the gun at the nearest body and reducing it to pulp.

"There's no way we can take them all!" Ben yelled from the storeroom.

"Maybe. But it'll be fun finding out."

The reloading of the shotgun began to sound rhythmic until he fired his last cartridge. All at once, the zombies retaliated. Those crippled from the shotgun crawled towards him. Those with their legs intact raced forward. Throwing the empty weapon aside, Frank wasted no time in retrieving the handgun. He brought the weapon up to meet the nearest face and fired. The gunshots began again, with Frank picking off those nearest to him.

He continued to pull the trigger until a clicking sound replaced the gunfire.

"I'm out!"

"Get down!"

Frank obeyed Ben's command as a shotgun boomed. The blast overhead created a high-pitched ringing in his ears as he hit the ground. He jerked back as searing gunpowder drifted onto the nape of his neck. He tried to complain, but the gunfire drowned his words.

"How many guns did you load?" Frank yelled, between the bursts of shotgun fire.

"The same as you."

Frank looked up from his prone position, straight into the wide eyes of an undead elderly woman. The corpse grinned as it crawled towards him, paying no heed to its shattered legs. Frank lurched away, crawling back until he found his discarded shotgun. He turned and swung the butt of the weapon down onto the zombie's forehead. The impact sent it crashing to the ground. Before it could rise, he struck again. The boom of the other shotgun diminished the dull thud, but he knew he had smashed through its skull. Not wanting to take any chances, he struck again, and again.

Jumping to his feet, Frank darted back into the storeroom, noting that Ben was no longer firing the shotgun. Instead, the cracks of a handgun resounded through the blood-spattered store.

"There's still too many!" Ben yelled over his shoulder.

Frank looked out and estimated at least a dozen more undead creatures standing in the main store. He turned back to the box of bullets and reloaded, the sound of Ben's gunfire still echoing around the room.

"I'm out!"

Frank rushed back to the storefront as Ben retreated. Seven zombies stood glaring at him. They charged forward, but the carpet of bodies slowed them down. Frank glanced at his feet. Satisfied there were no crawlers, he turned his attention to those still standing. He braced the shotgun against his shoulder and fired. Four out of the seven zombies fell in quick succession. He aimed at the fifth, but found the slide had jammed. He tried to rack it again. It was stuck.

"C'mon!"

He stepped back into the storeroom, where Ben snapped the magazine into his handgun and fired three shots out through the doorway.

"Thank God." Ben sighed, throwing the weapon down onto the counter.

"I told you we'd do it."

"Yeah, well, we still need to hurry. There'll be more on their way."

"At least now we have time to barricade the door. C'mon, let's get to it."

Frank walked past Ben toward the row of shelves next to the doorway. After testing the sturdiness of the metal structure, he pushed hard on the side until it tipped. A loud clatter accompanied the landing of the shelves as they blocked the entrance.

"There. Now nothing can get in."

Frank gave the shelves a harsh tug to verify his statement. The barricade remained still, completely blocking the doorway.

"Yeah, and *we* can't get *out,*" Ben said.

"Why would we want to do that?"

"So we can load the van."

"Have you not been here for the last ten minutes? The van is shot to hell. There's no way we can get away in that."

"Then what do you suggest?"

Ben followed Frank's gaze towards a row of heavy shutters. He looked back and shrugged.

"That's where the crates get unloaded," Frank said. "All we have to do is go and find another car, grab the guns and ammo, and get the fuck out of here."

"And it's gonna be that easy? How do we know there aren't hundreds of them behind those shutters?"

"We don't, that's why we load as much firepower as we can, first."

The pair stopped talking when a growl emerged from the barricaded doorway. They looked through the metal shelves, but the source remained a mystery amongst the scattered bodies.

"Let's just do this," Ben said.

They loaded the weapons in silence, each choosing two shotguns and two handguns. Once they had finished, Frank grabbed the chain operating the shutters.

"Are you ready?"

Before Ben could answer, he tugged hard, rolling the metal shutters up and out of sight. He jumped back, expecting to see a crowd of flesh-hungry faces staring up at him. What they saw was the back of an LGV.

"You must be blessed or something." Frank laughed. "I've never had so much luck."

He jumped off the ledge and down into the loading bay, approaching the driver's side.

"How am I blessed?" Ben watched as Frank tugged the door. It swung wide, allowing him entry. "So far, we've been shot at by looters, had our van destroyed, and re-enacted World War Two. There's no divine force looking out for *me,*" he continued.

"Oh no?"

Frank reappeared, dangling a set of keys from his finger. He jumped from the van.

"Let me tell you something," he said as he climbed back onto the ledge, "there's no way God is rewarding *me*. I'm the scum of the earth. I care for nobody but myself. I'd happily let the world go to shit as long as *I'm* still breathing at the end. I was in prison because I'm a murderer. I beat my wife to death, and d'ya know what? I don't regret a single thing. I'd do it again and again and again, a thousand times over, given the chance. I should have been the *first* to die when this shit happened."

He approached the work surface where they had loaded their weapons, and scanned their haul.

"Sorry, pal, but whether you like it or not, it's *you* who God favours," he continued.

Before Ben could answer, a growling noise at the barricade caught their attention. Only this time, they could see the source.

"To be honest, I don't think there is a god," Ben said as they looked on.

"No?"

"No. After all, what kind of god would let *this* happen?"

They both stared in silence as the little boy at the barricade reached through a gap. His blood-soaked romper suit revealed a hollowed-out torso as he pressed against the barrier. He growled quietly, eyeing the pair with an unwavering hunger and a tireless determination.

27

Lisa stepped out into the dark hallway. Despite the rifle in her hands, she couldn't help but feel vulnerable in the darkness. She continued down the corridor, glancing at the closed doors as she passed. Curiosity steered her towards the rooms, but the seven bullets in the rifle kept her on track. If they were going to survive the ordeal, she would have to shoot only when necessary. She reached the end of the hallway and found the top of a staircase. The foot of the stairs was a lot brighter. Apprehension displaced her relief when she considered the source of the light. If it was a window, they would be in trouble if a zombie were to stumble across it.

She crept down the stairs, aiming the rifle ahead, and reached the bottom without incident. Yet, a quiet shuffling nearby caused her heart to race. Somebody was around the corner. With an intake of breath, she propped the rifle against her shoulder and turned. She yelped in alarm as a hand seized the weapon.

"Wait, it's us!" Tina urged. She released the gun as Simon appeared behind her.

Lisa exhaled, shaking her head at the pair. "I almost killed you!"

"Well, open your eyes next time," the teenager retorted. She turned and pushed past Simon, walking back down the corridor.

"You know that alarm is going to be the death of us," said Simon.

"Relax, you can hardly hear it." She went to walk past, but he stopped her with an outstretched arm.

"It's quiet in here, but it's still screeching out *there.*"

"We'll deal with it. Now get out of my way." She made to move again, but Simon grasped her shoulder.

"I told you not to smash the window," he said.

"And I told *you* to get out of my way." She threw the rifle aside and grabbed him by the shirt. He gasped in alarm as she slammed him into the wall, pressing her forearm against his neck. "Touch me again and I'll blow your fucking head off, understand?"

Before Simon could respond, Tina turned the corner.

"Are you coming or—" She stopped mid-sentence as she observed the tense standoff.

"Yeah, we're coming now," Lisa snarled through clenched teeth, her eyes locked with Simon's. She turned and grabbed the rifle from the ground.

"Touch *me* again and I'll put you in your place, you little slut."

The man's outburst shocked Tina, who gasped in amazement. Lisa turned and smashed the butt of the rifle into his face. His head snapped back as he cried out in pain. She ignored his whimpering and joined Tina by the doorway.

"Good job," the teenager praised.

"He asked for it."

Lisa looked around the large warehouse. Colossal shelving units stood from floor to ceiling, stocking a variety of goods.

"You broke my nose!"

She turned to look at Simon as he cupped a bloody hand to his face.

"Step out of line again and I'll break your *legs.*" She made her way down one of the aisles, duly followed by Tina.

"So how are we gonna do this?" the teenager asked.

"Let's look for a trolley or something. Then we can wheel it to the van and load it in the back."

"Then what?" Simon grumbled. "Leap out of the window Dukes-of-Hazard-style?"

"Got a better suggestion?"

"Yeah, let's turn back the clock and not break the fucking window!"

"Idiot."

The two women walked to the end of the rows with Simon in tow. He had his head tilted back, pinching the bridge of his nose with his thumb and forefinger.

It was when they reached the far wall that Tina spotted the trolleys in the corner. "Something like that?" she offered.

"Exactly."

Lisa made for the row of trolleys but stopped short as a plank of wood swung through the air in front of her. She took a step back as the assailant stepped into view, swinging the board with greater ferocity.

"Get back!" the man snapped.

Lisa aimed the rifle at his head. "Drop the wood or I'll blow your head off."

The man stared at the trio, his eyes darting between each of them before he lowered the plank to his side.

"Who are you?" Lisa demanded.

"Adam."

"Well, Adam, I'm Lisa. This is Tina and Shithead." She motioned to the pair behind her.

"You're not one of them?" he asked.

"Nope."

"Have they bitten you?"

"Nope."

"But I'm guessing you're the ones who set off the alarm?"

"You got one right," Lisa praised. "It was the only way we could get in."

"You need a place to hide?"

"No, we need supplies."

"Oh, great. So you figured you'd go looting through my store and to hell with the consequences?"

"This is your store?"

"It is now. I had to kill my dad. He was bitten."

"I'm sorry to hear that."

Adam shrugged, but Lisa could tell he was concealing his sorrow.

"Look, we need supplies. It's the only way we're going to survive."

"I would've thought food was the most essential."

"We've got another group searching for food."

"Another group? How many of you are there?"

"A few."

"Really?"

"Yeah. We've got a farmhouse out in the countryside. If you give us some supplies, you can come with us."

"What do you need?"

"Anything we can use to barricade the house."

Adam nodded. "Okay, you'll need wooden planks and nails to start with. We've got nail guns here as well."

"Sounds good to me."

"We've got soldering guns, angle grinders, drills."

"We don't have any electricity, or at least not for long."

"Oh, right." Adam quickly scanned the rest of the warehouse. "There's a load of sandbags left over from the floods last spring?"

"We'll take them. Lead the way."

The trio followed Adam as he rushed down one of the aisles. He stopped halfway, at the series of planks.

"How many of these will your car hold?" he asked, turning to face Lisa.

"We've got a Transit van, so we should get a fair few in the back."

"Where is it?"

"Outside. We've backed it up to the window so it'll be easy to fill up."

"But judging by your expression, there's a problem," Adam muttered sceptically.

"Yeah. There are tons of zombies surrounding this place. We're going to struggle to drive it away."

He nodded, his gaze drifting as if lost in contemplation. "Okay," he said after a brief silence. "We'll fill the van first and then see what we can do afterward." He stooped down and retrieved a number of boards from the shelf.

"Good. Shithead, go and get a trolley." Lisa turned to face her bloodied companion.

"Get it yourself."

"What did I tell you about stepping out of line? Go and get a fucking trolley!"

Simon glared at her before trudging towards the back of the store. When he returned, they filled the metal container with the planks.

"Okay," Adam said once the trolley was full. "Lead the way."

"You two start filling another trolley."

Lisa left the pair and retraced her steps back to the passageway, with Adam and their goods in tow. She stopped at the door, trying to establish which way led to the van.

"Do you know where you're going?" Adam asked.

"Nope, I came in through the top window, but it should be near here."

"The only window leading outside is in the room to your right."

Lisa turned towards the door, which stood ajar. With her rifle at the ready, she kicked it wide and burst into the empty room. The alarm blared louder than ever, but the sound of the zombies outside was even more prevalent. The back of the van blocked out most of the light from the window as she turned to grab the trolley. The shattered glass crunched beneath their feet as she helped push the planks over to the window.

"I'll jump in the back, you pass the wood through."

Lisa stepped onto the window frame and climbed into the back of the van. Sensing her presence, the horde started to pound the sides, filling the echoic space with metallic thuds. Lisa dragged the boards into the back as more of the undead creatures joined the fray.

"Hurry!"

Adam passed the rest of the boards over. He stepped aside as Lisa jumped back in.

"How many are out there?" he asked.

"Too many."

She stepped back over to the door as Tina appeared with another trolley filled with wood.

"Where do you want this?"

"Leave it there, take this one back and fill it up."

Lisa took the trolley from the teenager and wheeled the empty one back into the corridor.

"How many more do we need?"

"I'd say two more before we start on the rest of the stuff."

Tina nodded and left.

"Right then, let's go again."

After twenty minutes of passing the trolleys back and forth, the van was almost full.

"This will have to be the last one," Lisa told Tina as she took the final trolley. "Any more and you won't be able to get in. Start loading this one while we come up with a plan to get us out of here."

She motioned for Adam to follow, stopping as she passed the warehouse.

"Shithead, go and help Tina; we're leaving."

She heard an inaudible grumble from Simon as she strode towards the stairs.

"So, what do you have in mind?" Adam asked as they bounded up to the first floor.

"I don't know. I've only got seven bullets left. I want to see how many are out there before we go any further."

She walked past the closed doors until she reached the room she had gained entry through.

"My dad's office," Adam said, following her inside.

"Where is he now?"

"In the next room along."

"And he's definitely dead?"

"I caved in his skull with a claw hammer. What do you think?"

"I'm sorry."

Lisa approached the broken window. The sight outside confirmed her fears. There were at least two dozen zombies crowded around the van. Some peered through the windows, while others pounded the side in frustration. She stepped back to give Adam a better look.

"Oh my God," he whispered, "I recognise some of those people."

"That's not going to help us get out of here. We need a plan. Any ideas?"

"There's a back door?"

"That's not going to help us get to the van," she replied.

"No, but there's an alley on either side that leads to the front of the store."

"So?"

"So, why don't I go out there, get their attention, and lure them away from the van? I can run back down the alley and get in through the back door."

"And when they're gone I can jump down, wait for you three to get in the back, and then drive us to safety."

"Exactly."

"It does sound like a good plan."

"But?"

"But I'm not keen on using you as bait. What if you trip? Or what if they're faster than you?"

Adam considered the possibility briefly before a smile spread across his face.

"The room next door has a window above the alley. You can cover me there. If any of them look like they're gaining on me, shoot them."

"I only have seven bullets left."

"So don't miss. Besides, I'll be in and out in thirty seconds."

Lisa chewed her lip. "Okay, are you sure?"

"I'll be fine. C'mon, let's go and tell the others."

Lisa followed him back down the stairs, where Simon and Tina waited.

"Do we have a plan?" Tina asked.

"Yeah," Lisa replied. "Where's the back door?"

"At the back of the warehouse," said Adam.

"Right." She turned to Simon and Tina. "I want you two to wait here for Adam. He's going out through the back to lure the zombies away from the van. Once we're clear, I'm gonna jump down, get behind the wheel and wait for the rest of you to get in the back."

"No chance," Simon snapped. "I don't trust you. You'll leave us as soon as the coast is clear."

"No, I won't. I'd leave *you* behind in a heartbeat, but Tina and Adam have their uses. I'm not leaving them behind. Once Adam is back inside, all three of you jump in the back of the van and off we go."

"How will you know we're in?"

"Just bang on the back or something. That'll be my cue to drive." The three silently considered the plan.

"Everyone ready?" she asked.

"Let's do it." Adam nodded.

"Good. So where's the window overlooking the alley?"

"Upstairs, first door on your right."

"Okie doke, good luck."

She turned on her heel and ran back up the stairs. She could feel the adrenaline coursing through her body as she made her way into the small, well-lit room. The first thing that struck her was the smell. The next was the dead body slumped in the corner. She aimed her rifle before noticing the odd shape of the corpse's skull. A claw hammer lay next to it, coated in blood and tufts of hair.

"You weren't kidding about your dad, Adam."

She tore her eyes away and approached the window. There were no creatures in the alley. All Adam had to do was get the attention of the crowd out front and they would be good to go. She threw the window open, waiting for the plan to unfold.

Before long, she saw Adam dashing alongside the alley wall. He stared ahead, scanning the road outside for potential threats. When he was level with the window, he glanced up, ensuring Lisa was in position. She gave him a reassuring nod as he passed, watching him until he disappeared around the front of the store. Her heart pounded hard against her ribs as she waited for him to get the attention of the milling zombies. She wondered how he was going to do it. Would he shout? Scream? Whistle? Or throw something in their direction? The answer came as Adam's voice reached her small enclosure.

"Hey, fuckfaces, over here!"

The excited shrieks of the undead followed his outburst. Lisa gripped the rifle and aimed into the alley. She could hear pounding footfalls, but there was no sign of Adam. She held her breath as another second went by.

"Come on," she muttered.

The screeching and wailing grew louder. The anticipation was almost too much. After what felt like an age, he sprinted into view with a crowd spilling into the alley after him. She aimed the rifle at the closest one and fired. The shot dropped the undead woman instantly, causing all those behind it to stumble.

Lisa felt a wave of relief wash over her. But the feeling quickly subsided when Adam suddenly stopped in his tracks.

"What are you doing?" she cried.

She fired again as the zombies drew close. Adam whirled around, looking up both sections of the alley.

"Adam!"

"Help me!"

She fired at another zombie, and another, until Adam's terrified eyes met hers. He remained still, staring in horror. Lisa quickly found the cause of his fear. She looked down his escape route and saw a series of undead men, women, and children dashing towards him. He was trapped. With only three bullets left, Lisa felt as helpless as he did.

"No!"

She shot the first zombie reaching out for him. The corpse fell at his feet. She looked the other way and fired at a child. Its head exploded, showering Adam in gore. She looked on, aghast, as the crowd closed in. Adam cried out as she swept her sight back and forth along the alley. Bodies packed both sides tightly as they grabbed their prey.

"I'm sorry."

Lisa looked down the scope, lined up her target, and shot Adam in the head. His body crumpled to the ground as a sea of hands and mouths consumed him. With a parting look at the grotesque display, Lisa left him behind and rushed to the top of the stairs.

"Guys, Adam's dead. Get in the van now!"

"What?" Tina shouted back.

"The back door is still open and the zombies are gonna get inside. Get in the van now!"

She didn't wait for another response. Instead, she sprinted down the corridor and burst into the room with the broken window. She looked down at the van, relieved to see an empty car park below. Using the butt of the rifle, she smashed away the rest of the exposed glass and stepped on the windowsill. The drop was a lot higher than she remembered. Yet, her fear was short-lived as a distant screech brought her back to her senses. Lunging forward, she soared out of the window and landed atop the van. The impact caused her to stumble. She pitched forward, rolling from the roof to the ground.

She hissed in pain as she landed awkwardly on her leg. Yet, a nearby growl left her no time to contemplate her injury. She limped towards the driver's seat and slid behind the wheel.

"Are you in?" There was no answer. She rapped on the back of the van. "Guys, are you there?"

A horrified cry came in response as a series of urgent taps sounded on the partition behind her. Lisa put the van in gear and raced forward out of the car park. She looked in the side mirrors at the diminishing depot, hoping she hadn't left her companions behind. A crowd of bodies poured out of the broken window. The undead creatures had got inside, but she was too far away to identify whether Tina and Simon were among them.

"Guys, are you back there?"

There was no response. A sick feeling formed in the pit of her stomach as she drove towards the designated meeting point. Part of her wanted to stop and check the back of the van, but it would be too dangerous without a weapon. Despite her reservations, she continued to drive.

28

Frank drummed his fingers on the steering wheel. Their rendezvous point had been deserted for the past ten minutes. With an agitated groan, he looked at his passenger. "How long since we split up?"

"Almost an hour," Ben said.

"Let me know when it's exactly one hour."

"What difference does it make? We can't go looking for them in this."

"Looking for them? Who said anything about looking for them?"

Ben stared at him blankly.

"If they don't turn up, we're heading back to the farmhouse," Frank continued.

"Like hell we are!"

"Hey. We told them *one* hour. After that, we turn back."

"I'm not leaving Amy behind."

"Fine, then you can wait on the street while *I* drive back."

The pair fell silent as a Transit van turned onto the road ahead of them. Frank recognised it as the vehicle Lisa had left in. He felt a flicker of relief as she came into view behind the wheel.

"Took your time!" he yelled out of the window, as Lisa rolled to a stop beside him.

"Fashionably late," she replied. "Nice wheels, by the way."

"You can thank Benny for that. He's the one with all the good luck."

Frank jabbed a thumb towards the stone-faced security guard. Lisa drove past them and performed a U-turn. It was then that Frank caught sight of the zombie clinging to the back.

"Hold up!"

Producing a handgun from within his jacket, he blasted the creature in the back of the head. The van slowed to a stop and Lisa got out of the driver's seat. He frowned when he noticed her limping around the back of the van. Jumping from the cab, he strode over to her.

"Have you been bitten?"

"No, I think I've sprained my ankle."

They both looked down at the motionless corpse. The gaping hole in the back of its head offered a clear view of its brain. The skin on its legs was gone, exposing muscle and bone.

"What happened to this guy?"

"If you're referring to its legs, that's a result of being dragged for a mile and a half."

The pair looked into the back of the van as Tina came into view. She shuffled past the pile of wood and jumped to the ground. Simon followed her out.

"You're okay?" Lisa gasped.

"Yeah, but we were almost zombie food back there. What took you so long?"

"I didn't know if you were in or not."

"Well, we were! Then these guys got in." She kicked the corpse at their feet.

"Where's Elaine?" Simon demanded.

"She's not back yet."

"What? I'll kill you!" He lunged at Frank, who sidestepped him with ease. In a quick motion, he swiped Simon's legs. The man hit the ground hard, wheezing as the air escaped his lungs.

"Try it, Porky," Frank spat.

"You should… never have… split us up." Simon slowly rose to his feet.

"Why not?"

"Because they might be dead because of you!" Ben snapped as he joined the group.

"Look, I want them to come back as much as you," said Frank.

"Bullshit."

"It's true."

"Why?"

"Because they've got our food supply, dickhead. I don't give a shit *who* comes back, as long as they bring food!"

"You bastard." Ben stepped forward, stopping only when Frank produced the handgun.

"I don't want to kill you. But I won't think twice if you leave me no choice." The two men locked stares as the rest of the group looked on. "Now sit down, chill out, we'll give them five more minutes."

"I'm not leaving Elaine," Simon muttered.

"Then stay! I don't care." Frank placed the gun back in his jacket and peered into the Transit van. "So what did you get?"

"Mostly planks of wood. But we picked up a few nail guns, hammers, and sandbags," said Lisa.

"Great, that should do the trick. Were there any problems?" Frank observed a hint of sorrow flash over Lisa's eyes.

"A few hiccups," she said, "but we made it out."

"Good."

The pair turned as the roar of an engine filled the silent street. A red sports car idled into view, slowing to a halt next to the van.

"Elaine!" Simon cried.

His wife jumped from the car. The pair embraced as Amy rose from the driver's seat.

"Ben?" Her eyes lit up.

"I thought they were dead," Frank admitted. He turned away from the joyful reunion to look at Lisa. "It makes you sick, doesn't it?"

She nodded. "Sure does. Let's go and see their haul."

They examined the array of food on the back seat.

"Is this it?" Frank asked.

"No, Glen has most of the food."

"Where is he?"

"I don't know," Amy replied. "He was behind us for a while, but then I looked back and he wasn't there."

"What was he driving?"

"A lorry. Bigger than that one." She pointed at the vehicle Frank and Ben had arrived in.

"A lorry?" Frank repeated. "How the hell do you lose a lorry?"

"I told you, he was behind us one minute, then he wasn't."

"We can't wait for him. If he doesn't turn up at the house by tomorrow, we'll have to go back and get more food."

"Well, you're going to have to do it without us," Ben announced. "This is where we part ways."

"What?"

"We told you from the beginning, we'll help you, but we're not staying."

"That's fine," Frank said. "Fat twat, you and your missus can take the Transit. We'll take the lorry, and I'm sure Tina wouldn't mind a spin in that car."

The teenager grinned as she approached the sports car.

"Whoa, hold on," Ben snapped. "We want our share."

"Your share?"

"Yeah, like we agreed."

"What we *agreed* was that you would help us get all this stuff back to the house. If you're going to leave us here, then the deal is off."

Ben and Amy exchanged a look.

"Fine," Ben conceded. "We'll take the stuff back and then we'll leave."

"Good man. Right, Tina and nurse can go in the car, the whales can take the van and we'll take the truck. Ben, you get in the back of the Transit."

He waited for the group to disperse before climbing into the LGV.

"How much stuff are you going to give them when we get back?" Lisa asked, climbing into the passenger seat.

"Whatever it takes to get rid of them." Frank started the van, waiting for the others to drive ahead.

"I wonder what happened to Glen," Lisa said.

"Who knows? But if he *does* turn up, he'd better have food."

***

Glen sped down the street leading to his home. It seemed like an eternity since he had stopped following Amy, but he guessed it had only been five minutes. A burgeoning feeling of guilt formed as he imagined the group looking for him. He intended to return with the food they had salvaged, but there was one thing he had to do first. With a newfound determination, he pushed the lorry further.

He soon realised that the small cul-de-sac he had lived in for five years would struggle to house an HGV. But he ploughed on, smashing cars aside and crushing the milling undead beneath the monstrous wheels. Before long, he pulled up alongside his house. He grabbed the shotgun and leapt from the vehicle. Leaving the engine idling, he marched up the garden path, scanning the area for any signs of the undead. There were none, but his door was open. He racked the shotgun, contemplating the horrors inside.

The hallway was empty as he stepped onto the threshold. He remained rooted to the spot, listening for any sounds within the house. After a few seconds of silence, he was sure it was empty. He closed the door behind him and stepped into the kitchen. It was there that he met his elderly neighbour.

"Mrs Cropley?" he stammered.

The old woman whirled around. She snarled at him, her eyes manic, until he blew her head off. Blood and brain matter spattered the kitchen as Glen rushed over to the cutlery drawer. He stopped as an eager cry came from the doorway. The two men who had pursued him earlier now rushed at him again. This time, Glen was ready. Resting the shotgun against his shoulder, he blasted the pair with a single shot. Both fell to the ground in a heap as he opened the drawer. He rummaged through the utensils until he found the sharpest knife he owned. Resting his shotgun on the counter, he placed his hand on the work surface.

"C'mon."

He held the knife above his injured finger, the blade trembling as he tried to muster the courage to go ahead with his plan. He let out an exasperated sigh as he stepped away from the counter.

"C'mon!"

His heart pounded against his chest as he paced back and forth. He glanced around the kitchen until he saw a towel. He snatched it from the worktop, bunched it up tight, and bit down on one of the bulky edges. He spread his fingers wide on the tabletop, lifting the knife above his injured digit once more. He breathed deeply and steadied his hand as he lowered the blade closer. He closed his eyes and began to count.

"One. Two. Three!"

The towel muffled his words, along with his screams, as he sliced into the finger. He tried to cut through in one fluid motion, but the bone remained strong. Screaming into the towel, he looked away as he pushed all his weight on the blade. Eventually, the bone snapped, allowing the knife to slice the rest of the way through muscle and flesh.

The room spun, bobbing up and down as his finger rolled away. He slumped to the ground, trying not to look at the bloodied stump left behind. Tears streamed from his eyes as he cradled his ruined hand in the towel. The white fabric turned red as he wrapped it up. He breathed heavily, keeping his eyes firmly closed. The pain was unbearable, but it was worth it if it saved his life.

On unsteady legs, he rose to his feet, aided by the shotgun, which he used to push himself upright. The world continued to spin as he made his way over to the medicine drawer. Swallowing a cocktail of painkillers, he remembered the second reason he had returned home. He glanced at the kitchen table, relieved to see his bag of cannabis was untouched. Wiping away tears, he grabbed the bag and his lighter and staggered out of the house.

The cul-de-sac was still relatively empty, except for a pair of undead Rottweilers. Red foam dripping from their fangs, they snarled at Glen from the other side of the street as he cautiously approached the lorry. One had its ribcage exposed, whilst the other stood on skeletal paws and had a huge portion of its shoulder missing. Both had fur matted with congealing blood. Wide eyes above mangled snouts watched him as he slowly reached for the door. Barking in unison, the pair dashed toward him.

Glen jumped inside and slammed the door shut as the two dogs bounced off the side. All at once, several zombies emerged from neighbouring buildings. They eyed him hungrily as he turned the huge vehicle around. A brief jerk as he went told him that one dog had fallen under the wheels. He ignored the yelp, swinging the vehicle around until it was facing the right direction. Putting the lorry in gear once more, he drove forward, pursued by the persistent undead.

It took him only five minutes to reach the countryside again, leaving the ruined town behind. He blinked hard, trying to focus his vision as he rolled the cannabis between his fingers. The road ahead was empty, barring the odd abandoned car at the side of the road. Glen cast a glance at the vehicles as he retrieved his lighter. Nobody was inside, at least not that he could tell as he raced past. He inhaled deeply, savouring the hot smoke that filled his lungs.

Despite waiting in anticipation for the high, he already felt lightheaded. He looked down at the sodden towel encasing his hand and couldn't help but wonder if he was safe. The hazy vision he attributed to blood loss. The slowing heart rate he blamed on the pills. Yet, it was too soon to blame his ravenous hunger on the cannabis. He looked at the remaining digits on his hand, surprised at how appealing they were starting to look.

***

"Okay, we've brought your stuff back. Now let's talk about splitting it."

"Fair enough," Frank said. "What do you want?"

"Half."

"Ha, you're pulling my leg."

"We don't want half," Amy said. "All we want are a few weapons, ammo, food, and that car."

"Now *you're* pulling my leg. I haven't even had a go in it yet."

The pair watched him, annoyed.

"Okay, fine, take the car. Start unloading it and we'll swap guns for food." Frank approached the rear of the lorry and swung the metal doors wide.

"Wow, look at *your* haul." Lisa beamed as she joined him.

"You should see some of the guns we picked up. We've got American imports and *handguns*. Our gun shop must have been doing some dodgy deals."

"Most gun shops do." She looked around at Frank's bewildered face. "What? I know a bit about guns."

"Yeah, and where to get them," he said. "How?"

"I used to hang out with the right people. You learn things. And I can tell you, you don't need to travel far to get your hands on illegal guns, it doesn't matter where you live."

"You learn something new every day. Either way, they're not getting their mitts on these imports. They can have two handguns, a shotgun, a rifle, and that's their lot."

"No grenades?"

"Funny enough, there weren't any there."

"It's a shame we're not in Manchester. I know a few places you can get them."

"Okay, smart arse, you know your guns. I get it. Stop trying to impress me." He jumped into the back as Tina appeared beside Lisa.

"They've emptied the car, now they want their weapons."

"Right, you take this, and this." He passed a shotgun and a rifle to Tina. The teenager disappeared from view as Frank retrieved two boxes of bullets.

"Two boxes each?" Lisa muttered. "How many have you got?"

"Loads, but they won't be able to carry many."

He passed the shotgun and rifle rounds to Lisa, along with a pair of handguns. Once she had left, he retrieved two boxes of handgun bullets, before jumping from the lorry and making his way over to the others. It was then that movement in the distance caught his eye. An HGV turned onto the road leading up to the farmhouse.

"Looks like our food has arrived."

"We want more than this," Ben said, rattling the boxes of bullets.

"Are you going to war or something? That's more than enough."

The thunderous roar of the HGV grew louder.

"We want more than this," said Ben. "I didn't risk my life for four boxes."

"Six, actually," Frank said, handing over two more. "And you're welcome."

"Hey, Glen!" Amy yelled. She held up a hand for him to slow down, but the driver ploughed on. "Glen!"

Amy stepped back as the lorry drew close. The rumbling engine caught the attention of the rest of the group.

"What the fuck is he doing?" Frank snapped.

They watched in horror as the lorry sped off the road, striking the Transit van, which tipped onto its side as the HGV roared past.

"Glen!" Lisa bellowed.

She rejoined the rest of the group as the lorry smashed into the farmhouse. The foundations crumbled around the solid metal frame as it finally came to a halt. They looked on as the upper level of the building collapsed, a plume of dust and grit bursting high into the air as bricks and mortar rained down on the lorry. The group retreated to a safe distance as the rubble scattered around. Only a small section of the house remained intact.

"I'm going to kill that little prick."

Frank marched forward as the driver's door swung open and Glen fell from the vehicle amid a cloud of dust.

Despite his distorted view, Frank fired twice into the smokescreen. A shriek told him he had hit his target.

"You shot him!" Amy gasped, running to Glen's aid. It was as she neared she realised he was long dead. Despite the dust, the unmistakable growl within was all she needed to hear. She turned away as Frank approached his vehicle. He looked out to the road as he went, his breath seizing in his lungs.

"Oh, fuck!"

The rest of the group turned and followed his line of sight towards the crowd that was making their way across the field.

"That idiot has brought them right to us," Lisa stammered.

"Ben, we have to go," Amy urged, grabbing him by the wrist and dragging him to the sports car.

"You three, get in the back, now!" Frank snapped at the remaining trio. Tina obeyed and rushed towards the rear of the lorry.

"What about Glen?" Elaine asked. "You've injured him, we can't leave him behind."

The dust cloud had cleared, revealing the crawling figure it had previously concealed. They stared at Glen's eager eyes as he tried to rise, but the bullet in his leg put paid to that. Collapsing in a heap, he began dragging himself towards them. He stopped as a loud bang accompanied a bullet in his head.

"Problem solved." Frank lowered his handgun. "Stay with him if you want. If not, get in!"

He strode toward the cab of the lorry, where Lisa was already waiting.

Frank put the lorry in gear and spun the wheel. The wide circle proved time-consuming as the horde of undead drew near. He watched the sports car race down the track ahead of them, past the approaching zombies.

"Looks like they got the better deal," he said, the lorry finally facing the right way.

"How? We've got the guns."

"They've got the food."

"Not all of it." Lisa moved her legs aside, revealing four bags of cans and boxes in the footwell.

"You really are a master thief, aren't you?"

"Sure am."

"But they still have the fast car."

"We've got durability. It'll take a lot to smash this thing up."

"They don't have Blob and Blubber to contend with."

Lisa looked at him thoughtfully. "Okay, they have the better deal."

As they looked ahead, it was clear the crowd would cut them off. They sprinted across the field as the lorry trudged on.

"Things are going to get bumpy," said Frank.

The zombies spilled onto the track ahead of them. He aimed the handgun out of the window, firing in quick succession. Two of the creatures fell, but the bullets whizzed past the majority. With one hand on the wheel, Frank continued to fire. A few more stumbled as the gun clicked empty. He sat back in his seat as the sea of undead roared closer.

"Hold on!"

He pushed the lorry harder, speeding towards the crowd until, at last, they collided.

The impact shook the LGV and it slowed as countless bodies fell beneath its wheels.

"Faster!" Lisa cried as the lorry slowed down.

"I'm trying!"

He had no idea how many corpses he had crushed, but the sheer number they were still to face was disheartening. As the lorry had almost ground to a halt, he decided on a different approach.

With a roar of the engine, he jerked the wheel sideways, bounding onto the bordering field. The zombies followed, crying out as the lorry moved past them. The trailer bucked over the uneven ground as they sped up once more.

"What the hell are you doing?" Lisa gasped.

"What? It worked, didn't it?"

Frank looked in his side mirror for confirmation. Sure enough, the zombies were now running alongside the trailer. The mass of mangled bodies left in the road had painted its surface red. He looked back as Lisa snapped at him.

"Are you forgetting what's back there?" She jabbed a thumb at the trailer behind them.

"Those three? They can live with it."

"I'm not talking about them; I'm talking about all the loaded guns!"

Frank's heart lurched as the magnitude of his actions became clear.

"The bouncing could set them off!" Lisa urged.

"I realise that."

Frank lurched towards the side. He smashed through a wooden fence before they were driving on the road once more.

"Thank God." Lisa sighed.

Frank stared ahead, scanning the area for anyone else in their path.

"So now our building's gone, where do we go from here?" Lisa asked.

"We go north."

"North? Why?"

"I'm going to collect on a bet."

29

Footsteps echoed around the large room as Gus Razor paced back and forth. He would stop now and then to frown at the gagged soldier in front of him before resuming his stride. The man's bound hands were bleeding from the constricting cable ties around his wrists. The soldier fought to speak through the soiled rag in his mouth, but only an inaudible muffle escaped.

"You want to speak?" Gus asked. The soldier nodded, his eyes fixed on the gangland boss.

"Fine, but it'd better be something useful. If you tell me you need a piss, you're gonna get another beating."

Razor strode over to the man and yanked the fabric from his mouth. He gasped for air as his captor crouched to his level.

"Now what's so important?"

"I need a piss."

Razor swung a punch at the soldier's face, causing his head to snap sideways.

"A soldier with a sense of humour? What did you clowns do in Iraq? Throw custard pies?" He rose to his feet and resumed his pacing.

"They're not coming back," the soldier said after a while. "They must've been gone for half an hour."

"This is a big place. It'll take a while to make sure everywhere's secure."

"It *was* secure until you lot tricked me into letting you in!"

"Yeah, keep telling yourself that, Murdock. There's no way you could have kept this place secure on your lonesome."

"Well, *you're* going to have to try. Your boys have either left you or they're dead."

"Willing to bet your life on it?"

The soldier fell silent as Gus turned to face him. He produced a large combat knife from a sheath on his belt.

"No?" Razor continued. "How about your peepers? Or those big cauliflower ears?"

The man remained silent, eyeing his captor with contempt.

"Here's the deal, G.I. Joe. You better hope they *don't* come back. Because if they *do,* I'm cutting something off."

"What? Why?"

"Why not?" Gus sneered.

"Look, I can help you. Let me out of this chair and you'll have a fourth gunner to protect this place."

"I gave you that chance yesterday. You responded by breaking poor Zielinski's nose. Do you remember?"

The man fell silent once more.

"No chance, Sunshine. You're only alive to serve as zombie chow if those things get in again, that's it."

It had been almost four hours since the undead had managed to gain access. Even now, Gus still felt the adrenaline pumping through his body. He slid the knife back into its sheath and resumed his pacing.

The sound of footfalls accompanied his own as the two men returned from their expedition.

"Well, Action Man, looks like you were wrong." Gus pulled the blade from its sheath again. "What do you want removed?"

"No, please!"

"Wait, Gus," Zielinski said.

"I'm busy." Razor yanked the soldier's ear and started to slice.

"You might wanna see this!" Zielinski shouted over the soldier's screams.

Razor turned to face the two men. "What's that?" He eyed the bundle of documents in Zielinski's hands.

"Read them."

"Fuck off, Zielinski. You know I don't read." He turned back to his victim and made to continue slicing until Zielinski spoke again.

"Fine, but there's something else you need to see."

"What's wrong? Have you found how they got in?"

"Yeah, we've sorted it. The base is secure."

"So what do I need to see?"

"Look outside."

"Don't fuck with me, Zielinski!" Gus spat, pointing the blade at him. "Just tell me what's out there."

"A lorry. And it's heading straight for us."

***

Amy rubbed her forehead as their car raced along the Yorkshire moors. The roar of the engine was all she could hear as they sped through the desolate landscape.

"Something up?" Ben asked.

Amy looked around and found concern in his eyes. "No... I just..."

"Just what?"

"Do you think we should have left them back there?"

Ben looked back at the road. "No, you were right. We had to move. If not, the zombies would have caught us."

"I know, but we could have made space. Some of them could have got in with us."

"Amy, by the time we'd have done all that, it would've been too late. Besides, in all the confusion, I think they would have jumped in the lorry regardless."

Amy looked away and stared at the passing countryside. She had watched in the wing mirror as the lorry had ploughed through the crowd of undead. She remembered the sick feeling in her stomach as the vehicle slowed. Then came the sweeping guilt as the lorry disappeared from sight. Despite barely knowing the group, and despising the criminal leading them, she couldn't help but feel responsible for their demise.

"We don't even know if they *were* killed," Ben said, as if reading her mind. "They might have made it out."

"I guess we'll never know."

"Are you okay?"

"Yeah. We've got guns and food now, right? At least we stand a better chance of surviving."

"Right." Ben smiled.

The sun was at its highest. Its radiant beam covering the countryside, raising the temperature of the car.

"It might be a fast car, but the air con sucks." Amy sighed as she opened her window.

"Yeah, well, we don't have to endure it much longer, we're almost there."

They were nearing a large facility on the other side of the neighbouring field. She found it reassuring that there were no undead creatures nearby. Yet, she still felt apprehensive about entering the slaughterhouse. Her trepidation intensified as the smell of death drifted through the open window.

"Oh god." She gagged, putting a hand to her mouth.

"Looks like this place was hit pretty bad." The metal door that led into the building was dented out of shape. Ben reached behind him and produced the shotgun propped against the back seat. "Where are the bullets?"

"Here." Amy handed him the boxes they had taken from Lisa earlier.

"We should've got more," Ben said. He sifted through the boxes until he found the shotgun shells.

"We were lucky to get *out* of there." Amy watched him thumb the cartridges into the gun before handing it to her.

"Here, you take this. This place might be quiet, but we don't know what's inside."

She took the weapon from him as he retrieved the rifle from the back. She stared at the entrance to the building as Ben loaded the rest of the weapons. The indentations in the door signified a lot more than undead humans. She held the shotgun with trembling hands as Ben passed her a handgun.

"Just in case," he said.

She took the weapon and followed him as he swung the door wide. Standing in the open air made her stomach turn. The buzzing of flies was the only sound as they approached the building.

"Are you sure we should do this?" she whispered, as Ben peered into the confines of the room. Satisfied they were safe, he turned back to Amy.

"I need to see if he's alive. I owe it to Fran."

"Okay."

She followed him as he crept through the doorway. The thud of his boots echoed as he walked deeper into the slaughterhouse. Amy breathed through her mouth in an attempt to dispel the rank odour which seemed to worsen as they went. She scanned the area, trying to detect movement within the shadows. Ben stopped in his tracks.

"What's wrong?"

He didn't answer.

She looked past him towards the shattered confines ahead. The large gate, which must have imprisoned the animals, now hung loose on a single hinge. Amy felt a flicker of dread in her stomach as the notion of undead farm animals filled her mind. She aimed her shotgun toward the enclosure.

They edged forward, stepping through pools of blood and gore until they arrived at the holding pen. The lack of livestock was unsettling.

"Where are all the animals?" she whispered.

"Look behind you."

The carcasses lay scattered next to one of the huge machines. The gangway above had collapsed, sending those standing on it down into its metallic maw to be ripped to shreds.

"What is that thing?"

"A meat-separation device. The largest in Europe, actually; my dad's pride and joy."

Amy didn't want to know any more. She tore her gaze away and scanned the rest of the area.

"So where's your dad?"

A gunshot answered her question, ricocheting off the ground next to their feet. She shoved Ben to safety as another shot sounded.

30

"Wait here."

"No way," said Lisa, "I'm coming with you." She grabbed Frank's arm as he made to leave the lorry.

"We don't know what's in there. If things go bad, I want to be able to make a quick getaway."

"And I don't want to risk you being ripped apart. I'm not protecting those little shits on my own."

She jerked a thumb towards the trailer, which housed Tina, Simon, and Elaine.

"C'mon, then."

He leapt from the carriage and waited for Lisa to join him in front of the military base. The barriers leading up to the huge building lay in ruin, making it easy for their lorry to gain access. Frank half expected their vehicle to succumb to machine-gun fire as they neared, but it soon became clear the army was no longer around. With that in mind, he drew his handgun as they stepped toward the barricaded door.

"Do you think there's anybody here?" Lisa whispered.

"*Someone* is."

Frank motioned towards the barricaded windows. "Whether they're still alive is another question."

As they neared, Frank heard a familiar voice.

"Frankie!"

They looked up to see Gus Razor peering out of an upper-floor window.

"I'll be right down!"

With that, he vanished from sight.

"What was this guy put away for again?" Lisa asked.

Frank sighed, shaking his head. "It'd be easier to tell you what he *didn't* get put away for."

They fell silent as an angry outburst from Razor accompanied muffled thuds.

"That's heavy, you tosser!"

A loud bang caused the pair to step back.

"See, now look what you did!"

Before long, the large doors swung open.

"Frankie!" Gus stepped towards them with open arms.

"How you doing, Gus?"

"Not as good as you," he said, looking Lisa up and down. "You didn't wait long, did you?"

"Fuck you," she said.

"Oh, got a mouth on her as well. You've got yourself a right little treasure there, Frankie, m'boy."

"Looks like I'm not the only one making new friends," Frank retorted, nodding towards the two men behind Gus.

"Well, you already know our little Polish friend."

"What happened to you?" Frank frowned at the sight of Zielinski's distorted nose.

"Pissed off an army cadet," said Gus. "Now, this evil-looking bastard is Lurch."

He pointed towards the hefty man on his right. Eyeliner and black lipstick adorned his face, whilst countless piercings shimmered in the sunlight. His long black hair fell loosely over his leather jacket. A chain hung from his jeans, which also sported a sheathed combat knife. His menacing stare softened when he spotted Tina coming up behind the others.

"Fuck me, Frankie. You didn't tell me you'd brought Morticia to this little gathering. What is this, Addams Family Reunion?"

"This is Tina," Frank said. "Tina, this is Gus, Zielinski, and Lurch."

"Hi." She locked eyes with Razor's gothic henchman.

"Hi." The man smiled.

"Okay, that's enough from you, Tainted Love," Gus snapped, rapping the man on the shoulder. "Go and see if our army cadet is still yapping."

"He's fine."

"Then go and keep a lookout."

Lurch's menacing glare returned as he slunk back into the building.

"Where the hell do you find these guys?" Frank asked. "He's almost as big as Tony."

"We found Lurch doing some Kung Fu on a pensioner."

"You sure know how to pick 'em."

"So do you," Gus said as Simon and Elaine appeared. "What the fuck are you doing? Smuggling immigrants?"

"What the hell are we doing here?" Simon asked.

"We're here to put your piloting skills to the test," said Frank. "Gus, please tell me you've got planes in there."

"The best fighter jets money can buy. The only problem is we can't fly them."

"This guy can."

"What?" Gus and Simon snapped in unison.

"I can't fly a fighter jet!"

"Why not?"

"I've never even been in one."

"It can't be that much different. Keep your finger off the missile button and you'll be fine—"

A series of thunderous gunshots sounded overhead. Frank looked up and saw Razor's henchman firing from a top window. He was aiming at the destroyed barrier, where countless zombies sprinted towards them.

"I think we'd better take this reunion inside," Gus offered.

The group ran indoors, congregating in the hall. Gus and Zielinski blocked the entrance with large metal drums. Frank produced his handgun as the gunfire continued overhead.

"Where the hell did you get a shooter?" Gus demanded, as he produced his own gun. Not waiting for a response, he turned to his companion. "Zielinski, guard this door with your life. If you let those fuckers in, I'll chop your knackers off!"

With Frank close behind, he jogged away, up a flight of stairs, and rushed into a nearby room.

"I'm sure I don't need to remind you to shoot them in the head."

They crouched beside a window. The glass was already shattered, with wooden boards hammered over the frame. Gus removed a loose board and aimed through the gap. Frank followed his example and pointed his handgun at the crowd. The pair fired in succession. The zombies were quick, but the bullets proved quicker. Before they had wasted half of their rounds, bodies littered the grass.

"So where did you get the gun?" Gus's handgun clicked empty. He retrieved a second magazine, reloaded, and took aim once more.

"We raided a gun shop."

Frank followed the progress of a young female as she sprinted towards the building. As soon as the sights were level with her head, he pulled the trigger. He lowered the gun, watching as the machine gun crippled the remaining zombies.

"Did you get much?" Gus asked.

Frank snarled as a bullet from the machine gun clipped the top of his lorry. "We won't have anything if boy-wonder hits that trailer again!"

Gus looked at the vehicle, his eyes widening. "That's full of guns?"

"And ammo."

"Fuck me," Gus groaned. He staggered to his feet, yelling up at the floor above. "Watch out for the lorry, you dickhead!"

The machine gun continued to rattle.

Frank jumped to his feet as a second bullet ricocheted dangerously close to the fuel tank.

"Oy!" Gus shouted.

He raised the handgun aloft and fired two rounds into the ceiling. The gunfire ceased as a cloud of plaster rained down on the pair. Frank leapt back as the fragments crashed around them.

"Oh, fucking hell," Razor spluttered, brushing the white dust out of his hair.

"Great job, Gus."

"He stopped, didn't he?"

"Of course he did, you probably shot him!"

Razor's face dropped. "Lurch?"

A tense moment of silence passed before a voice answered.

"What?"

Gus breathed a sigh of relief. "Get your arse down here."

He strode out of the room, reloading his handgun with a new magazine as he went. Frank followed as they retraced their steps back down to the waiting group.

"What the fuck is he doing here?" Gus demanded, as he set eyes on the soldier.

"I untied him," said Lisa.

"Why?"

"We're fighting for survival here. We need every man we can get, and a trained soldier is a valuable asset."

"My thoughts exactly," the soldier snarled. He held a hand to his bloody ear, his unblinking eyes fixed on Gus.

"Don't try anything funny," Gus said. He turned as Lurch rejoined the group.

"You almost hit me!" he snapped.

"And you almost blew up our lifeline. That was a truck-load of ammunition you were firing at!"

"Look, can we stay focused here?" Lisa urged. "Why don't you show us these planes?"

"Did you get them all, Lurch?" asked Gus.

"One or two might have got behind us, but I got most of them."

Gus laughed indignantly as he led the group through another doorway. They stopped at another barricaded door.

"Right then, you can go first," he told Lurch.

"What?"

"You let them past; you go and check if they're out back."

"Fine."

"Wait," Tina said. "I'll come with you."

Lurch turned to look at her, a slight smile adorning his face.

"Isn't that cute? Nice knowing you, sweetheart." Gus moved the barrels aside until the doorway was clear.

"Here, you can't go out there without a weapon," Lisa said, offering the handgun to Lurch.

"I have a weapon." He pulled the combat knife from the sheath on his belt and turned towards the door.

"A knife?" Lisa gasped, looking at Gus. "He's going out there with a knife?"

"He's a crazy bastard."

They all looked on as Tina and Lurch swung the doors wide, sunlight flooding the room. The two in front stepped outside, scouring the open courtyard for a threat. When nothing came, they turned back to the group.

"Looks empty."

Gus strode forward with the others in tow. The first thing Frank saw was the procession of fighter jets towards the end of the courtyard. But once he had taken in their route to freedom, he also noticed the large metal dome in the centre.

"What exactly is this place?" He scowled, turning to face the soldier.

"A barracks for overseas operations. But its primary use is for weapons research and development."

"We don't need to hear all this," Gus insisted. "Let's see if Maverick can get those birds in the sky." He winked at Simon, who didn't return his affection.

"Actually, why don't we tell them more about this place, Gus?" Zielinski said. Razor shot him a menacing glare.

"What's going on?" asked Frank.

"Gus doesn't want you to know about this place. If you did, you'd know how this whole zombie thing started."

The gangland boss clenched his fists as Zielinski turned to look at the others.

"And more precisely, you'd learn how Gus Razor caused the end of the world."

31

Amy gasped as another shot ricocheted nearby. “What’s he doing?”

“He’s a prick.”

“But doesn’t he know it’s you?”

The machine behind which they had sought refuge clanged as a bullet struck it.

“Probably,” Ben said. “He did say if he ever saw me again, he’d shoot me in the face.”

He shrugged as another shot hit the ground near their feet. Silence fell as the man reloaded.

“Let’s move.”

The words had barely escaped Ben’s mouth before he disappeared around the side of the machine. Amy ran after him, stopping in the middle of the factory, where Ben aimed the rifle at his father.

“Stop!”

Ben watched through the scope as the elderly man fumbled with a handful of bullets.

"I said stop!"

He fired a shot at the wall beside his father. The man flinched, dropping the bullets and magazine onto the metal walkway.

"I taught you to shoot better than that!" he said.

"That was a warning shot. Stop trying to kill us."

"Have you been bitten?"

"No."

"Then get up here, I haven't got all day."

They watched the man scoop up the magazine and the few bullets that had not fallen through the grates. Muttering to himself, he stormed towards his office. They walked across the factory floor, stepping over innumerable dead animals and factory workers. Amy realised with horror that some of the men had no other afflictions apart from a bullet hole in their head.

"You don't think he killed them *before* the outbreak, do you?" she asked.

"I wouldn't put it past him."

A sick feeling started to form in the pit of her stomach as they ascended the stairwell. They took one last look at the carnage below before heading into Gordon Chesterfield's office.

"What are you waiting for?" demanded the old man as they appeared in the doorway.

Ben stepped into the room with Amy at his back. They watched as Gordon poured a tumbler full of whisky.

"Is this all you've been doing?" Ben asked, "sitting here getting drunk for the past two days?"

"Three days, actually."

"Three?"

"Yeah, I was gonna be in deep shit with the law. I could've gone away for quite a while if it wasn't for this fabulous blessing."

"Blessing? What do you mean blessing?"

"I mean, I'm a free man. They can't put me away if there are no coppers left." Gordon beamed as he raised the glass to his lips.

"Yeah? Well, your *blessing* took your daughter's life!" Ben yelled.

Gordon placed his glass back on the desk, staring at his son in horror. "Frances?"

"Dead."

"Are you sure?"

"She was eating people, Dad! So yeah, I'm pretty fucking sure!"

The elderly man's face contorted. He let out an agonised cry and crumpled in his seat. Tears streamed down his face as he held his head in his hands.

"She's gone. Gone, and it's my fault."

"What?"

Gordon's breathing became heavy and a growl replaced his sobbing. "It's *my* fault!" He lunged to his feet. "All my fault!"

He snatched the tumbler from the table and hurled it against the wall. The glass shattered into a hundred pieces, showering the carpet in whisky-coated shards. He slumped back in his seat, staring blankly out of the window behind his desk.

"What do you mean it's your fault?" Ben stepped forward, taking a seat opposite his father.

"Everything," Gordon replied. "It's all my fault. All the death. All the chaos. All those *things*!" He pointed an accusing finger out of the window. Ben followed his gaze, groaning when he spotted the herd of cows approaching the factory.

"We need to go."

"What do you mean?" Amy pressed, ignoring the urgency in Ben's voice.

"I spread it across the country."

"Wha—how?"

"I helped an old friend. His entire livestock was slaughtered. Eighty cows! He was going to go bust unless I helped him."

Ben fixed his father with a stern look. "What did you do, Dad?"

"I told him to bring them down. We stripped the meat and sent it out."

"You sold infected meat?"

"I didn't know it was infected! This was nearly two weeks before all this shit started. I told him I'd sell it on for him without any fuss. Then I started getting emails from different shops. They said their customers were reporting food poisoning. They were questioning my product and demanding an investigation. Every day, more and more complaints kept coming in. Then, they stopped."

"How far did you transport it?" Ben asked.

Gordon looked up, tears rolling down his face. "Nationwide."

"With eighty cows? How did you manage to spread it that far?"

"Mince," Gordon muttered. "We minced it with the other meat we had stored to cover it up."

"So this entire thing started because of you?"

Gordon nodded. "I was just trying to help him out. I didn't know it would turn people into cannibals!"

"The food poisoning!" Amy gasped. "The hospital was overrun with cases of food poisoning. *That's* how it started."

Gordon nodded, staring at the desk.

A delighted screech resounded from the entrance of the factory. The undead animals had arrived.

"Right, c'mon, we need to go," Ben said. Amy leapt from her seat as he grabbed his father's arm. "Dad, c'mon."

The old man smiled knowingly.

"C'mon!" Ben snapped.

Gordon slipped his arm out of his son's grasp and reached for his bottle of whisky. "It's poetic, isn't it?" he mused, more to himself than the others. "Almost like a form of justice."

"What?"

"I've been slaughtering animals for thirty-five years. I built an empire from killing. Now it's time for the animals to get their revenge."

"Revenge? What are you talking about?"

"You'd better leave, son. As we speak, those delightful bovines will be making their way up the stairs."

Amy glanced out into the factory. The undead cattle were ascending the stairwell. “He’s right, we need to get out of here.”

Ben looked back at his father.

“Go on.” Gordon smiled, shaking his son’s hand. “I’d rather be in heaven with your mother and Frances than running around this shithole with you two.”

Ben smirked. He nodded and released his father’s hand. The metallic clatter of hooves on the walkway sounded as he stepped out of the office. The first of the crazed heifers was only a few metres away. It snarled at the pair before its head splattered under a hail of shotgun fire.

The couple retreated, firing at the animals approaching the office door.

“Stop wasting your bullets and get out of here!” Gordon bellowed.

The pair continued to unload their guns, leaving behind a procession of mangled animals. With Gordon’s safety secured for a while longer, they turned and ran to the end of the walkway. A large circular window looked out onto the moors below.

“The car is just down there,” Amy said. “If we lower ourselves down, the drop won’t be that high.”

Ben nodded and stepped back as Amy swung the butt of her shotgun at the window. The glass shattered, leaving a jagged exit into the countryside. She knocked the remaining glass out of the frame and scrambled onto the window ledge.

“It looks pretty high,” he said. “Are you sure you want to do this?”

"Feel free to go first. You can catch me."

Ben laughed as he looked back at the walkway. "We best hurry. If we wait around any longer, my dad will start taking pot-shots at us again."

Amy smiled as Ben lowered himself off the ledge. "Be careful."

Unable to tell how far away he was from the floor, she watched with bated breath as he hit the ground hard. His legs buckled as he landed, but he made a sharp recovery and jumped to his feet.

"Are you okay?" she called.

"Yeah, c'mon."

Ben shouldered his rifle, firing twice into the building. A startled screech came from within until a third shot silenced it. Amy took a deep breath and lowered herself over the edge. Holding the shotgun and clinging to the ledge proved difficult; she tried to adjust the weapon as she eased herself down. Her arms trembled, aching as she tried to correct her grip. The shotgun fell as she slipped and let out a shriek, falling through the air, a weightless experience that ended abruptly when she hit the ground.

"Shit, are you alright?" Ben cast a concerned glance over his shoulder. He fired another shot into the building as Amy rose to her feet.

"Yeah, I'm fine."

She gently applied weight to her throbbing ankle. The pain was prominent, but not enough to prevent her from walking.

"Let's get out of here."

She hobbled to the car as Ben shot the last cow that had ventured outside. The rest, they assumed, were in the building. Amy looked back towards the circular window in Gordon Chesterfield's office. There was nobody there. She wondered whether he was still alive or if the cows had administered his warped view of justice. She glanced at Ben and found him staring at the window too.

"I'm sorry, Ben."

"No sweat."

As they entered the car, Ben handed her his rifle. She placed both weapons in the footwell as he turned the car around. With a roar of the engine, they raced away from the gore-filled slaughterhouse. Amy couldn't help but feel sorry for the old man they had left behind, but something about his story didn't seem to add up.

"Y'know, I don't think your dad *did* start all this."

"What do you mean? He sent infected meat all over the UK."

"I know, but how did the meat become infected?"

"His friend's cattle were slaughtered."

"Yeah, but by *what*?"

She knew the realisation had hit as soon as Ben's eyes widened.

"So we know how it spread across the country, but what started it?"

***

Gordon remembered the phone call like it was yesterday.

"Gordon, it's Harry." The elderly man had fought back tears as he spoke.

"Harry? What's wrong?"

"It's my cattle. They've been slaughtered."

"Slaughtered? By who?"

"A fucking lunatic. He's torn them apart!"

"What?"

"I came out to check on them and they've all been ripped apart. Some were still alive, but I had to kill them; their guts were hanging out. Then I saw the psycho crouched next to one. He was eating it! He looked up when I got near, and just… smiled at me. He was covered in blood and still had raw meat in his mouth."

"Harry," Gordon said, "is this a wind-up?"

"Does it sound like a fucking wind-up, Gordon? I blew his head off!"

"What?"

"He got up and came at me. I had to shoot him. It was self-defence, Gordon, I swear!"

"You need to ring the police, Harry."

"The police? He was unarmed. They'll do me for murder!"

Harry had sobbed down the phone. Gordon had sat back in his chair, staring out at the moors.

"It doesn't make a difference, anyway. I had over eighty cows. All gone. I'm ruined."

"Look … I can help you out. I'll suspend all deliveries today. Load them up and start bringing them here. I'll get them treated, chopped up, and distributed."

"What? Really?"

"Yeah. But listen, I'm putting my neck out for you here. You can't tell a soul, understand?"

"But how will you do it? Some of them have been completely stripped."

"Just bring them all down. I'll work something out when I see them."

"What about the crazy bastard I shot?"

"Dig a big hole and bury him. If somebody comes looking, feign ignorance. I'll do the same."

"Thanks, Gordon. You have no idea how much this means."

"You'll obviously make a loss, Harry. But if it keeps you from going bust, then that's all that matters, right?"

"Right."

"Good, start bringing them down and I'll see what I can do."

He had hung up the phone, poured himself a drink, and pondered long and hard.

Gordon held the new bottle of whisky to his mouth and took a hefty swig. He considered how things could have been different had he not helped Harry. Was he still alive? Was he aware he'd played a part in creating the chaos? Or was he now partaking in it?

The first undead animal stepped into the office, breaking his contemplation. He looked at the young cow with a sneer.

"You gotta be bigger than that if you wanna take me."

The cow took another step before he shot it between the eyes. He looked back out of the window as the undead creature crumpled to the floor. The sports car was no longer in sight, leaving the vast landscape completely still. He stared out at the endless fields, thinking about his daughter. Despite a stomach full of whisky, he felt empty inside. A guttural growl announced the arrival of a second cow.

"No chance."

He shot the animal before it stepped into his office. He looked down the neck of the bottle as he took another swig. The sloshing whisky cast an amber tint over the next animal that entered. Gordon set down the bottle and stared at the large cow.

"Well, you're a beauty, aren't you?"

The crazed heifer watched him with wide, staring eyes. Its lipless mouth formed a permanent snarl as it stepped over the dead cows. Gordon turned, busying himself with another bottle of alcohol. The undead animal stepped forward, like a tiger stalking its prey.

"I think me and you should go down in a blaze of glory."

Gordon soaked his handkerchief in the potent mixture. The liquid dripped from the fabric as he stuffed it into the neck of the bottle. Turning back to the animal, he produced a lighter and lit the end of the cloth. The flame devoured the handkerchief as the cow attacked. It rushed toward the desk as Gordon hurled the cocktail.

The bottle smashed on the cow's skull, showering the office in glass as the alcohol ignited and a sea of flame engulfed the room. The undead cow was oblivious to the searing heat as it clambered onto the desk. It darted toward Gordon, who now held a gun to his temple.

"Good luck, Benjamin."

His head jerked sideways as the bullet entered his brain and he fell in a heap. An enigmatic shriek escaped the cow as it pounced on the motionless body. It wasted no time in tearing flesh from his lifeless form, but it meant little to Gordon. As soon as the bullet had entered his brain, he faced an eternity of darkness.

32

"Shut the fuck up, Zielinski!" Gus Razor spat.

"Wait, what's going on?" Frank asked.

"It's him," Zielinski continued. "It's his fault all this started."

They watched as Gus went nose-to-nose with the Polish man.

"I swear to God, Zielinski, shut it, or I will kick your arse back to Krakow!"

The two men locked stares until the click of a gun caused them both to turn.

"Tell us what happened," Frank said, aiming the shotgun at them.

"Well, it started when—"

"*I'll* tell the story!" Razor bellowed, pushing Zielinski aside. He turned his back to the group and looked towards the military complex.

"A few weeks back, one of my boys got word of a military cargo being transported. He found out it was the same routine every week. He was certain it was guns. Maybe confiscated weapons, or prototypes that hadn't matched the specification, I don't know. Either way, I gave the order to intercept the cargo on its next run."

"And I'm guessing they were transporting corpses?" Lisa said.

"Don't ask me, I wasn't there."

"Yes, they were," the soldier said. "*We* had no idea either. Our orders were to keep the base secure and destroy the medical waste every week. It was the scientists in the complex that knew what was going on."

"Did you not get suspicious when the *cargo* started moving and eating people?" asked Frank.

"They were never alive. They were dead before the experiment, as far as I know; bodies donated to science and that kind of thing. The corpses transported were experimental failures. But we weren't authorised to know what they were doing down there."

"Down *where*?"

The soldier motioned towards the large dome in the centre of the courtyard.

"Wait, there's a lab under there?"

"An entire medical facility. I told you: the base is used for weapons research and development."

"Why were they experimenting on corpses?"

"Probably trying to create a super-soldier or something," Tina muttered.

The group turned as one and looked at the teenager, who crossed her arms. "What? That's what they always do in the films."

"Not quite," Zielinski said. "Me and Lurch found a bunch of paperwork in one of the filing cabinets. They were trialling bioweapons."

"Bioweapons?"

"Yeah, It's all here."

He produced a wad of folded sheets from his pocket and handed it to Lisa.

"Oy!" said Gus. "Where did you get that?"

"We tried to tell you," Zielinski said. "You *don't read,* remember?"

Gus Razor snarled at the pair. He made to speak, but Frank interrupted him.

"I still don't understand how this all started. So, Razor's boys ambushed the truck, yes?"

"Yeah," the soldier replied.

"Then what happened?"

"I have no idea. I was never a driver. All I know was what the lads told me when they got back."

"And what did they say?"

"They were attacked by a group of blokes in a blacked-out van. They were trying to ram them off the road. Both vehicles got smashed up pretty bad. In the end, those guys gave up and fell back. But when they went to destroy the bodies, they found that the hold was damaged."

"So the zombies escaped?"

"Their report said the cargo was accounted for, but one of them told me later that there was a corpse missing."

"But you said they were dead when they were being transported. Rejects, right?"

"Yeah."

"So it would've been a corpse at the side of the road? How could it have spread the virus?"

The soldier shrugged. "I don't know. Maybe this one *wasn't* a reject after all, or maybe a fox took a bite of it and became infected, who knows. What I *do* know is that it wasn't long after that when the shit hit the fan."

The group glared at Gus Razor.

"Oh, grow up, you little specks of shit! You're all giving me evils just because a hijack went wrong? It was these cunts that created the virus. *They* started it."

Frank glanced at Lisa, who was studying the unfolded documents. "Find out anything?"

She raised a hand to silence him, keeping her eyes on the pages.

The soldier made for the door. "I've had enough. I'm off to make a brew while you lot sort this out."

He reached for the handle before the door swung open. A wild screech accompanied an undead woman as she dived onto him.

"Shit!"

Frank levelled his shotgun at the grappling pair, but his aim wavered when he heard yet more shrieking coming from the side of the building. Ignoring the potential threat, he looked back at the soldier as the zombie tore a chunk out of his hand. Lisa's rifle drowned out his scream of pain as the attacker lurched back with a bullet in its head. The soldier scrambled to his feet and rushed inside.

"You said you'd got them all, Lurch!" Razor snapped.

"No, I didn't. I said one or two might have got past."

"Well, there's more than one or two here, you dumb fuck. Can't you count?"

The group readied their weapons as a series of zombies rounded the corner. A hail of gunfire echoed around the courtyard. They banded together as the undead ran straight at them from both sides of the building. As each corpse fell, another took its place in the endless assault.

"One or two!" Gus raged over the gunfire. "You need your fucking eyes tested."

Lurch scowled. He gripped Tina's hand and ushered her away as the gunfire continued.

"How many bullets you got left, Frank?" Gus shouted.

"Enough." He blasted a woman as she drew close, reducing her top half to a bloody mush. "I think that's the lot."

"Good, because I'm out." Gus returned the weapon to its holster.

"Do you have any more guns?" Frank asked.

"I think there are some back inside."

"Right, Pinky and Perky," Frank said, turning to Simon and Elaine. "Go inside, get some guns, and bring them out here. We need to make sure the rest of this place is secure."

He turned back to the others, but stopped in his tracks when he heard the click of a handgun.

"No. We're not following your orders anymore!"

Frank turned, to see Simon brandishing the handgun, which shook in his chubby hand.

"Where the hell did you get that?"

"From the back of that bloody lorry. You're not going to order us about anymore. Me and Elaine are getting the hell out of here."

"Fuck me, you sure know how to pick 'em, Frankie." Gus chuckled until Simon's wavering aim rested on him.

"Fuck you!"

"Now hold on a minute," Gus started, raising his hands as he stepped forward.

"No, *you* hold on!" Simon lurched toward him, aiming the handgun at his head.

"Oh, you fat twat. I'm bored with this. Frankie, kill him."

Simon aimed at Frank, whose shotgun remained by his side.

"Frank, shoot him!" Gus repeated.

"I can't, I'm out of bullets."

"What? You just said you had *enough* bullets!"

"I did. I used it on that last zombie."

"Oh, well, fuck a moose on a winter's night!" Gus spat. "Blondie, you shoot him."

"Nobody is going to shoot us," Simon snapped. He aimed the gun at each of them as he and Elaine backed away.

"What are you gonna do, Simon?" Lisa asked.

"We're getting in one of those jets and we're getting away from here."

"But where? Everywhere's fucked."

"We'll go to France, Spain, Italy. Anywhere but here."

"Have you forgotten about the Channel Tunnel?" Frank asked, "Europe is gone. Asia is gone."

"Then we'll go to Africa."

"Africa?" Gus laughed. "Even if they're not infected, they'll still eat you."

"Then we'll go to America. I can fly us there."

"Pull the other one. You'd never make it to the Yanks in one of those."

"We'll take our chances." Simon swung the weapon from side to side as he steered Elaine back with his free hand.

"We need to stick together," Lisa protested.

"*We* are."

"You're being stupid."

"Am I?"

The pair reached the side of the building. Simon made to speak further, but a startled gasp from his wife stole his tongue and he whirled around as two undead soldiers rushed at them from behind the wall.

"Shit!"

The group looked on at the unfolding events. Simon shot one of the men, sending him crumpling to the ground. Elaine held out a hand to keep the remaining attacker at bay. She shrieked as it lunged for her, grabbing its face as it snapped toward her neck. Her palm blocked the zombie until it ripped into the flesh between her thumb and forefinger.

A second shot drowned her screams as Simon killed the creature. He wrapped Elaine in his arms as the group rushed over.

"Stay where you are!" He aimed the gun at the group.

"Simon, you need to kill her," Lisa urged.

"Like hell I do!"

"There's no cure!" She brandished the folded pages. Simon aimed the weapon at Lisa as she glared at him. They locked stares before another series of shrieks filled the air.

"Fuck it, I'm off," Gus stammered.

He turned on his heel and ran back to the military base, with Frank and Lisa close behind. The trio bounded over the corpse near the doorway and rushed inside.

Frank looked back, watching the fleeing couple. Simon fired at the zombies as they rushed towards the jet. Some fell to the ground, others ploughed on, determined to reach them before they escaped.

A straggling zombie turned the corner. After weighing up its options, it attacked the army base. Frank pulled the door shut, seconds before the creature crashed against it. It cried out in frustration, slamming itself against the wooden pane.

"Did they get away?" Gus asked.

"I'm not sure."

"Fuck me, I've never seen a fat twat run so fast."

Frank shook his head as he joined Lisa and Zielinski next to a gap in one of the windows.

"You'd think McDonald's were giving out freebies," Razor continued.

He stepped away from the door as the zombie continued its relentless assault.

"Shut up, Gus." Frank strained his neck to see more of the airfield, but the wooden planks obstructed most of his view.

"Do you think they made it?" Lisa whispered.

"I don't know."

"There really isn't a cure. These scientists have created a bioweapon, a nerve agent to infect the enemy."

"What?"

"It's all here." Lisa handed the paperwork over. "Apparently, gaseous agents are too easy to identify. They've manufactured a new strain which is transmitted via fluid."

"So it turns them into zombies?" Frank asked.

"Not at first. It's designed to kill them. But it continues to release neurotransmitters after death. The brain is reactivated, and they become those things."

Frank studied the sheet as she continued.

"The enemy spreads the virus within their camp. Before long, their army is decimated. Kind of like a Trojan horse."

"Will you drop this shit?" Gus spat.

"So it's spread by fluid?" Frank asked, ignoring the request.

"Bodily fluid."

"So as long as we don't wank these guys off, we should be fine." Gus snorted.

"Shut up, Gus. This whole thing started because of you."

"Spit and blood," Lisa said. "It's spread through a bite. It's why you didn't turn into one when Louise scratched you."

Frank touched his cheek, tracing the scabbed flesh with his finger.

"Oh ho, you've had *another* woman, Frankie? Fuck me, you get about."

Frank rounded on the gangland boss. "I won't tell you again, Gus. Shut the fuck up. New bodyguard or not, I'll still kill you."

Gus looked around the room.

"Hang on, where *is* Lurch?"

"Tina?" said Lisa. "Where's Tina?"

"I think I saw them run round the side," Zielinski offered.

Razor's eyes widened. "The little shits better not be in your truck!"

He bounded to the front of the building, followed by Frank and Lisa. They each found a gap in the barricaded window. Frank pressed his eye to the hole. The lorry was still there, surrounded by a sea of motionless corpses.

"Well, they didn't steal our truck."

"Thank fuck," Gus muttered, wiping sweat from his brow. He leaned back against the wall until the sound of an engine roared nearby. "Oy! They've only gone and nicked my van!"

"You mean *our* van," Zielinski said.

"Zip it, Polak. I don't share with narks."

Frank looked through the window. The prison van came into view as it trundled away towards the main road.

"I guess I'm not the only one who knows how to pick 'em," Frank sneered, looking at Razor's grimace.

"Yeah? Well, that's our only transport out of here."

"Relax, we've got food and guns in the lorry. We'll be fine for now."

"Yeah, but—"

"What happened to the soldier?" Lisa asked.

The men exchanged a glance as they stared at the open doorway nearby.

"Got any bullets left, sweet-cheeks?" Razor asked.

"Yeah."

"Good. You lead. If he looks at you with anything more than a smile, you shoot the bastard, got it?"

"I think I'll manage."

Lisa stepped forward, closely followed by the three men.

As they entered the room, they spotted the injured soldier. He sat in a small wooden chair beside a powerless vending machine.

"What happened to the rest of you?" He glanced up with a dazed look in his eyes.

"The kids have hijacked the prison van," Frank said. "And the fat twats were heading for one of those jets."

"Can they fly?" the soldier murmured.

"Apparently, but I'm not sure they made it."

"Elaine was bitten," Lisa added. "She'll be one of them soon."

The soldier nodded, looking down at his bloodied hand. They all fell silent as the sound of a jet engine rumbled overhead.

"I guess they made it."

"Who cares? I told you there's no chance they'll reach America," Gus snorted.

"America?" The soldier frowned.

"Yeah, Bonnie and Clyde are en route to the almighty USA."

"Can it be done?" Frank asked. "Can they do it?"

The soldier nodded. “It’s possible,” he said, staring at the wall.

“What?” Gus spat.

The soldier blinked, breaking his reverie, and stared at the group. “Those are the new-issue Hawk fighter jets. They’re state-of-the-art machines. They’ve got three fuel tanks, which I’d wager is more than enough to get them across the water.”

“But how can he fly one of those?” Zielinski asked.

“Jets these days practically fly themselves. They need little input from the pilot once they’re off the ground unless it’s performing a manoeuvre or firing a missile. As long as he has basic flying experience, he’d be able to pilot it.”

“But that’s good, right?” Zielinski suggested. “He can explain to the Americans there are still survivors and they’ll come and save us.”

Both Frank and Gus scoffed at the idea, shaking their heads at the Polish man.

“But what about the virus?” asked Lisa, after the indignant muttering had ceased.

“What about it?”

“He’s flying with Elaine! She’s infected. What if they *do* make it across?”

“Then what’s left of the world is going to die.”

Epilogue

Tyler Lincoln sucked on the Marlboro Light clasped between his lips. He looked around at the countless jets situated along the runway. His aircraft, the Lockheed Martin F-22 Raptor, absorbed the sun's powerful rays into its sleek, grey body. The black-tinted cockpit concealed the interior, but Tyler knew the layout like the palm of his hand.

He took another drag, contemplating the chaos that the rest of the world had fallen into. The US military's decision not to respond to the outbreak had left him shell-shocked. But the more he considered it, the more thankful he was that he didn't have to fly overseas to try to quell it. The prospect of leaving his family behind didn't bear thinking about, yet the idea of their succumbing to the virus was even worse. Despite his reservations, he was happy to contribute towards defending US airspace.

He exhaled a cloud of smoke through his nose and flicked the cigarette butt away. He was grinding the smouldering remains beneath his boot when he heard hurried footsteps approaching. He turned in time to see his long-time friend, Eddy Frankland, running towards him.

"C'mon, Lincoln, wheels up!" he yelled as he rushed past.

Tyler wasted no time asking for an explanation. He sprinted over to his aircraft and climbed into the cockpit.

"What have we got?" he asked, pulling on his headgear.

"Bogey entering our airspace in less than five minutes," Frankland's static-filled voice replied through the headset. "We need to take it down before it gets over US soil."

"Take it down? What if it's a friendly?"

"There are no more friendlies."

Tyler shook his head as he busied himself assessing the controls. Before long, the engines roared to life and he prepared to take off.

"Pre-flight check complete. Are you with me?"

"Shit!" Frankland spat. "One of my engines isn't responding."

"What?"

"Get up there, dude. We don't have time."

Tyler looked over at Frankland's motionless jet. He couldn't see inside, but he knew his friend would be frantically checking the displays. Without waiting for any further prompts, he taxied towards the runway and took off, listening to the instructions through his earpiece.

"Don't waste any time, Raptor One. Shoot it down on sight."

"Where is it?" Tyler asked, scanning the sky in front of him as he ascended higher.

"Co-ordinates being sent."

Tyler looked at the screen to his right. The display showed the target was only two minutes from land. He banked hard to the left, setting himself on an intercept course.

"Got him."

The distant target came into view. He soared past and performed a quick turn. Within seconds, he was behind the jet with missiles locked on target. His thumb hovered over the switch as he watched the aircraft. Its shape was unfamiliar, yet it looked capable of greater speeds. That, coupled with the unsteady flight pattern, gave him the impression a novice was piloting it.

"What's the status, Raptor One?"

He ignored the query as he pulled alongside the jet and established a communication link.

"This is the United States Air Force. You are about to enter restricted airspace. Turn back immediately." He listened, awaiting a response. When none came, he spoke again. "This is the United States Air Force. Do you copy? You are entering restricted airspace. Turn back now or you *will* be shot down."

A clatter came over the transmission as the hurried gasps of a man became clear. "Hello? Hello?"

"Do you copy?" Tyler repeated.

He looked at the display, which showed they were thirty seconds from land. He dropped back, once again tailing his target. His thumb hovered above the switch once more as the man's pleading cries filled his headpiece.

"Please, help! My wife is sick. She needs medical attention!"

Tyler's thumb faltered. Images of his own wife at home filled his mind. His heart hammered as a growl sounded from the jet. The man let out a frightened whimper.

"Please!"

Tyler's heart pounded against his ribs. He knew he had to destroy the aircraft, but his conscience forbade it. His hand trembled, tormented by the choice.

"Raptor One!" The voice from air traffic control sounded over the speakers. "He's going to be over land any second. Take him out!"

Tyler glanced at the display and knew they were right. He had to act fast.

"I'm sorry."

He locked the missile's senses onto the aircraft.

"What? Please, no!"

"I have to."

"No!"

"I'm sorry."

"*No*!"

The jet suddenly nosedived right before his eyes. Tyler blinked and followed its rapid descent. Alerts beeped from his control panel as the force of the manoeuvre threatened to overpower his aircraft. He felt a tightness in his chest as the pressure started to cripple him. He knew he had to pull up. His target was a lost cause. Even if the man could pull out of his suicidal dive, there was no way he could do it in time to regain his altitude.

Tyler dragged the jet back into a horizontal position. Assessing his elevation, he noted he was only a thousand feet from the ground. If he had gone any closer, his attempts to pull back up could have failed. He felt a wave of relief wash over him, but also a flicker of guilt. The man and his wife had perished in what must have been an almighty crash. He breathed deeply, waiting for confirmation of the wreckage. Seconds passed, with no notification from air traffic control. Tyler's brows creased. There were only a few seconds to spare until impact. The jet had to have crashed by now.

He cast an appraising eye over the wreckage as he descended back to base. Fire burned ferociously as black plumes billowed towards him. The jet had crashed towards the end of the runway. As he watched, his colleagues dashed over to the blazing inferno. The carnage that ensued would stay with him forever.

***

Eddy Frankland ran after his comrades as they sprinted towards the wreckage. He knew nobody on board could have survived, but the raging fire burned dangerously close to a fuel supply. If the flames drew closer, more explosions would ensue. He turned as the high-pitched whine of the fire truck announced its arrival. He recognised the stocky man behind the wheel as Arthur Morris, one of the oldest officers still in active service.

"Morris!"

He waved to halt the vehicle's progress. The man slowed to a crawl as he drew alongside Frankland, allowing him to jump onto the side. Clinging onto the rail, he looked ahead as the vehicle took off once more.

"Your boy Lincoln is gonna be in deep shit for this one!" Morris yelled through the open window. "His days flying birds are over."

"No. We're on red alert and Tyler's a great pilot. If anything, they'll have him scraping shit out of the engines for the next two weeks."

"I hope you're right."

Frankland mopped his brow as they neared the wreckage, seeping with sweat. He wiped his free hand over his face as the vehicle skidded to a halt.

"Let's hose her down."

Morris sent a blast of water onto the wreckage as more trucks arrived. Frankland leapt from the side as the men grabbed the handlines, adding to the burst of water. He looked into the orange screen in a daze. He often found fire mesmerising, and despite its destructive capacity, he couldn't help but feel calmed by its allure. A sudden movement within the flames dragged him back to earth. He looked away from the inferno at a smaller fire burning to the side, staring hard as a charred arm emerged from the wreckage.

"Morris! Get that hose over here!"

He turned back to the vehicle and retrieved a fire blanket as Morris aimed the spray overhead.

"What is it?"

"A survivor!"

Frankland rushed over to the body as it scrambled away from the flaming debris. He tried to get near, but the heat was too intense. He turned as Morris raced over in full PPE. The firefighter grabbed the blanket and darted forward. Frankland looked on in horror as the flames devoured the survivor. He guessed she was a woman based on the remains of her clothes, but the flames engulfing her made it difficult to judge. He watched as Morris pounced on the human fireball. The woman screeched and jerked as he smothered her in the grey cloak.

"It's okay!" he yelled, scooping her up in his arms. But still, the woman screamed, squirming in his grasp. He raced back to the truck with Frankland in tow, before laying her on the ground.

"She's alive. Help me, will you?"

Frankland stooped down beside the woman. The heat within the blanket was almost overpowering. The woman had ceased her struggles and lay dormant on the ground as the two officers looked on. A loud crack from the wreckage spurred Morris into action.

"I need to put this out. The medics are on the way."

Frankland nodded, concerned by the woman's still form. As his comrade dragged the length of hose closer to the crash site, he stooped down next to her face, the smell of burnt flesh stinging his nostrils as he drew closer. He stared at the blanket covering her head, wondering what horrors it concealed. If the rest of her body was anything to go by, he imagined her face was a blackened mess. His heart thumped against his ribs. With a trembling hand, he reached forward, grasping the edge of the blanket. It was then that the woman's head emerged from the folds. It all happened in a flash, his hand inches away from her head, her face darting out of the blanket and snapping at his fingers.

Frankland yelped in pain. He jumped back, examining the bloody gash on his smallest finger. Blood ran down the side of his hand, reaching his wrist before he wiped it away. He looked back at the woman, who lay prone once more. Her blackened face was worse than he had expected. All her features had burned away, leaving a charred, pulpy mass. Her nose, eyelids, and lips had all perished in the flames, giving the woman a skull-like appearance. Despite her immobility, she fixed him with a hungry stare, watching as he tried to stem the blood flow from his hand.

"Well, those guys can sort it now," Morris announced, motioning towards the other emergency vehicles that had arrived. Frankland glanced over, watching as they doused the wreckage in geysers of water.

"Are you alright?" Morris nodded towards Frankland's cradled hand. Before he could reply, a convoy of vehicles arrived.

"It's about time you guys showed up," Morris said, stepping towards them. Frankland looked down as the man's boot came close to the woman's head. He tried to voice his concerns, but she was too quick.

"What the—" Morris staggered as the crazed woman seized his leg. "What's she doing?"

"Move!" Frankland snapped, but it was too late.

The woman dragged herself closer and clamped her teeth into his leg. The man's scream echoed around the runway. He hobbled away as the other officers opened fire with semi-automatic rifles. The bullets ripped her remains apart, leaving behind fragments of bone and ash.

"He's infected." A senior officer stepped forward, eyeing Morris sternly. "Get him to quarantine, now."

"What?" he gasped, his panic-stricken eyes darting back and forth between the officers. The men stepped forward and grabbed him. "Wait!" Morris stumbled as he was escorted to a waiting vehicle.

"Frankland, are you injured?" the senior officer asked.

"No, sir." He concealed his injured hand behind his back.

"Good. Get in. I need you to file a report."

Frankland stepped forward as the door to the armoured vehicle swung open. He jumped inside and sat beside an officer. As the vehicle drove away, he looked down at his clasped hands. He knew what they would do to Morris. It would be the same thing they would do to him if they found out. He also knew what he would become. If their intelligence was correct, it was only a matter of time before he turned into a monster. He closed his eyes and shook the notions out of his head. He had never believed in monsters, nor had he ever believed he might become one. He felt perfectly healthy. His fever he blamed on the sun. His dizziness he blamed on the fumes from the wreckage. And he assumed his insatiable hunger was down to not having eaten that day, something he planned to rectify as soon as they returned to base.

The End

A LETTER FROM THE AUTHOR

Dear Reader,

Thank you so much for purchasing my debut novel. I sincerely hope you enjoyed reading it half as much as I did writing it!

As a new author, I don't have an extensive following that will help promote my book far and wide. Every review I receive is a massive help in getting my novel noticed. Amazon prioritises books with lots of interest as 'recommended reading,' so every little helps. On that note, I would be thrilled if you would be kind enough to leave a review. It doesn't have to be an essay, just a line or two with a rating will be more than enough.

Without a host, *The Virus* can't spread, so thank you again for reading!

Damien Lee

The journey doesn't end here…

Get ready for… THE HOST

The army base had been an ideal refuge, secure and well-stocked. But with supplies running low and Gus Razor's worsening mental state, Frank and Lisa leave in search of pastures new, only to end up in the worst place imaginable — the one place Frank vowed he would never return to.

Amy and Ben should have been safe in the secluded cottage. But they're not the only survivors. Some mean no harm, struggling to survive. Others, though, have a far more sinister agenda.

Book Two of The Virus series is a brutal, graphic journey through a post-apocalyptic world, where zombies aren't the only evil to contend with.

EXCLUSIVE ADDITONAL CONTENT

Want to find out how Gus and Zielinski met Lurch, and how the three of them managed to secure the army base?

Get your FREE, exclusive novelette by signing up to my newsletter at www.damienlee.co.uk

You can unsubscribe at any time, but there will be plenty of bonus content, giveaways and freebies for all who remain signed up.

Printed in Great Britain
by Amazon

22231932R10218